PRAISE FOR JOHN McFETRIDGE

BLACK ROCK

"Canadian author/screenwriter J
Everybody Knows This Is Now
but is still looking for a 'break
drama and dynamic historical b
the one."

"[An] excellent historical procedure . . . Well done history and a really good plot line."　　　　　　　　　　　　　　— *Globe and Mail*

"[McFetridge]'s prose remains stripped back and forceful, the action propelled by laconic dialogue and the likeable Eddie Dougherty's refusal to allow politics to interfere with his personal pursuit of justice . . . It's a fascinating backdrop, too."　　　　　　　　　— *The Irish Times*

DIRTY SWEET

"McFetridge is an author to watch. He has a great eye for detail, and Toronto has never looked seedier."　　　　　　— *Globe and Mail*

"McFetridge combines a tough and gritty story populated by engagingly seedy characters . . . with an effective use of a setting, Toronto."
　　　　　　　　　　　　　　　　　　　　　　— *Booklist*

"The dubious fun is in the dialogue and details of a very entertaining and libidinous local debut."　　　　　　　　　— *Toronto Star*

"If more people wrote the kind of clean-as-a-whistle, no-fat prose McFetridge does, this reviewer would finish a lot more of their books."
　　　　　　　　　　　　　　　　　　　　　— *National Post*

EVERYBODY KNOWS THIS IS NOWHERE

"Amid the busy plot, McFetridge does a good job depicting a crime-ridden Toronto (a.k.a. the Big Smoke) that resembles the wide-open Chicago of Prohibition days with corrupt cops, gang warfare, and flourishing prostitution."　　　　　　　　　— *Publishers Weekly*

"This is McFetridge's second novel, and once again, Toronto is a leading character in a fine crime-novel. The city's sprawling growth, its ethnic diversity, and its 'almost American' focus on money are all ongoing motifs that enrich a novel already rich in on-the-make immigrants, edgy cops, and charming, devious women. Sex. Dope. Immigration. Gang war. Filmmaking. In McFetridge's hands, Toronto might as well be the new L.A. of crime fiction."   — *Booklist*

SWAP

"[*Swap*] grabs you by the throat and squeezes until you agree to read just one page, just one more page."   — *Quill & Quire*

"In just three novels . . . McFetridge has demonstrated gifts that put him in Elmore Leonard territory as a writer, and make Toronto as gritty and fascinating as Leonard's Detroit. . . . [McFetridge] is a class act, and he's creating fictional classics — maybe even that great urban literature of Toronto the critics now and then long for."   — *London Free Press*

TUMBLIN' DICE

"He's the guy with just the right balance of grit, humour, and rock'n'roll knowledge to do the job."   — *Toronto Star*

"Dialogue that sizzles and sparks through the pages, providing its own music, naturally of the hard-rocking kind."   — *Toronto Sun*

"Each of John McFetridge's . . . novels has a rhythm to them, mixing taut dialogue, spare description and a dark sensibility with the cool calm of a master bass player."   — *National Post*

"John McFetridge is — or should be — a star in the world of crime fiction."   — *London Free Press*

"Like [Elmore] Leonard, McFetridge is able to convincingly portray flawed figures on both sides of the law."   — *Publishers Weekly*

A LITTLE MORE FREE

A LITTLE MORE FREE

AN EDDIE DOUGHERTY MYSTERY

JOHN McFETRIDGE

ECW PRESS

Published by ECW Press
665 Gerrard Street East, Toronto, Ontario, Canada M4M 1Y2
416-694-3348 / info@ecwpress.com

This is a work of fiction. Names, characters, places, and incidents either are the product of the
author's imagination or are used fictitiously, and any resemblance to actual persons, living or
dead, business establishments, events, or locales is entirely coincidental.

Library and Archives Canada Cataloguing in Publication

McFetridge, John, 1959–, author
A little more free / written by John McFetridge.

Issued in print and electronic formats.
ISBN 978-1-77041-264-4 (pbk)
ISBN 978-1-77090-793-5 (pdf); ISBN 978-1-77090-794-2 (epub)

I. Title.

PS8575.F48L58 2015   C813'.6   C2015-902791-8
C2015-902792-6

Editor for the press: Jen Knoch
Cover design: Scott Barrie | Cyanotype
Cover images: Bluebird Café © Dennis Robinson/The Globe and Mail;
    foggy club © KN/Shutterstock; hand with gun © katalinks/Shutterstock;
    burning document © Rob Hyrons/Shutterstock
Author photo: Jimmy McFetridge
Printed and bound in Canada by Webcom   5   4   3   2   1

The publication of *A Little More Free* has been generously supported by the Canada Council
for the Arts which last year invested $153 million to bring the arts to Canadians throughout
the country, and by the Government of Canada through the Canada Book Fund. *Nous
remercions le Conseil des arts du Canada de son soutien. L'an dernier, le Conseil a investi 153
millions de dollars pour mettre de l'art dans la vie des Canadiennes et des Canadiens de tout
le pays. Ce livre est financé en partie par le gouvernement du Canada.* We also acknowledge
the Ontario Arts Council (OAC), an agency of the Government of Ontario, which last year
funded 1,709 individual artists and 1,078 organizations in 204 communities across Ontario,
for a total of $52.1 million, and the contribution of the Government of Ontario through the
Ontario Book Publishing Tax Credit and the Ontario Media Development Corporation.

   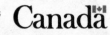

For Laurie, always

I only wanted to be just a man fulfilled
but a little more free
A little more free, a little more free.

Chicago, "Flight 602"

CHAPTER
ONE

Friday afternoon before Labour Day weekend, 1972, Constable Eddie Dougherty gave evidence in the trial of three women charged with being naked in a public place. The week before he'd been temporarily assigned to the Morality Squad and was one of the cops who'd gone in plainclothes to a *discothèque* on St. Catherine Street and arrested the women who were dancing in the window.

At first it had been fun, his first undercover work — the club was lively and the girls were having a good time. Dougherty figured, Of course they were dancing in the window, they were trying to get more customers in the place, but the guys he was with, Morality Squad regulars, weren't having any fun.

Now at the trial one of the other cops, Trépanier, was saying, "They wiggled their posteriors towards the window," and Constable Quevillon said, "It was shocking — the women appeared bottomless as well as topless."

When Dougherty was on the stand the prosecutor showed him the bright orange and red costumes, a thin strip of material, and said, "Is this, in fact, what this woman was wearing?" and motioned the G-string towards the blonde at the defence table sitting between the other two women.

Dougherty said, "Well, it looks like it, but I'd have to see her wearing it again to be sure."

Pretty much everyone in the courtroom burst out laughing and when the judge finally got them quieted down the blonde winked at Dougherty and blew him a kiss.

The judge said, "I'm afraid that's a little out of the question," and adjourned the trial until the next week when he said they'd hear from defence witnesses.

One of the reporters looked at Dougherty then and said, "You might as well just stay on the stand, Constable," and everyone laughed again.

In the hallway outside the courtroom the blonde came up to Dougherty and said, "Hi, I'm Erin Mulvaney."

"Yeah, I remember from the arrest report."

"Oh yeah. Anyway, I have to work tonight."

Dougherty said, "So do I."

"But sometimes when we finish we go to Dunn's for a bite."

"Oh yeah?"

"If you're, you know, hungry."

"Maybe a little cheesecake."

She was giggling then and said, "Yeah, maybe some cheesecake."

Dougherty said okay, maybe, and then he watched Erin walk away with the other two women.

That night he was back driving a squad car out of Station Ten. Captain Boisvert of the Morality Squad said Dougherty wasn't going to work out and Dougherty was okay with that.

A little after eleven, Dougherty was standing beside his squad car having a smoke with the doorman at Rockhead's on St. Antoine, and a call came over the radio about a fire at the corner of Dorchester and Union.

The doorman, a Joe Louis lookalike named Jones, looked up the hill towards downtown and said, "Union? By Phillips Square, that the Blue Bird?"

"Or the bar upstairs."

"Wagon Wheel," Jones said. "Country western."

"You know all the clubs." and Jones said, "Gotta know what's what in this business." and he leaned in a little, winked and said, "and who's who."

"Yeah," Dougherty said, "like this business," nodding his head a little towards the open window of the squad car. "Maybe it's a kitchen fire."

"Maybe."

The radio squawked out another call for the fire and Dougherty said, "Sounds like something." He was looking up the hill then, too — downtown was blocked by the expressway, but he saw smoke rising. Starting around the cop car he said, "Keep the peace tonight, all

3

right?" Jones said, "Will do, boss."

Dougherty drove fast up Mountain and turned right onto Dorchester. It was only a few blocks to Union, the radio going steady, every cop and fireman on duty called in. As soon as he saw the place, Dougherty knew it was bad.

A little two-storey building right on the corner, used to be a garage, now flames were pouring out the front door. Dougherty knew that behind the door were the narrow, rickety stairs going up to the nightclub.

And no one was coming out that door.

Dougherty jumped out of his squad car and saw a man hanging from the big neon sign on the side of the building for a couple of seconds and then he watched the guy fall onto the roof of a car and bounce onto Union Street. People were falling from the sky, climbing out the window behind the sign and jumping.

There was a fire escape on the other corner of the building and dozens of people were coming down it as fast as they could, tripping and falling. Fire trucks pulled up, and guys dragged hoses towards the building and hooked them up to hydrants. People were screaming and black smoke was pouring out of the building.

Chaos.

There was a loud crack and the wrought-iron fire escape gave way and collapsed. People were thrown off and people were crushed underneath.

Dougherty saw a rookie getting out of a squad car looking like he was going to faint and grabbed him and said, "Stay on the corner and keep Dorchester clear, make sure the fire trucks and the ambulances can get through. Start getting these people to hospitals."

People who had gotten out of the fire were standing by the building yelling back for people still inside and Dougherty tried to move them all farther away. He heard a guy calling his name, saw the bouncer and managed to make out something about the back door. Locked.

Dougherty ran around the building to the parking lot and the back door, ran up to it and heard screaming. Women screaming. Pounding on the door.

There was no handle on the outside.

Dougherty looked around on the ground for something to pry open the door but didn't see anything in the dark. The screaming died down and for a second Dougherty thought the panic was ending but then he realized the people trapped inside were just passing out from the smoke.

Then the doorframe busted and the door slammed onto the ground and three or four guys staggered out, coughing and trying to breathe.

Dougherty pushed past them into the stairwell and saw the bodies piled all the way up the stairs. One of the guys who'd broken the door and gotten out was right behind Dougherty and headed back in, saying, "My brother," and grabbing bodies and pulling them out. The stairwell was full of thick black smoke, it was impossible to breathe. Dougherty picked up a body, looked like a teenage girl, rushed outside, rushed back in, grabbed another.

A couple minutes later there was a fireman at the top of the stairs yelling down, saying, "*Tout le monde est sorti?*"

Dougherty tried to speak but his throat was closing

up so he just stood there nodding and waved and the fireman rushed back into the club.

Outside a guy grabbed Dougherty by the arm and said, "My fiancée's in there."

Dougherty was doubled over and gasping, trying to get air into his lungs, and he looked up at the guy and said, "We've been taking . . . people to hospitals."

The guy let go and ran off.

Dougherty took a few steps to a car, leaned back against it and looked back at the club. The Blue Bird Café on the ground floor was dark but there were still flames coming out of parts of the second floor, the Wagon Wheel. The fire trucks' ladders extended over the roof, firemen in the buckets pointing hoses at the building. The flames were getting smaller, going out.

Now Dougherty realized the crowd was growing. It wasn't just the people who'd been in the club, it was people showing up looking for friends and relatives. He closed his eyes and heard voices . . . my sister . . . my husband . . . it was a birthday . . . a party . . . we were celebrating . . .

There were more cop cars on the scene then, cops moving people away from the building.

Dougherty got some breath into his lungs — it tasted like soot — and tried to push himself off the car and stand up. He heard a voice that sounded far away but he focused harder and saw a man inches from his face.

"Are you okay?"

Dougherty realized it was a reporter he knew, Logan, and saw he was covered in black ash.

"They're all out of the stairwell, they're out."

"Good."

Logan leaned back against the car beside Dougherty and said, "It looks like they've got it under control." Then he looked at his watch and said, "That place went up fast."

Dougherty said yeah. He pushed himself off the car and walked back towards the building. As he pushed through the crowd he saw people with blood on their faces and hands and smashed glass all over the ground and figured they'd gotten out through the small windows. He'd been to the club a few times since it had become the country bar, almost everyone there was English from Verdun or the Point or the West Island. Lots of women who worked in Place Ville-Marie or the Sun Life building a little farther down Dorchester, secretaries, and guys from the custom brokers and shipping companies down the hill by the port. A working-class crowd.

Around the front of the building, Dougherty stopped and stared. The firemen were carrying out bodies, handing them from one fireman to another and cops were loading people onto stretchers and into ambulances and police cars.

The crowd was staying back but there was panic in the air.

Dougherty pushed his way past a couple firemen, one of them looked like the captain, and he heard him saying, *"Bien sûr, on sent le gaz dans tout l'escalier,"* and realized right away it was true, he could smell the gasoline, it was arson. He pushed his way up the stairs into the club.

A couple of firemen were shining flashlights into

the far corner of the room, past the dance floor, and Dougherty saw that was where they were picking up the bodies. He went over to help and caught unconnected words: "Women's bathroom," "*fenêtres brisées*," "kids." He took his turn picking up a body from the floor and walked across the club to the stairwell and handed it — him, Dougherty was thinking, a man about his own age, probably someone he'd seen when he was in the club — to a fireman.

Then he went back for another.

When the bodies had been cleared, Dougherty and the rest of the cops went down the stairs and left the firemen to do whatever it was they did.

Out front Dougherty had no idea how much time had passed since he'd first seen the flames coming out of the building — an hour? Three hours? There was still a big crowd all the way up Union to Phillips Square, and in the other direction Dougherty saw the rookie he'd told to direct traffic still standing on Dorchester waving cop cars in and out. He went up to the kid and said, "How you doing?"

"It's bad, isn't it?"

"The worst."

"Probably fifty trips to the hospital so far." The kid waved another cop car out onto Dorchester and looked at Dougherty. Dougherty didn't think he'd ever seen skin so white. He thought maybe that was just because every other face he'd seen for hours was covered with black soot but then he thought, no, this kid looks like he's going to pass out.

"Okay," Dougherty said, "keep the cars moving, we've got to be coming to an end."

The kid looked unsteady on his feet but he nodded and looked glad to have something to do.

Dougherty wandered back around the front of the Blue Bird and saw Logan talking to a couple of guys, saying, "He played the drums?"

One of the guys said, "Yeah, he plays drums. We're Don and Curly and the Dudes."

Logan was writing in his notebook. "You were the first one to see the fire?"

"Curly saw it, he stopped playing, he put down his guitar, told everybody not to panic."

Dougherty took a few steps away, the voice fading, ". . . tried to get everybody out, the windows were boarded up with plywood . . ." and he saw the night sergeant from Station Ten, Beauchamps, talking to a couple of detectives and the bouncer, guy named Riley, who was saying, "Around ten, ten thirty."

Riley saw Dougherty and said, "Eddie, you know that guy, Gaetan . . ."

"Gaetan who?"

"I don't know, sometimes he's in here with his brother, you had to straighten them out a couple weeks ago."

"Gilles Eccles."

"It was him I threw out tonight, him and a couple of his buddies."

"His brother?"

Riley thought for a second and said, "No, two other guys. They were all drunk, they came in and tried to sit with people they didn't know, they didn't want them, I had to get them out." He looked up at Dougherty and shook his head and said, "Eddie, man, the place was packed."

9

One of the detectives, a guy in his fifties Dougherty didn't recognize, said, "Do you know the other two?"

Riley said, "They're in here all the time, I don't know their names," and looked at Dougherty who said, "I've picked them up before, sometimes Eccles with his brother and another guy, O'Brien."

"That's right — Jimmy," Riley said. "He was one of them."

"But you don't know," the detective said, "if it was them who started the fire?"

Riley shook his head, he didn't know.

The detective looked at his watch and said, "*Bon*, it's after three, bars are closing." Then he looked at Dougherty and said, "Call the station, get addresses on these guys. Try to remember the other name."

"It'll be in one of the arrest reports," Dougherty said. "They've been picked up a few times."

He turned and took a step before he realized he didn't know where his squad car was, and as he was standing there one of the bartenders from the Wagon Wheel came up to him, looking like he wanted to say something, but Dougherty had to say, "What is it?" before the guy would say, "I don't really want to bother you, but . . ."

"But what?"

"Well, somebody rifled the cash register."

"What?"

"And a bunch of purses were stolen, the girls are talking about it over there."

Dougherty said, "Okay, well, tell them to come into the station tomorrow, okay? There's nothing we can do now."

The bartender said okay and started to walk away and Dougherty said, "Hey."

"What?"

"Try and keep them calmed down, okay?"

The bartender nodded, said okay and walked back towards the crowd. Dougherty watched him go, thinking the guy was still in shock, but hoping he could talk to the regulars, at least.

Then Dougherty saw his squad car on Dorchester, the front wheels up on the sidewalk, and he went to it and got on the radio to Station Ten and asked the only guy in the building to look up the arrest report on Gilles Eccles. "Drunk and disorderly back in July, I think."

"That's all you got?"

"There was one in the winter, too," Dougherty said, "fight in Atwater Park, with a drug dealer, I think, coloured guy, I chased him down St. Catherine, he broke a window in that store," Dougherty thought for a second and then said, "Cargo Canada. In the D&D there was another guy with him, Jimmy O'Brien, and probably another guy, I don't know his name but I need an address for him, too."

Over the radio the cop said, "That's all?" Sarcastic even now and Dougherty said, "As fast as you can."

The cop at Station Ten said, "Okay." Then he said, "How bad is it?" and Dougherty said, "Bad."

"They're saying on the radio more than a dozen killed."

"Yeah," Dougherty said, "more than a dozen."

Dougherty was standing beside the car holding the handset, the wire connecting it to the big radio on the dash stretched as far as it would go, looking over the scene. The two westbound lanes of Dorchester were blocked with squad cars, Union Street was filled with fire engines and there were hundreds of people just standing around.

A few minutes later the cop at Station Ten was back on the radio saying, "Okay, I got an address for Eccles: NDG, below the tracks, no surprise there."

"What about the other guys?"

"O'Brien is in Verdun but there's no one else on the report. I'll keep looking, last winter, and back."

Dougherty said, "Okay. What're the addresses you have?" The cop read out the street addresses and Dougherty ran back to the detectives.

"One's in NDG and one in Verdun."

"The third?"

"Still looking."

"Okay, get another officer and you each go and wait — maybe they'll go home. If they do, bring them in."

The other detective said something and then the two of them spoke quietly to each other for a moment. Dougherty couldn't make out what they were saying. Then the first detective nodded and said to Dougherty, "We'll get a coroner's warrant — with that we don't need to charge him with anything right away. You pick him up and bring him to Bonsecours Street. We'll find out if it was him."

"Okay." Dougherty ran to his squad car. He found the rookie who had been directing traffic standing under a streetlight looking dazed and gave him the address in Verdun and told him to go and wait there. "Park around the corner, try and stay out of sight, but watch the building. If anyone goes in radio right away." The kid nodded and got into a squad car and Dougherty watched him drive away, hoping he wouldn't crash.

Then Dougherty got into his squad car and backed out onto Dorchester. As he pulled away he looked into the rear-view mirror and saw firemen still working while some stood in small groups with cops, people wrapped in blankets sitting in the street.

It was bad.

Dougherty drove fast, the streets deserted at three in the morning, and got to Grand Boulevard in less than fifteen minutes. On the other side of the train tracks it was a wide, tree-lined street with nice, old brick houses, especially once it crossed Sherbrooke, but below the tracks Grand was a single block of three- and four-storey low-rent apartment buildings and some old fourplexes and walk-ups. Dougherty dumped his squad car behind some trucks in the parking lot of a landscaping company on St. Jacques and waited in the shadows across the street from Eccles's building.

He didn't have to wait long.

A grey Comet pulled up, and Eccles got out just after three thirty. Dougherty grabbed him. There was no fight, no struggle. Eccles had been drunk earlier but now he looked like he was in shock.

Dougherty said, "So, you know how bad it is."

Eccles started crying, saying, "We didn't want to hurt anybody."

Dougherty cuffed him and dragged him across St. Jacques to his squad car, put him in the back seat and then got on the radio and called it in.

The cop at Station Ten said the detectives would

meet him at HQ and Dougherty said okay.

He drove all the way to Bonsecours Street in Old Montreal with Eccles sobbing in the back seat.

An hour later Dougherty was standing in the parking lot behind the building having a smoke when Detective Carpentier pulled up in his own car, a Bonneville, and got out saying, "*Mon Dieu.*"

Dougherty had known the homicide detective for a few years, had been with him when they'd arrested a man they thought had killed five women, and he'd never seen him so shaken.

Carpentier looked at Dougherty and said, "*On dit peut-être plus de trente?*"

Dougherty spoke French, too, saying, yeah, it looked like more than thirty, and the detective said again, "*Mon Dieu.*"

Then Carpentier switched to English and said, "You have a suspect?"

"Yes. There are two more: we've got a man waiting at one of the apartments and this guy" — he motioned towards the building — "will give up the other one."

"They were thrown out of the club earlier?"

"They were drunk — the bouncer threw them out."

"And you're sure it was them?"

Dougherty took a drag on his cigarette and tossed the butt on the ground. "He's been crying since I picked him up, saying how they didn't mean to hurt anyone."

Carpentier nodded and walked past Dougherty to the doors of the police station saying, "Well, they did."

The sun was coming up then, and a little while later the parking lot started to fill up with people coming to the morgue to identify bodies. Dougherty recognized a few people, had nodding acquaintances with them, a couple he'd been in classes with at Verdun High School.

Then it was quiet for a few minutes, and Dougherty was thinking about going home when a car pulled up and a guy got out. Dougherty recognized him but couldn't place him. The guy was by himself and as he came towards the back door and saw Dougherty he said, "She wasn't at the hospital, she wasn't at the Royal Vic or the General or the St. Luc."

As he was talking, Dougherty realized he'd seen him the night before, outside the Blue Bird looking for his fiancée.

"They told me to come here."

Dougherty said, "Downstairs," and as the guy pushed past him into the building, Dougherty touched his arm and said, "You by yourself?"

The guy said yeah, and they looked at each other for a moment and then the guy went inside.

A little while later Detective Carpentier came out and stared up at the blue sky. He lit a cigarette and said, "Do you know where they bought the gas?" and Dougherty said no.

Carpentier didn't look at him, he just kept staring at the sky and said, "A gas station on de Maisonneuve." He took a drag and exhaled slowly, smoke coming out of his nose, and said, "Where his father was working. His father told him he was drunk and he should go home. One of the other guys . . ." Carpentier turned and looked at Dougherty and said, "You were right, he gave them up: it was O'Brien and another, Jean-Marc Boutin."

Dougherty nodded, "Yeah, I know him."

"Oh yes, they are what the newspapers will call 'known to the police.' Going back years."

Dougherty said yeah.

"They spent the day drinking, the three of them, on the South Shore, then they came to the club."

"Riley told me he kicked them out."

"They went to Club 67 — do you know it?"

"On Crescent."

"Yes, that's the one. They had a few more drinks and came up with their plan. The first gas station they went to wouldn't sell them any so they went to where Eccles's father was working. Eccles talked to him while Boutin filled the, how you say, *canne de gaz, rouge?*"

"Jerrycan."

"Jerrycan. And they went back to the Blue Bird."

"Where are the other two?"

"He doesn't know, he says he left them at Torchy Wharf, you know it?"

"La Tortue, yeah. It's in Verdun, bottom of Allard Street."

"He doesn't know where they were going — he thinks out of town."

Carpentier finished his cigarette and tossed the butt on the ground. Then he turned around and went back inside.

A couple of cops came out and squinted into the sun. One of them said, *"Tabarnak, je suis fucking fatigué."*

The other cop, an older guy probably in his late forties, looked at Dougherty and spoke English, saying, "There were two birthday parties in that club. One guy was turning thirty-nine, he was there with his wife." The cop moved his head a little, the smallest of motions towards the building and said, "They're both here. Four kids at home. Orphans now. The other one was turning twenty-one."

The other cop, the tired one, said, "*Deux filles là, quatorze ans.*"

Dougherty didn't say anything but he wasn't surprised to hear there were fourteen-year-old girls in a bar. Montreal, always a party town. Then he wondered if this would change that but didn't think it was too likely.

Then the older cop said, "*Bon*, better get some sleep," and looked at Dougherty. "You work tonight?"

"Yeah."

The other cop said, "You working the game?"

"What game?"

"*Quelle partie?* Come on."

Dougherty shook his head and said, "Right, shit." Then he said, "No, I'm on patrol."

"Me too, we're watching it at the bar in the plaza, Alexis Nihon."

"Not Toe Blake's?"

"Hey, we might get a call, and it would be too crowded, too tough to get out of there."

Dougherty said, "That's very conscientious of you," and the other cop said, "Eh?"

"That's good thinking."

"Oh well, it won't be much of a game, but fun to smack some commie bastards around, eh?"

Dougherty said yeah, and the other two cops walked through the parking lot towards the Métro station. He'd forgotten about the Summit Series, as it

17

was being called. After years and years of watching the Soviet so-called amateurs beat up on Canadian university kids at the Olympics and World Championships, Canada's pros were finally getting their chance at some revenge. Four games in Canada and then four games in Moscow. First one tonight at the Forum in Montreal. Be good, Dougherty figured, give people something to cheer about.

He walked to where he'd parked his squad car a few hours earlier when he brought in Eccles and as he opened the door he looked back at the building and saw a man coming out with his hands over his face. He was stumbling and shaking and Dougherty went to him, grabbing him by the arm and holding him up.

The guy was crying, sobbing, and Dougherty realized he was the one who'd been looking for his fiancée.

They stood there for a minute by the door and then Dougherty said, "Where do you live, where's your family?"

"I'm okay, I'm okay."

"Come on," Dougherty said, "where do you live? I'll drive you."

"No, it's okay." The guy took a deep breath and got himself under control. "I'm okay."

"Your parents, man, where are they?"

The guy took a couple more breaths, struggling to get air in and out, and then he said, "LaSalle, it's okay. I'm okay."

"I'll follow you."

The guy said he was okay again and walked to his car in a daze. Dougherty got into the squad car and followed him, onto the expressway at Berri, west through the Ville-Marie Tunnel and then to de la Vérendrye Boulevard through Verdun and into LaSalle.

When the guy pulled up in front of a two-storey duplex on 9th Avenue, Dougherty pulled over, too, and watched the guy go into the house. There were other people inside. It was quiet for a minute and then Dougherty heard the crying.

"Sixty-five cents for a pint? We should arrest you."

"You'd like to try, you would." The waitress had an Irish accent and Dougherty thought she sounded a little like his grandmother, but the wench outfit with the low-cut white blouse and the short skirt took away that image pretty quick.

Gagnon, who'd complained about the price, was saying, "It's fifty cents at the Royal," and the waitress said, "Ah, but they don't treat you so well," and Dougherty had a feeling her joking around was just about over as she put down six pint glasses, three in each hand. The place was packed with guys watching the game and the waitresses were hopping.

Dougherty handed her a couple of two-dollar bills and a single and said, "It's my round, thanks."

Canada had scored thirty seconds into the game, Phil Esposito banging the puck out of the air and past a Russian goalie nobody'd ever heard of.

Dougherty started his shift at six but got sent on a call right away and by the time he finally parked his squad car on Atwater across from the Forum he heard the eighteen thousand people inside cheer the second goal. It was looking like the rout everyone

19

predicted, but by the time he got to the Maidenhead bar at the Métro level of the Alexis Nihon shopping plaza across from the Forum, the Soviets had scored to make it 2–1.

Now Gagnon was saying it was great to see the commies get put in their place but one of the older cops, a guy named Duclos that Dougherty had never seen outside the station, said, "They're starting to look better, look at the way they move as a unit." Every guy at the table, half a dozen cops all in uniform, told him he was crazy.

Then just before the first period ended the Russians scored a short-handed goal off a two-on-one and Duclos said, "How do you get a two-on-one killing a penalty?"

The cops made Duclos buy the next round.

Dougherty got sent on another call. He had his walkie-talkie on his belt and when the call came in he looked around and saw he was the only one with a radio.

Duclos shrugged and said, "If you lose it or if you break it, you have to buy a new one out of your own pay," and Dougherty said, "Yeah, I know the rule," and Duclos said, "So, leave it in the station like everybody else."

The call was actually in the plaza — a couple of kids had grabbed some jackets from the Jean Junction and run. Dougherty brought Gagnon with him and they ended up chasing the kids up three flights of stairs and then back down, past the Miracle Mart and the Steinberg and the Vieille Europe food store and the poster shop and the movie theatre and finally caught them at the turnstiles to the Métro, almost at the doors to the Maidenhead.

Gagnon said, "You made us miss the game," and one of the kids said, "Screw you."

They were both teenagers, boys with long hair wearing t-shirts with images of rock stars with long hair, confident that they were still minors and nothing serious would happen.

Dougherty told Gagnon to take the jean jackets back to the store and he took the kids to Station Ten and dumped them in a cell. They were mouthy when he dragged them out of the Alexis Nihon but they got quieter in the squad car and had nothing to say at all in the cell. Dougherty figured it might make an impression and it might not, hard to tell these days, but it was pretty much all he could do. He phoned the manager of the store and sure enough the guy was just happy to get the jackets back and didn't want to have to go to court if it looked like the kids' parents could afford a lawyer. Dougherty told him, "Yeah, it looks like they can, addresses are in Westmount," so he let them go and drove the couple blocks back to the Maidenhead.

And was shocked to see the Soviets were leading 4–2.

The bar was quiet, shocked silence.

Duclos said, "It's 110 degrees in there and Sinden is only playing three lines."

Canada got one back but the Soviets scored three more and the game ended 7–3 for the commies. Huge upset. Unbelievable.

Gagnon said, "So much for eight games to none." The prediction every hockey expert had made. Eight easy wins for the Canadian professionals.

One of the other cops said, "Well, they've been training all summer, we've been playing golf," and a few guys tried to agree but it was half-hearted. The game hadn't been close.

"Oh, we'll win a couple," Duclos said, "but the bubble has burst."

"We'll win the next seven games."

"All right," Duclos said, "we have to do some crowd control," and he led the way out of the shopping plaza and onto Atwater.

The crowd was coming slowly out of the Forum. The people were upset about the loss but it looked to Dougherty like they were more in shock. And maybe when they got out of the steam bath that the inside of the Forum had become and into the cool night air they calmed down. Whatever it was, the crowd wasn't rowdy — they looked like the living dead.

Dougherty's radio crackled again and he took it off his belt and pressed the button, saying, "Go ahead."

The sergeant at Station Ten, Beauchamps, told him there was something suspicious on the stairs coming off Mount Royal at Peel and Dougherty said, "Suspicious?"

"That's what the call said, yeah."

"On the stairs?"

"That's right."

"Okay, I'll check it out."

He got into his squad car and was amazed that eighteen thousand unhappy people could disperse so easily and quickly. The bars had filled up, no doubt, and the Métro would probably be crowded for a while, but the streets were surprisingly empty.

Dougherty drove up Atwater to Pine, halfway up Mount Royal. He parked at Peel and stood for a moment looking at the cobblestone path leading to the stairs, the black iron railings on either side cutting through dark forest all the way up. He figured if it was an office building, the stairs would probably go up ten or fifteen storeys — the lookout at the top higher than any of the big downtown buildings, higher than the nearly fifty storeys of Place Ville Marie, and then there was the huge cross on top of that.

It was almost midnight by then and the area was dark and quiet so Dougherty turned on his flashlight and lit up the first section of stairs as far as the landing — maybe twenty stairs.

Nothing suspicious.

As he started up the stairs, trees on either side, he was hoping he wouldn't have to go all the way to the top, and then he realized he wouldn't.

Right there in the trees beside the first landing was the something suspicious.

Dougherty got out his radio and called in, saying, "I found it."

The sergeant said, "It is suspicious?"

Dougherty said, "Yeah, it's suspicious."

"What is it?"

"It's a dead body."

CHAPTER
TWO

"Male, white, mid-twenties."

"You sure it's a male, with that hair?"

"Yeah," Dougherty said, "he's got a beard."

"Of course."

Dougherty was standing on the landing looking down at Detective Carpentier. They were waiting for the assistant coroner and one of the other cops now on the scene to get the stretcher out of the black station wagon.

Carpentier said, "There's no blood."

"Not that I can see," Dougherty said. "Maybe on his back?"

Another flash went off, lighting up the area for a second, and the photographer, Rozovsky, said, "Maybe he broke his neck, maybe he fell."

The assistant coroner, LaPointe, was coming up the first set of stairs then, pushing past Carpentier and carrying one end of the stretcher, and he said, "Is that your expert opinion?"

"Oh no," Rozovsky said, "we'll have to wait days or weeks for an expert opinion."

LaPointe said, "Have you got enough pictures for *Allo Police?*"

Rozovsky climbed up a few steps and took a picture of the two police cars, Carpentier's unmarked car and the coroner's station wagon, and said, "Not much of a crime scene, *Allo* will only pay if this guy turns out to be famous."

LaPointe was at the body then and he looked up at Rozovsky, not sure if the police photographer was serious about selling pictures to the tabloid or not.

Dougherty said, "Maybe he was drunk."

"We'll find out," LaPointe said, "in a couple of weeks."

Carpentier said, "*Bien.*" Then he said, "Is Dr. Michaelchuk still at the morgue?"

"There was one more death," LaPointe said. "A woman who was crushed under the fire escape, she died today in hospital. That's thirty-seven."

Carpentier shook his head. There was nothing to say, it was overwhelming.

LaPointe and the other cop worked in the light from Dougherty's flashlight to get the body onto the stretcher and down the stairs.

Rozovsky said, "Here comes the press," and Dougherty looked down to see a man with curly red

25

hair down to his shoulders and a beard getting out of an old Ford.

"Logan," Dougherty said, "he's all right."

From the landing Dougherty watched the reporter, Keith Logan, look at the body on the stretcher and maybe recognize the guy but then maybe not. Dougherty looked out at the city. Even halfway up Mount Royal he was looking down on the top of a lot of buildings, the big black towers of Westmount Square, Alexis Nihon Plaza and the Forum, the searchlight on top of Place Ville Marie making its slow turn around downtown.

Logan climbed the stairs and said, "The call said something suspicious, I thought maybe it was a bomb."

Dougherty said, "We haven't had a bomb in this city in two years," and Logan said, "Last month, at the Forum, the Rolling Stones equipment truck?"

"Oh yeah, I forgot that," Dougherty said.

Rozovsky was packing up his camera and he said, "It didn't do much damage."

"We had a quote," Logan said, "somebody called the guy the world's dumbest bomber."

Dougherty shrugged. He watched Carpentier standing by the station wagon talking to LaPointe.

"We used the Mick Jagger quote, 'Why didn't that cat leave a note?'"

Dougherty said, "Yeah, that would've been good." and Logan said, "But now you have more info."

Dougherty shrugged again and said, "Not really."

"But something, what?"

"It's nothing you can put in the paper."

Rozovsky said, "Not in the *Gazette*, anyway."

Logan said, "I don't write for *Midnight* or *Allo Police* or any of them."

"Okay." Rozovsky started down the stairs.

Logan looked at Dougherty and said, "But I'd still like to know, I'm going to the Forum on Monday, what are the chances of another bomb?"

"What show is that?" Rozovsky said, "Alice Cooper?"

"And Dr. John," Logan said. Then he looked at Dougherty and said, "So what do you know about the bomb?"

"No one will care," Dougherty said. "It doesn't have anything to do with the Rolling Stones."

"The Forum?"

Dougherty turned and looked at Logan and said, "It's just a rumour, but it could be something to do with the trucking company they were using."

"Oh," Logan said, "union stuff?"

"Maybe, but not here. Company's based in Philadelphia. Anyway, it's just a rumour."

Logan nodded and said okay. He looked tired. "Wasn't even that big a deal on their tour, when they left here they got arrested in Rhode Island."

Dougherty said, "You don't know that guy, do you?"

Logan glanced at the stretcher being loaded into the station wagon and said, "I thought maybe I did, I thought I'd seen him around. Who is he?"

"Don't know yet, there was nothing on him."

"You think he got mugged?"

"No idea."

Logan said okay and turned to walk back down the

stairs, saying, "I just stopped by because the call said suspicious. I'm still talking to people about the fire." He stopped on the bottom step and looked back up at Dougherty and said, "Any word on the other two arsonists?"

"Not yet."

"Okay, well, see you around." Logan got in his car and drove away and the coroner's station wagon left a few seconds later.

Dougherty came down the stairs and stood beside Detective Carpentier.

"It didn't work out with the Morality Squad?"

Dougherty said, "You heard? Yeah, I don't know, they're just a little too . . ."

"Moral?"

"Something like that."

Carpentier nodded a little and said, "Well, it's serious business, it seems like there is a new topless joint every week in this city."

"Gotta check them all," Dougherty said.

"Yes." Carpentier let it go then and Dougherty was glad. Joking around was all well and fine but Dougherty, only five years on the force, was feeling his career stall. Not that he'd had any idea about a career when he signed up — all he wanted then was to drive fast and get a little action in — but here he was, overnight shift driving a squad car and every time it looked like he might get a promotion something screwed it up.

Now Dougherty was starting to feel he screwed it up himself. He just wasn't sure how.

A couple of years before, when bombs were going

off in Montreal every couple of weeks and when the British Trade Commissioner was kidnapped and the Deputy Premier of the province was kidnapped and murdered, Dougherty had worked pretty closely with Carpentier trying to catch a man they thought had killed five women. After that, Dougherty thought he'd get promoted to detective right away but instead he was sent back to driving patrols.

Now Carpentier was saying, "If this turns into something, I'll give you a call," and Dougherty said, "Thanks."

Carpentier got in his car and drove away. Dougherty stood there for a few minutes looking down at the city, the strange mix of shiny new fifty-storey office towers and two-hundred-year-old stone buildings, the three bridges crossing the wide St. Lawrence River and the South Shore suburbs beyond where Dougherty's parents had bought a duplex and settled in.

He figured it was after three a.m., checked his watch and saw it was three twenty, figured he could head back to Station Ten and by the time he wrote up his report it would be close to six, end of shift. He could get some sleep and then drive over the Champlain Bridge, have an early Sunday dinner with his folks before two days off and then days for a couple of weeks.

Or he could finish his shift and sleep until the next one started.

Dougherty got into his squad car and started it up and before he even put it in gear there was a call on the radio, a robbery at the Museum of Fine Arts.

"Is anybody else available?" Dougherty said. "I'm still at the crime scene on the mountain."

"Why are you still there, the body is long gone. Anyway you're three blocks away, you can be at the *musée* in two minutes."

Dougherty said, "Yeah, all right, on my way," and clipped the handset back to the big radio on the dash.

CHAPTER
THREE

The Montreal Museum of Fine Arts was on the north side of Sherbrooke between Bishop and Crescent, a fifty-year-old granite building about three storeys high. Dougherty drove around, past the big marble pillars in front of the doors, some architectural style he thought he should know but didn't, to the loading doors in the back.

A security guard was standing by the open garage door. Dougherty parked, got out of his squad car and said, "Are you all right?"

"Bastards tied us up, took us an hour to get free."

"How many?"

The guard spoke English with no accent, saying, "Three. I saw two of them, long hair, ski masks. One was French and the other one was English."

"And the third?"

"I'm not sure, I heard them talking but it was too far away to make out. I was doing my rounds on the second floor and then there they were. I have no idea where they came from."

"Two of them?"

"That's right, they told me to lie on my stomach and when I refused they fired two shots into the ceiling."

"You're okay?"

"I'm mad as hell."

"Are you working alone tonight?"

"No, Sam and Hughey are here, they were on the first floor, they heard the shots and came upstairs. The bastard thieves brought us all down here and tied us up."

"How did they get in?"

"I don't know."

Dougherty heard a car and turned to see another squad car. Behind it a big sedan pulled in and a man got out.

"That's Mr. Bantey," the security guard said. "Everybody else is out of town."

Another squad car pulled up then and Duclos got out. He looked at Dougherty and said, "Hey Eddie, long time no see," and Dougherty said, "That game seems like a long time ago. There was no trouble at the Forum?"

"No, but since the bars closed we've been getting more calls."

Constable Gagnon and a rookie Dougherty didn't recognize got out of the other squad car.

The guy who'd pulled up in the sedan, Bantey, came up to Dougherty and the security guard saying, "George, are you all right? How are Sam and Hugh?"

The security guard said, "Same as me, mad as hell."

"But they're not hurt?"

"No."

"That's good."

Dougherty said, "When did the alarm go off?"

The security guard, George, said, "After they tied us up they went and got some paintings and some jewellery, they were stacking it by the loading dock and one of them opened the side door, over there," and he pointed to a door beside the garage door. "The alarm went off then and they took off, maybe an hour ago."

"Why didn't we get the call then?"

Bantey said, "That door is just on an internal alarm, it only rings in the building."

Dougherty said, "So how did they get in?"

"I don't know yet."

Another car pulled up then, and two detectives got out. Dougherty recognized them as a couple of guys from the Night Patrol, the squad of detectives that worked all over the city, not connected to any particular station and not specializing in homicide or armed robbery or anything like that, just any crime that happened overnight. A couple of decades before, when they were cleaning up the city after the war, taking down the gamblers and bootleggers and pimps that had moved in to supply the soldiers and sailors on their way to Europe, the Night Patrol was legendary, like something out of a Hollywood movie.

Now Dougherty was thinking they were still like

something out of a Hollywood movie but there's a new Hollywood — *Easy Rider* and *Five Easy Pieces* and *The French Connection* — and there hadn't been a new detective added to the Night Patrol in a long time.

As Dougherty watched the two detectives walk up and start talking to the museum guy, Bantey, he figured the way his career was going, he might end up on the Night Patrol.

After a quick conversation Bantey turned and started towards the museum and the Night Patrol detectives motioned for Gagnon and the other rookie to follow them.

When they were out of earshot Duclos said, "How did you get put in with the old guys so soon?" and Dougherty said, "I don't know."

Duclos leaned back against the squad car and got out his cigarettes, offered one to Dougherty and they both lit up. Duclos blew smoke at the night sky and said, "Burglar alarms changed everything, you know."

"No, I didn't."

"We used to walk the streets, the beat, you know?"

"I walked a beat."

"Sure, for a parade or some special occasion. We used to walk all the time, we talked to people, we knew them all. Eyes and ears on the street."

"Then we got cars," Dougherty said.

34   "No, then we got burglar alarms. Wired right into the station houses. The alarms would go off and we'd have to check it out right away. Almost always it was nothing, a strong wind would shake the doors and set off the alarm. But we'd have to check."

Dougherty took a drag on his smoke and thought

he was glad to be driving around in a squad car instead of walking a beat, but he didn't say anything.

"At first it was just the big buildings, you know, and the big houses, rich people. But then everybody started getting the alarms. The insurance companies sold them, you know."

"I guess so."

"So now we drive around in cars and check burglar alarms and we don't know any of the people. Do you know any cab drivers?"

"Just the ones I arrest."

"My first arrest," Duclos said, and Dougherty noticed he was smiling, "was in the Point, you know it?"

"I grew up there."

"No kidding? Well, my first arrest, the first night I was walking my beat by myself, you know that *casse-croûte* on Rue Charlevoix?"

"Corner of Colerain, yeah, Paul's."

Duclos was nodding then, still smiling, "A cab driver called to me, said somebody was breaking into the store so I ran. There was a guy, older than a teen-ager but not much, climbing out the window from the basement. He had cartons of cigarettes, as many as he could carry. I grabbed him by the collar and I said, 'You're under arrest.' And then we just stood there, the two of us, and then the guy said, 'What are you going to do?' and I didn't know." Duclos laughed.

"Then," he said, "I saw the cab and I waved him over and I said, 'Drive us to the station house,' and we got in."

"Oh yeah," Dougherty said, "that's better than a squad car."

35

Duclos inhaled on his cigarette and let the smoke out slowly. "Maybe you're right, I don't know. I'm getting too old for this."

Dougherty said, "Me too," and wasn't sure if it was a joke or not.

Another car pulled up then, a Volkswagen Beetle, and a middle-aged woman got out. She walked up to Dougherty and Duclos and said, "I'm one of the museum curators of decorative arts. Mr. Bantey called me — there was a robbery?"

Dougherty said, "That's right, Mr. Bantey is inside with the detectives. What's your name?"

"Dorothy McIntosh."

"Okay Mrs. McIntosh," Dougherty said, "come on, I'll take you in."

"Miss McIntosh."

As soon as they walked into the big room on the main floor of the museum, Miss McIntosh stopped and said, "Oh my God."

The place was torn apart: there were broken frames and backings all over the floor, the display cases had all been smashed.

Dougherty and Miss McIntosh walked through the museum — every room had paintings missing, cut out of frames that were scattered on the floor — until they found Bantey and the detectives on the top floor and Miss McIntosh said, "Oh my God, Bill, it's devastation, they've completely cleaned it out."

"There's a lot piled on the first floor," Bantey said, "it looks like they opened the door accidentally and set off the alarm before they'd loaded everything. They just grabbed what they could then and ran."

Miss McIntosh said, "How did they get in?"

Bantey pointed up and said, "Looks like the skylight."

"But what about the alarm?"

"It was turned off during the repairs."

"They knew that? Someone told them?"

Bantey looked at the detectives and then back to Miss McIntosh and said, "I can't imagine that, we think it might have been someone on the construction crew. If it had been someone from the museum, as unthinkable as that is, then they would have known about the alarm on the door."

"Of course."

"We'll have to figure out exactly what's missing, come on."

Bantey and Miss McIntosh left then and Dougherty stepped up to the Night Patrol detectives and said, "*C'est vrai ça, à propos de l'alarme?*"

The detective shrugged and said, "Maybe. But maybe they did get what they wanted and set off the alarm so it wouldn't look like an inside job."

Dougherty said yeah and realized he wouldn't have thought of that.

Then one detective said, "Go outside and see how they got on the roof."

There were more cars by the loading dock then: Dougherty recognized a couple of reporters standing with Duclos and then he saw a van from CBC Radio setting up.

Next to the museum was a church and in the lane between the two buildings Dougherty found a ladder, probably left by the construction crew, and was able to lean it against the building and climb up. On the roof he walked towards the skylight and saw something he recognized — the same boot picks his father used to climb poles to install telephones. Dougherty walked back to the edge of the building and saw that the big tree was close enough for a guy to have climbed and then jumped to the roof. Then he could have put down the ladder and all three would be up.

Back at the skylight Dougherty realized it had been opened — not broken — and that a tarp was over part of it.

He went back in and told the detectives what he'd found.

A couple hours later Bantey and Miss McIntosh held a press conference on the front steps of the museum, a Beaux Arts building Dougherty had found out from a reporter, and they had a list of what had been stolen — eighteen paintings and thirty-nine pieces of jewellery and silver. The quick estimated value was about two million dollars. One of the paintings, which Bantey described as a "landscape oil, *Evening Landscape with Cottages*, by Rembrandt," was valued at a million dollars.

Dougherty was back at Station Ten a little after nine a.m. and told the desk sergeant he was checking out and he'd write up his reports later. It was Sunday morning and Dougherty was starting two days off before coming back for two weeks of day shifts.

The desk sergeant said, "The reports have to be handed in by this time tomorrow morning," and Dougherty said okay, but he'd still do them later.

When he'd first started working shifts the older cop who was training Dougherty, Gauthier, had said that when going from nights to days, the thing to do was stay up all day after finishing an overnight and go to bed as late as possible. Gauthier had laughed saying, "When I was your age that was eleven o'clock or midnight. Now I make it to eight, I'm lucky."

So Dougherty had some breakfast and went home and did some laundry and in the afternoon drove across the Champlain Bridge to Greenfield Park for dinner with his parents. As he pulled off the main drag, Taschereau Boulevard, into the suburb, he saw the Burger Ranch was closed and he thought that was too bad. It had been a kind of California-style drive-in, one of the first places Dougherty had gone when he got his driver's licence in his last year of high school. He didn't know many of the other kids there — his parents had only recently moved into the red-brick duplex in the subdivision and he was finishing high school on the island of Montreal in Verdun, but he met a few people that night.

Less than ten years ago and already it seemed like another era, a distant memory.

As he drove up Patricia Street, Dougherty saw his little brother, Tommy, and some other boys playing road hockey and heard one of them shout, "Car," as they pulled the nets to the curb to let him pass. He parked in front of the house on the corner, got out and heard one of the kids say, "All right, I'll be goalie, I'll be Tretiak," and he thought, Shit, one game and the kids want to be the Russians. Wait till they lose the next seven.

Going into the house, Dougherty realized it was Tommy being the Soviet goalie.

The first thing his mother said, standing in the kitchen with a dish towel in her hand, was, "Those poor people." She looked tired, her face drawn and her shoulders slumped.

Dougherty said, "Yeah, it's terrible."

"A fire like that is the worse." Her French accent was heavier than usual, she was so upset.

Dougherty said, "Yeah, it is," and she said, "All those people."

Then Dougherty's father came up the stairs from the basement, saying, "Son, maybe you can give me a hand," and Dougherty said sure.

In the unfinished workshop half of the basement Dougherty's father had the vacuum cleaner taken apart, and he said, "If you could just hold this wire while I get the screw in."

He didn't really need the help, of course, Dougherty knew that, and after a couple of minutes without either of them saying anything Dougherty realized that was the plan — a few minutes without talking.

When the new wires were spliced in, Dougherty's father thanked him and closed up the vacuum cleaner. Then he said, "You haven't had a minute to yourself, have you?"

"Not really, no."

"You get a drink with the other cops?"

"We watched the game."

"That's good."

Dougherty said yeah. He watched his father wind the cord and put the vacuum down beside the furnace and then he said, "I don't know how I'm going to sleep when it's dark."

His father said, "I know."

Neither one of them made a move to go upstairs. Dougherty wanted to say something but he couldn't come up with anything, and then his father pulled his pack of cigarettes out of the breast pocket of his shirt and held it out.

Dougherty took the smoke, and they both lit up.

Then his father said, "It never goes away. After a while it's not the last thing you think about when the lights go out."

Dougherty said, "You saw a lot of guys killed, didn't you?"

"Well, D-Day, yeah."

Dougherty didn't say anything and then his father said, "But before that, a few times. The *Charlottetown*, a Corvette I was on, sunk by a U-Boat."

"In the North Atlantic?"

Dougherty's father smiled and said, "No, just off Gaspé, in the Gulf of St. Lawrence. We were only going from Quebec City to Sydney, Nova Scotia." He paused for a moment and Dougherty waited — his father hardly ever talked about his experiences during the war and Dougherty realized he'd never really been interested before. He was a little ashamed of that but he just stood and waited, and finally his father said, "A torpedo hit us."

Dougherty had been expecting more and he looked a little surprised. His father said, "It was dark, we weren't expecting it. Torpedo hit and the explosion lit up the sky." His father shrugged a little and said, "Split the hull right down the middle. The ship just broke apart — guys were jumping off grabbing whatever they could." He paused and motioned with his hands and then turned them palms up and said, "The rest of the convoy went after the U-Boat. Never did get it."

"How long were you in the water?"

"A few hours, till the sun came up. It was a few more hours before we found out we lost eight men."

Dougherty didn't say anything, he just nodded and his father said, "Eight guys you knew, spent every minute with."

"Yeah."

"More after that, every time a convoy got hit, a few times in the North Atlantic."

"When I went into the Wagon Wheel," Dougherty said, "I saw the bodies under the tables. They looked like they were passed out."

"I can imagine."

Dougherty said yeah. "Some of them, you know, looked a little like Cheryl."

"I don't think she likes country music."

"Yeah, but . . ." and Dougherty realized it was a joke, a little gallows humour from his dad. Sure, his sister, Cheryl, twenty years old and still playing hippie music, still listening to Janis Joplin and Neil Young.

But the fire could've been in the Laugh-In or the Yellow Door or any club. It could've been in one where Cheryl and her friends were hanging out — Dougherty knew that and his father knew that.

Then Dougherty's mother was calling them for dinner and he and his father looked at each other and didn't say anything else, they just went upstairs. In the kitchen his mother said, "*Édouard, vas chercher Tommy,*" so Dougherty went out onto the front steps and saw the kids had stopped playing hockey and a couple were sitting on the curb and a couple of others were standing on the street holding their sticks like guitars, pretending to play.

Dougherty called for Tommy and his little brother stood up, grabbed his stick and ran into the house. As soon as he got in he said, "Are you working the Forum tomorrow night?" and Dougherty said, "No, why?"

"The Alice Cooper concert."

"You want to see that?"

"Yeah."

"Why?"

Tommy was past him and inside by then, shoes and coat off and sitting down at the kitchen table.

Dougherty said, "Where's Cheryl?" and his father gave him a look so he dropped it.

During dinner Tommy told them he was going to buy the new Jethro Tull album, *Thick as a Brick* — he heard it at Timmy Keays's house and it was better than *Aqualung*. Dougherty said, "Better than *Aqualung*?" and it took Tommy a couple of seconds to realize Dougherty was making a joke.

Then Dougherty said, "Are you going to watch the game?"

Tommy said, "You think the Soviets will win all eight?"

Dougherty gave his father a *kids today* look, shook his head and motioned to Tommy.

After dinner Tommy went into the basement, and a few minutes later his mother yelled at him to turn down the music, and Dougherty couldn't tell if he did or if the next song was just a little softer.

43

As soon as he could leave without looking like he was running off, Dougherty said he'd been up for over twenty-four hours and needed to get some sleep to start his day shifts and he left. It wasn't quite nine and he knew there was no way he'd fall asleep when he got home, no matter how tired he was, but he didn't know what to do so he stopped at the Fina station on Taschereau and got some gas and drove around.

He drove for a few hours, expressways mostly, and bridges, the Champlain, Jacques-Cartier, Victoria. He drove until the sun was coming up and then went home and fell asleep for a few minutes at a time all day.

Monday evening Dougherty went back to the Maidenhead tavern and watched Canada win the second game in the series 4–1 in Toronto. So much for either side winning eight games. Dougherty figured at least now it looked like it might be a series. Duclos had been right, the bubble had burst, the amateur Soviets were as good as the Canadian professionals, now they'd have to see who wanted it more, as the cliché went.

When he left the Alexis Nihon plaza Dougherty walked across the street to the Forum and asked the cop by the loading dock how Alice Cooper was doing, and the guy said, "*Y'a pas encore commencé.*"

Dougherty went inside and spoke to another cop who was standing in the hallway outside the dressing rooms who said, "*Il regardait la partie,*" and Dougherty said, "Guy wearing makeup, with that hair, wearing nylons and those boots? He's got a snake around his neck and he's watching the hockey game?"

"Apparently he's from Detroit."

Dougherty was thinking he'd grab a program or something for Tommy but he didn't see anything like that. He tried to hang around to see a little of the show so he could at least tell his little brother what it was like but the noise was too much. Maybe it was the bad sound in the Forum, but it didn't sound like music to Dougherty.

School's out, forever.

Tuesday the funerals started for victims of the fire, and late in the afternoon Dougherty was sitting on a stool at a lunch counter on St. Matthew finishing a souvlaki and watching the small TV on a shelf above the cash.

Pete Spirodakis was standing behind the counter, a white apron around his waist and a little paper hat on his head, and he was saying, "Can you believe this? And we're next."

Dougherty said, "What do you mean?" On TV was the scene at the Olympic Village in Munich. Some Israeli athletes had been taken hostage and cops and military guys were everywhere.

Pete said, "We're the next Olympics, in '76, this'll be going on here."

"You don't think it'll be all over by then?"

Pete laughed and said, "What, the Middle East? You've never been, have you?"

"No."

"How's it going in Ireland?" Pete said. "That all over now?"

"I don't know," Dougherty said. "I've never been there, either."

"You gotta see more of the world."

"Not if it's all like that."

Pete said, "It's not like that all the time." Then he looked up at the TV and said, "But you will be busy when that's happening here."

"If I'm still here."

"Ha, you'll still be on that stool — where do you have to go?"

"That's true."

Pete poured more coffee into Dougherty's mug and then went back to looking at the TV. The screen showed what looked like an apartment building, a window on the second floor, a guy wearing a white undershirt talking to someone on the ground.

Then a guy beside him in the window said something and was clubbed with the butt of a rifle.

Pete said, "AK-47."

Now the TV cameras were showing a man on the balcony, wearing what looked like a homemade ski mask. He stood on the balcony for a minute, looked down over the edge and then went back inside.

Dougherty said, "When did this happen?"

"This morning," Pete said. "They've been showing this all day."

An older guy came out of the kitchen then, shorter than Pete and wider, a fringe of hair around his bald spot, and he said something in Greek, waving his hands, and Pete said something in Greek and they went back and forth a bit. Then the older guy went back into the kitchen and Pete looked at Dougherty and said, "You're lucky you don't have to work with your father."

Dougherty said, "You like it," and Pete smiled a little and said, "Sometimes, yeah."

Then as Pete went and got a big bag of sugar and filled up the glass jars with the silver tops and little flaps over the spouts, Dougherty watched the TV reporters — sports reporters because that's who was covering the Olympics — explain that very soon the hostages and the kidnappers would be transported by helicopter to a nearby NATO air base where they'd get on a plane and travel to Cairo. The kidnappers had demanded the release of 234 prisoners being held in Israel and two members of the Red Army Faction being held in Germany, Andreas Baader and Ulrike Meinhof.

Dougherty lit a cigarette and dropped the match in the ashtray on the counter.

Pete said, "You think they're really going to let all the prisoners go?" and Dougherty said, "I don't know."

Then Pete said, "How many did the FLQ want released here, thirty?"

"Something like that."

"Bank robbers mostly, weren't they?"

"Guy who made the bombs," Dougherty said, "couple guys who killed the two clerks at the sporting goods store on Bleury."

"Oh yeah, I remember, they were robbing the place, shotguns and hunting rifles."

Dougherty watched the TV and Pete put a piece of pie down on the counter in front of him. Dougherty said, "Oh, no, that's okay." and Pete said, "On the house."

The two of them drank coffee and watched the TV until a reporter said that the German forces had attacked the kidnappers at the air base and freed all the hostages.

Pete said, "All right, this calls for a celebration, where you going tonight?"

"I'm going to bed."

"Oh, come on, you need to go out and get a drink. Where do you go, the Cock 'n' Bull?"

"No."

"They had their amateur night last night," Pete said, "did you hear about it?"

"No, what happened?"

"Turned into a wake, you know, for the people at the Wagon Wheel, went on all night, some of them came in here this morning when I opened up."

Dougherty nodded but didn't say anything and then Pete said, "The Clover Leaf?"

"I don't go to Irish bars."

"Not the John Bull? The Irish Lancer?"

"Where's the Irish Lancer?"

"In the LaSalle Hotel, on . . ."

Dougherty said, "Drummond."

"That's it."

"Not tonight," Dougherty said, "I'm going to get some sleep — I'm working in the morning."

Pete said, "Okay, but when I open my club, you're coming."

48   On his way out the door Dougherty said, "You got it."

He had nowhere to go, really, so he walked up and down St. Catherine Street a couple times, and he did stop for a drink, but not at one of the Irish bars — he stopped at the Rymark, a tavern. It was quiet on

Tuesday night, and Dougherty was surprised when one of the waiters climbed up on a chair and turned on the TV on the wall in the corner. There wasn't a hockey game, Dougherty knew that, and he was pretty sure if the Expos were playing the game was over. Then he saw the scene on the TV was the Olympic Village again, and the guy from *Wide World of Sports* was talking. He was looking bad.

Someone in the tavern yelled, "Turn it off," but the waiter turned up the volume and Dougherty heard the sportscaster say, "It's official now, we have the official word. We just got the final word . . . you know, when I was a kid, my father used to say, 'Our greatest hopes and our worst fears are seldom realized.' Our worst fears have been realized tonight. They've now said that there were eleven hostages. Two were killed in their rooms yesterday morning; nine were killed at the airport tonight. They're all gone."

There weren't many guys in the tavern and there wasn't much reaction. The waiter who'd turned on the TV was still standing on the chair and he said, *"Câlisse."*

Dougherty left thinking maybe Pete was right, maybe they would be busy in four years when the Olympics came to Montreal.

The next morning when Dougherty got to Station Ten to start his day shifts Sergeant Delisle told him there was some undercover work if he wanted it and Dougherty said, "What's it about?"

"Call CIB."

Dougherty stood at the front desk on the phone with a detective in the Criminal Investigation Bureau, being told there would be surveillance on some employees and a couple of art students who'd been working at the museum, when a woman came in to report a missing person.

Delisle took down the woman's information, and Dougherty was only half-listening, but when he hung up the phone, Delisle was saying, "*Comme tous les autre hippies ici,*" and Dougherty said to him, "*Oui, mais nous en avons trouvé un,*" and Delisle said, "*Ah oui, je l'avair oublié lui.*"

The woman said, "What is it?"

Dougherty said, "It might be bad news."

She frowned and nodded and Dougherty thought she looked like she'd gotten herself ready for it. Still, he knew when it actually sunk in it would be different.

"I have to go to Bonsecours Street now anyway, I can give you a ride if you don't have a car."

"What's at Bonsecours Street?"

"It's police headquarters," Dougherty said. "And the morgue."

CHAPTER
FOUR

Colleen said, "Yes, that's him. That was him."

Then she looked at all the other stretchers, more than a dozen, each with a body covered with a white sheet and said, "It's like on TV, except they're not covered in flags."

"These are the last," Dr. Michaelchuk said, "they'll be moved to funeral homes today."

Dougherty said to Colleen, "If you're okay, I can take you upstairs to talk to a detective."

In the police car on the drive over, after the awkward bit where she'd started to get into the back seat and Dougherty motioned to the front and she'd said that was usually how she rode in cop cars, she'd told him that she'd come to Canada with the guy they were likely going to see.

Dougherty said, "Where are you from?" and she said, "Before here, Wisconsin, Madison, you know it?" and Dougherty shook his head. He knew she wanted to talk and had learned the best thing to do when someone wanted to talk was to let them. It took a few minutes but then she said, "Before that I lived all over. My father's a professor. Well, he is now. David and I, we weren't really a couple, not really, not for long. High school sweethearts, I guess. I moved to Madison my senior year, didn't know anybody. David was nice to me. But by the time we got here, it was just, you know," and Dougherty said, "Yeah."

Then she'd brightened and looked at Dougherty and said, "It might not be him," and Dougherty'd said, "Yeah, might not be."

Now, in the elevator, she started to cry.

When the doors opened on the third floor, Dougherty took her by the elbow and moved her down the hall and said, "There's a washroom," and she nodded a little and went in.

Dougherty waited a minute and then lit a cigarette and leaned back against the wall.

"Changer l'uniforme pour des jeans déchirés et voilà."

Dougherty said, "Detective Boisjoli."

The detective switched to English then, saying, "You look just like a student, standing around with nothing to do."

"I brought a woman from Station Ten to identify a body," Dougherty said and motioned to the washroom door. "She knew him."

"*Je suis désolé.* Someone close to her?"

"Yes."

"All right," the detective said, and then, motioning down the hall, "Is it a homicide?"

"Looks like it."

"*Bon.* Then come and see me."

"Yes, sir."

Dougherty watched Boisjoli walk down the hall and into the CIB office. He'd known the detective when the guy was working out of Station Ten, before his promotion.

When Colleen came out of the washroom she said, "Thank you," and Dougherty nodded and led the way to the homicide office. He could tell she'd been crying but it looked like she'd pulled herself together.

In the office Detective Carpentier stood up from his desk as they approached and Dougherty said, "Detective Carpentier, this is Colleen Whitehead, she just identified David Murray as the man who was found on Mount Royal."

Carpentier pulled a chair closer, saying, "Please, sit down." Then he said, "Would you like a cup of coffee or tea or something?"

Colleen said, "No, I'm fine."

Dougherty started to leave, but as Carpentier was sitting down he motioned for him to stay so Dougherty did, standing behind Colleen's chair.

"*Bien,*" Carpentier said, "I am very sorry for your loss, Miss Whitehead."

"Thank you."

"May I ask, what was your relationship with Mr. Murray?"

"We were friends. I was telling officer . . ." she looked up at him and Dougherty said, "Constable Dougherty. Édouard." Then he smiled and said, "Eddie," and she said, "I was telling Constable Dougherty here that David and I came to Montreal together from Wisconsin."

"When was that?"

"Two years ago, November sixteenth, 1970."

"You remember the day?"

"When you leave your country and you know you're never going back, it's a big day."

Carpentier nodded as he was getting out his notebook, but Dougherty didn't really get it.

Colleen pulled a pack of Du Mauriers out of her purse, and slid out a cigarette. Dougherty lit a match and held it for her as Carpentier said, "Mr. Murray was a draft dodger?"

She tilted her head back a little and exhaled smoke at the ceiling. Then she said, "No, he was a deserter."

Carpentier wrote it down and Dougherty was a little shocked she could say something like that so easily.

She took another drag on the cigarette and said, "It sounds awful, that word, deserter," and Dougherty heard himself say, "Yeah."

She turned a little and looked at him and said, "It's a lot more complicated than that."

54 Dougherty didn't say anything. He was thinking, Yeah, it must be, but he didn't really believe it.

"When he enrolled at the University of Wisconsin he got an education deferral from the draft, but after a couple of years he dropped out and he got his notice."

Carpentier wasn't writing anything down but he

nodded and said, "That's when you came here?"

"No, David went to basic training. He could've registered at some other school, got another deferral, got a note from a friendly doctor, tried to fail his physical, claimed to be a homosexual — there are all kinds of ways."

She paused then and Dougherty watched her smoke and waited and then she said, "David said he didn't want to lie."

Carpentier was nodding but Dougherty didn't get it: why didn't the guy just do his duty?

"By then a couple of his friends from high school had gone and come back. Well, one of his friends, Stephen, didn't come back, but the ones who did, they told him not to go."

She took another drag and leaned closer to Carpentier's desk so she could reach the ashtray.

Carpentier said, "He couldn't be a conscientious objector?"

"No," Colleen said, "he's Catholic. He was Catholic. The Church isn't opposed to the war so the government wouldn't grant him objector status. We were pretty deep into the anti-war movement by then, that's why David dropped out of school — he was always organizing and going to demonstrations and marches."

"So he left his basic training and you came here?" 55

"He was going to finish it," Colleen said, "and do his tour and come back and join the VVAW, the Vietnam Veterans Against the War, or something like that, but he couldn't do it."

"The training?"

"Basic Killing, he called it. He said you really have to get kids young to train them for that. But he was really torn, he didn't want to break the law but he didn't think the government should be able to force him to go to another country and kill people."

"It's good to have a country to come back to, though," Dougherty said.

Colleen turned a little to look at him and Dougherty realized she was probably about his own age, twenty-six, maybe a couple of years younger, and she said, "Do you feel threatened by some peasants in rice paddies ten thousand miles away?"

"They're communists," Dougherty said, "and they're getting a little backup from some bigger countries."

"Are they?" She turned back and looked at Carpentier and said, "Anyway, David said it was a matter of personal liberty, the government didn't have the right to make him kill people."

Carpentier said, "We have had our issues with forced conscription here, too," and he glanced at Dougherty and said, "*Te souviens-tu des croix de guerre?*"

Dougherty had a vague memory of history class at Verdun High, something about conscription during the First World War and French-Canadian families, rural families, farmers, putting up crosses asking God to save their sons from the army recruiters, but he just shrugged and shook his head.

Carpentier was already looking at Colleen and said, "But whatever his reasons, you came to Montreal."

"Yes. We weren't a couple by then, we were just friends — close friends, part of the same group — and

56

we felt the same way about the war and about our government and we decided to come here and protest the war from here."

"That was two years ago."

"Yes." She paused and even Dougherty could tell there was something else that she didn't want to say.

Carpentier looked at Colleen and waited and finally she said, "David didn't get his landed immigrant status."

Carpentier said, "He didn't," and Colleen said, "No." She paused again and then she said, "We weren't really sure how it worked — we just drove here. We told people we were going to Cape Cod and then when we got to Vermont we just crossed the border and came to Montreal. When David went to the Council, they told him he had to apply before he came into Canada."

"What council is this?" Now Carpentier was writing something in his notebook.

"The Council to Aid War Resisters. This is before there even was the Deserters Committee."

Dougherty said, "The deserters have a committee?"

Carpentier ignored him and said, "So what did you do?"

"The Council has volunteers. I became one myself, so did David. We drive guys back over the border and they tell the truth." She glanced at Dougherty and then looked back at Carpentier. "Each immigration official at each border crossing has their own discretion. There's a point system they're supposed to follow."

Carpentier said, "Supposed to?" and she said, "Well, they follow it for things like education level and work experience and that kind of thing, but there's a

57

lot of points at their discretion."

Dougherty said, "Do you lose a lot of points for being a deserter?" There was more of a sarcastic edge than he'd wanted and Colleen looked at him for a moment and then looked back at Carpentier and said, "No."

Then she took a last drag and stubbed out the cigarette in the ashtray and said, "Since Kent State and the invasion of Cambodia there've been so many more coming that the immigration guys at the borders have really tightened up."

Or, Dougherty thought, started doing their job.

Carpentier said, "But regardless of his immigration status, David was in Montreal?"

Colleen nodded. She looked around the office and then she said, "We crossed back into the States. I thought we'd go back to Wisconsin, but he didn't want to go to jail. He said he wouldn't be able to protest the war from a prison cell."

"So," Carpentier said, "you snuck into Canada?"

"I was accepted as a landed immigrant and finished my degree at McGill. David came in through the underground. There was talk about going to Sweden, but it seemed so far away. For a while David said he was going to go back to the U.S. and try to get in legally, but he was working for the Council and then the Deserters' Committee, he was busy."

"How did he make money?"

"I don't know."

Carpentier said, "It could be important."

"I really don't know."

"I understand you don't want to get anyone in

trouble but someone killed David and we need to find out who that was."

Colleen got out another cigarette, but this time Dougherty watched her get out her own matches and light up. She took a deep drag and exhaled and then said, "At first I worked, I got a job at McGill, in the library, and we lived with other people, other Americans." She took another drag and said, "But after a while David started disappearing for days at a time. I don't know what he was doing."

"Was he still living with you and the others?"

"I moved out last year, but as far as I know David was still in the house."

Carpentier said, "When was the last time you saw him?" and Colleen said, "Before this morning?" Carpentier didn't say anything and she said, "I don't know the exact day, last week, before the fire at the club."

"What did you talk about?"

"Nothing really."

"How did you know he was missing?"

"Oh, well, he wasn't there, at the house, on Sunday. It was a potluck, we were planning a rally for McGovern."

Carpentier said, "In Montreal?"

Colleen blew out a long stream of smoke and said, "Yes, on the McGill campus. There are a lot of American students here who can vote."

"But David wasn't at dinner?"

"No."

"And," Carpentier said, "none of his roommates reported him missing?"

"Well, like I said, he disappeared for days at a time."

"But there was something about this time that was different?"

"Just that," she paused, started to lift the cigarette to her mouth and stopped and said, "just that he said he would be there and usually he was good for his word."

"But the roommates didn't think it was unusual?"

"We talked about it," Colleen said, "but to be honest, they don't trust the police. Any authority. There are FBI agents in town, CIA, that kind of thing."

"I don't think the FBI can work in Canada," Carpentier said and Colleen took a drag on her cigarette and blew out smoke saying, "Maybe not officially."

Carpentier nodded and said, "*Bien*. What is the address of the house and the names of people living there?"

Dougherty watched Colleen, and he thought she looked like a suspect who didn't want to give up an accomplice, and then Carpentier said, "We're not interested in anyone's immigration status, we're homicide."

She nodded and smoked and then said okay and nodded again. "They really don't like dealing with police."

She glanced at Dougherty and then Carpentier said, "We won't wear uniforms when we visit the house."

Now Colleen was smiling and she said, "You think that'll make a difference?"

Carpentier smiled, too, and said, "I suppose not."

CHAPTER FIVE

Dougherty figured there were probably three or four thousand people in the park and at least half of them were carrying candles. There was a stage set up at one end and serious-looking men were giving speeches.

The guy Dougherty was following had left his basement apartment in a squat, three-storey red-brick building on St. Kevin near the corner of Côte-des-Neiges Road and walked a few blocks through the neighbourhood. Dougherty was sure the guy hadn't seen him, hadn't seen him since he'd left the museum a couple hours earlier. Now as they got to the park, the ceremony, or whatever it was, was already going and it took Dougherty a few minutes to realize it was a vigil for the athletes killed in Germany. He heard a man onstage saying, ". . . a senseless, barbaric massacre of innocents. Their only crime was to compete for their nation. What sort of victory is this, this slaughter?"

Then he noticed the flags, Canada, Quebec and Israel, all over the crowd.

When the guy had left his apartment, Dougherty'd hoped he was going to a bar to watch the hockey game, Canada and the Soviets in Winnipeg.

Now there was a guy on the stage giving a much more fired-up speech, but the audience wasn't really going for it. The guy ended by saying, "Never again, never again, never again," but barely anyone clapped for him.

Dougherty looked around, not sure exactly what was going on, and then he heard the click of a camera and saw Rozovsky coming up to him saying, "Nice you came, but you're not JDL, are you?"

"What?"

"Jewish Defense League." Rozovsky motioned towards the stage and then said, "No one's in the mood for it, these people came to mourn."

Dougherty said yeah, and then moved a little closer to Rozovsky and said, "I'm working," and Rozovsky nodded, understanding, and said, "Bomb threats?"

"No," Dougherty said, "not this, something else."

Rozovsky shrugged and said, "I'm working, too."

"Oh yeah, which newspaper?"

"Don't know yet, *Canadian Jewish News* probably, maybe get some out on the wire." He looked around at the crowd, mostly older people, some kids, not many in their mid-twenties like Dougherty, and Rozovsky said, "It's not a student rally, that's for sure," and Dougherty said no.

Onstage a rabbi was leading a prayer and then the crowd sang a song Dougherty didn't know. Rozovsky said, "'The Hope,' Israeli anthem," and Dougherty said okay. Then the crowd sang "Oh Canada," and Dougherty sang along a little with "True north strong and free" and "We stand on guard for thee."

As the crowd was walking away, Dougherty heard a man with a beard and a yarmulke saying, "It's terrible — young men with their whole lives ahead of them, victims of a war older than they were," and a woman saying, "We came from Poland to escape the hate, can't we ever have peace," and then he heard men's voices saying that they should invade Lebanon and Jordan and bomb them into dust, finish it.

Rozovsky said, "We can still catch the third period, hear Foster Hewitt mangle the Russian names." and Dougherty said, "No worse than he mangles Yvan Cournoyer."

"Where did you park?"

"I can't," Dougherty said, "I'm working."

"Oh yeah, you said."

"I can't talk about it."

Rozovsky said, "Sure, sure, top secret, very important," backing away. He snapped Dougherty's picture and then turned and walked into the crowd.

Dougherty shook his head and watched him go, then watched the guy he'd followed to the vigil, Norm Mullins, a janitor at the museum, make his way through the crowd towards Queen Mary Road. He was an older guy, and Dougherty figured he was the same age as his father, mid-fifties. When Detective Boisjoli had given Dougherty the assignment he'd told him everything they knew about Mullins — his schedule at the museum, his address, the fact he lived alone. And that was it. Boisjoli said he thought the guy had been in the infantry in the war, but he wasn't sure.

Now Dougherty followed Mullins through the neighbourhood, mostly two-storey brick houses, duplexes and some apartment buildings. On Côte-des-Neiges, Mullins went into a *dépanneur* and came out a few minutes later with a paper bag that looked to have a couple of quart bottles in it — Dougherty guessed Molson Ex, but he couldn't be sure.

Then Dougherty followed Mullins to his apartment building and watched him go inside, saw the light in the basement window come on and then the flicker of the TV and then, standing on the sidewalk across the street from the apartment building, Dougherty felt that everyone was looking at him, that there were faces in every apartment window and every car that drove by was going too slow.

Crazy.

He walked back to Côte-des-Neiges and went into the first bar he saw, just in time to catch the third period, the game already tied 4–4. The place was crowded and Dougherty stood at the end of the bar closest to the door and ordered a draft.

The bartender brought the beer and said, "You don't want to see it, anyway," and Dougherty realized he'd been looking out the window of the bar across Côte-des-Neiges to the apartment building.

"Not bad, 4–4."

"We were up 3–1," the bartender said. "could have been 8–1 if it wasn't for that goalie, and their first two goals were short-handed. How do you do that?"

Dougherty said he didn't know, and the bartender said, "You watch them move, they're always moving, and they throw the puck around all the time, all those short passes — you know what they look like?"

"Organized?"

"They look like Eddie Shore's teams in Springfield." He looked up at the TV on the shelf behind the bar and said, "Except they're in a lot better shape than Eddie's teams ever were."

An old guy sitting at the bar said, "We'd be in better shape, too, if it wasn't pre-season — you think they could get away with this in March?" and the bartender said, "Yeah, I do."

There wasn't any scoring in the third period and when the game ended the old guy said, "Well that's okay, we're just getting our legs, we're going to win the rest of the games."

"In Moscow?" The bartender was shaking his head.

Dougherty had been keeping an eye on the apartment building across the street, but he'd seen enough of the game to know the bartender had a point, the four games coming up in Moscow would be tough.

"We win the next one in Vancouver," the old guy said, "and go to Russia up two wins to one with a tie and that'll do it."

The bartender looked at Dougherty as he was picking up his empty glass and said, "One for the road," and Dougherty said no, put a two-dollar bill on the bar and said, "Keep the change."

"Thanks, boss."

Outside the bar, Dougherty took another look at

Mullins's apartment, the light from the TV still flickering, and figured that was it for the night. He got on the bus and rode it down the hill to Sherbrooke, and then walked a couple blocks to Station Ten and was surprised to see the place hopping — half a dozen cop cars lined up out front on de Maisonneuve and plenty of guys coming and going.

Dougherty walked into the station and a young cop, the rookie Dougherty had directing the traffic at the Blue Bird fire, saw him and said, "'*Eille, t'as manqué tout le fun.*"

Dougherty said, "What happened?"

The rookie spoke French, telling Dougherty everybody on duty had gone on a drug bust at an apartment on Lincoln and the haul was huge.

Dougherty tried to remember the kid's name but he couldn't, and the kid went on, saying there were five people in the apartment when they got there and two more came in while they were there, "*Mauvais timing, eh?*"

Dougherty said, "Yeah, some bad timing. What did you get?"

"Liquid hashish, *beaucoup.*"

One of the detectives, Lamothe, said, "*Plus de cent mille dollars.*" and Dougherty said, "Really? A hundred grand just in the apartment?"

Lamothe said, "No, but we found a key to a locker at Gare Centrale, and it was there. Thirty pounds."

"And that's a hundred thousand dollars' worth?"

"Ten bucks a gram," Lamothe said. "On the street."

Dougherty said wow, but was thinking ten bucks seemed too much. He didn't say anything and then the kid said, "*Et aussi quatre livres de hash noir et du LSD, plus d'une centaine de tabs.*"

"All that was in the apartment?"

"*Oui.*"

Then Lamothe said, "Hey Dougherty, we're processing them now and they're all English. You want to play detective?"

Dougherty said, "Okay." He was still on duty, his shift had started at four when Mullins finished at the museum and would continue overnight. Then he remembered the rookie's name and said, "Unless Aubé wants the practice." and the kid said, "*Non, ça va.*"

The drug dealers, the alleged dealers, the way Dougherty knew the detectives would say it, were in the cells at the back of the station house, six men and a woman — a girl, really. She looked like a teenager.

Dougherty walked back and said, "Who's next?" and no one said anything so he pointed at the guy closest and said, "Come on, write a confession, you'll feel better."

The guy said, "I have nothing to confess."

"Of course not," Dougherty said, unlocking the cell.

At an empty desk in the bullpen, Dougherty put the blank report into a typewriter and rolled it into place. Sitting there in his jeans and old Leo's Boys football jacket Dougherty felt like a detective. The guy sitting across from him was trying to look bored and annoyed, but Dougherty knew a few hours in the station and the guy would start to get nervous. Spend the night in Parthenais jail and he'd be a wreck. Dougherty said, "Name," and the guy said, "Wilson, Duncan."

"Where do you live, Wilson, Duncan?"

"The Holiday Inn."

"Not where you're staying," Dougherty said, "what's your permanent address?"

"That's it, that's where I live."

"The one on Sherbrooke?"

"Yeah, just up the street."

"What's the address?"

The guy said he didn't know, and Dougherty typed in *Sherbrooke Street* and figured he'd get the numbers out of the phone book later. Then he said, "You're American, aren't you?" and Duncan Wilson just shrugged.

"How long have you been in Canada?"

"A few months."

"Are you a draft dodger," Dougherty said, "or a deserter?"

"That's not on your form."

"Are you here on a student visa?"

"No."

"Are you a landed immigrant?"

"No."

Now he was starting to look a little nervous, so Dougherty said, "Well, that's okay, you're American so your embassy will take care of you," and Wilson, Duncan nodded, admitting that was true and maybe not liking the idea very much, but sitting in a police station he'd take it, and then Dougherty said, "Do you know a man named David Murray?"

It caught him off guard and he shook his head and said, "No," but Dougherty was sure he'd seen a reaction to the name.

"Okay. Date of birth?"

Ten minutes later Dougherty had all the basic information from Duncan Wilson and he took him back to the cells and brought out another guy and filled out his form.

When all the arrest reports had been filled out and the suspects were piled into a paddy wagon and taken to Parthenais jail in the east end, Dougherty looked at the addresses and saw there were five Americans altogether: Duncan Smith, the girl and one other guy were from Brooklyn, another guy was from Clintondale, New York, and another guy was from Bethel, Vermont. One of the other guys lived on Prud'Homme in NDG and one guy said he was an engineer from some place called Gernersgade in Denmark.

It was a little after midnight, Dougherty's shift was over but before he clocked out a call came in about a dead body in the Atwater tunnel and he said, "Some rummy get run over?"

The desk sergeant starting his overnight shift said, "No, the call said a young guy, still has the knife sticking out of his chest."

CHAPTER
SIX

The body was in the curb lane on Atwater, just as it came out of the underpass below the raised Ville-Marie Expressway.

Detective Carpentier said, "If these guys were territorial I'd say this was a message," and Dougherty said, "But these guys are — oh, I get it."

"St. Henri Dead Men," Carpentier read, touching the dead man's leather jacket with his toe. "Appropriate name. More than he wanted it to be, I would expect."

Dougherty said yeah. He was looking through the underpass and up the hill towards St. Catherine Street and the Forum and Atwater Park. "I guess they were moving up from St. Henri into downtown."

"It would be very tempting for them," Carpentier

said. "A bigger market for their hash and speed."

The dead guy, the Dead Man, was on his back, a big knife still buried in his chest but there wasn't much blood on the street so Dougherty said, "He was killed somewhere else and dumped here?"

"Looks like it," Carpentier said. Then he looked at Dougherty in his jeans and football jacket and said, "You're not on duty?"

"I was on surveillance but he went to bed. I was at the station house when this call came in."

"Now you want to work this one, too?"

"I wanted to talk to you about something else, about David Murray."

Carpentier moved away from the body and towards his car. The two northbound lanes of Atwater had been blocked by a patrol car and the traffic, what there was of it, diverted into one of the southbound lanes through the underpass. A couple of uniformed cops were direct-ing the cars, keeping one lane moving in each direction.

At his car, Carpentier lit a cigarette and said, "We haven't even spoken to the roommates yet, what did you find out?"

"Nothing really," Dougherty said. "But I helped process some drug dealers who were picked up tonight and most of them are Americans."

"Oh, I see," Carpentier said, "and David Murray had no status, no landed immigrant papers, no student visa."

"He had to make a living somehow."

"He was already in the underground."

"He was already sneaking back and forth across the border."

Carpentier smoked and said, "They were all Americans with the drugs?"

"No, there was a guy from NDG and another guy from Denmark, but all the others, five of them, are Americans."

"It's interesting," Carpentier said.

Dougherty was glad the detective agreed and said, "It's worth looking into."

"Yes," Carpentier said. He leaned back against his car and looked around and said, "All these drugs, it's not good."

"No," Dougherty said, "it's not." He looked at the detective, thinking for the first time that Carpentier was looking old, and the next thought that came into Dougherty's head was that he was counting on Carpentier to get him a promotion. He felt a sharp pang of guilt for being so selfish. Standing over a dead guy around the same age as he was and all Dougherty could think about was how that could help him at work. Shit.

Then Carpentier said, "*Bien*, do you want to come with me tomorrow, talk to the roommates?"

"If you want."

Carpentier smiled and said, "Come on, it could be good for you, do a little detective work."

Dougherty said, "Okay." Then he motioned back to the Dead Man and said, "What about him?"

Carpentier said, "*Un à la fois, novice,*" and Dougherty thought, Yeah, sure, one at a time, but I'm not a rookie anymore.

The next morning, Dougherty was called in to Bonsecours Street at eight a.m. along with the other cops who were working surveillance of the museum staff and the detectives who were running the investigation.

They were told there hadn't been any new evidence, but now the museum staff was saying maybe the thieves had been more selective than they'd thought.

Standing at the front of the room Detective Boisjoli spoke French, saying, "The museum director has now, grudgingly, admitted that the burglars chose," and he checked his notebook and read, "an interesting selection from an interior decorating point of view." The cops in the room chuckled and Boisjoli said, "So, it appears they were working to order. Likely the men who entered the museum were local but know nothing about art."

Dougherty was looking around the room at the other young cops in plainclothes, all as excited as he was about their surveillance assignment and all trying to look just as blasé about it. A couple of guys he'd never seen before really did look like they could be university students, their hair was already touching their collars, and they hadn't shaved in days.

"It's the Rembrandt," Boisjoli said, "that's the key. In the past few months Rembrandts have also been stolen from museums in Worcester, Massachusetts, and Tours, France."

One of the student-looking cops held his hand up a little, and when Boisjoli nodded at him, he said, "Do either of those look like inside jobs?"

Boisjoli nodded. "In Massachusetts two men walked into the museum when it was open, put the Rembrandt, two Gauguin, and a Picasso into bags, put on ski masks and walked out. They weren't reported immediately because people thought they were part of the construction crew."

There was a lot of murmuring about another museum under construction and then Boisjoli said, "Both museums being under construction may be coincidence. There was no construction in Tours, they simply smashed a window." He checked his notebook again and said, "At that time a Rembrandt and a Jan van Goyen was stolen."

"So," one of the other detectives said, "we're looking for a fan of Rembrandt?"

Cops laughed and Boisjoli said, "The museum director said these paintings would be appropriate in a single collection. Also, there have been some recent arrests of art thieves, one in Italy and one in London, England, an art dealer, William Horan, who was selling stolen paintings, two of which belonged to Queen Elizabeth."

The cop next to Dougherty leaned closer and said, "*Volés à ta reine,*" and Dougherty said, "She's not my queen," but the guy didn't seem to get it — Irish, English, all the same to him.

"The paintings are probably in the collection of a Greek tycoon or a Texas oil millionaire, something like that," Boisjoli said, "but the thieves are probably still in Montreal." He looked at the detective who'd made the joke and said, "Anything on the men who were watching the museum?"

A couple of guys said, "What?" so the detective said, "We have been told that for a couple of days there were some men on the roof of the apartment building next to the museum, sitting on lawn chairs, smoking cigarettes." He shrugged, clearly not putting much weight to the report. "We did find a lot of cigarette butts on the roof, but that's all. No one in the building knows anything about it, and the only description we have is that they were wearing sunglasses."

"So," Boisjoli said, "someone who worked in the museum was likely paid off by the thieves. Keep looking."

Then Boisjoli and the other detective gave out some new assignments, and Dougherty and the others were told to keep their surveillance routines.

The meeting broke up, and Dougherty went down the hall to homicide to look for Carpentier. The big office was almost empty except for one detective sitting at a desk by the window, tapping at typewriter keys one at a time in a slow, deliberate march. He looked up when he saw Dougherty and said, "*Retourne au hall, à la salle de défilé.*"

"No, the meeting is over," Dougherty said. "I'm looking for Detective Carpentier."

The typing man swivelled a little in his chair and looked at Dougherty and said, "*À cette heure?*"

Dougherty said, "*Oui.*"

"*C'est les homicides ici.*"

Dougherty was thinking, You're here, but he let it go and the detective switched to English saying, "Homicides usually happen at night."

"I know," Dougherty said, "I was with Detective Carpentier last night at the scene."

"He was up all night with the mother of that biker,

hearing stories about what a nice young man he was, how he loved dogs and kids. You were there?"

"No, he did that with Detective Marcotte. This is for a different homicide, David Murray."

The detective nodded and said, "Oh yes, the American," and he picked up some folders on his desk and looked through them saying, "Not much in that file."

"Not yet."

Then the detective looked at Dougherty and said, "You're going to fill this?" He held up a folder.

"I'm going to work with Detective Carpentier, yeah."

"Bonne chance."

The woman said, "You don't remember me?"

Dougherty said no.

"You arrested me last year."

"I can't remember everyone I arrest."

"Yeah, I guess, you bust so many people."

"Just the ones that break the law." And then, before she could say anything Dougherty said, "And it wasn't last year, it was the year before."

They were standing on the sidewalk in front of the house on Hutchison Street, three storeys with an iron staircase coming straight down from the second floor, not the winding stairs more common on old Montreal houses. The McGill students who lived in the neighbourhood called it "the ghetto," but Dougherty had a feeling the permanent residents raising their kids didn't think of it like that.

"You and the army, you dragged us out of bed."

Carpentier, standing on the sidewalk beside Dougherty, said, "Why does every person say the army was in their house when we all know every arrest was made by the Montreal police."

"It was in St. Henri," Dougherty said. "We had a tip an American wanted for murder was staying there."

The woman said, "Murder? I don't think so."

"His bomb killed a man," Dougherty said, "at the University of Washington."

"Wisconsin."

"You see," Dougherty said, "you know all about it."

"And so do you."

Dougherty nodded a little. That was true, he'd recognized her right away. It was the workboots she was wearing, probably the same ones she'd been wearing when he'd brought her in along with the other members of the St. Henri Workers' Collective, though then, and now, it looked like she was doing most of the work herself. Today she had a bag of groceries in one hand and a stack of mimeographed posters in the other.

"You've changed," Dougherty said. "Moving up the hill has been good for you."

"And arresting innocent people has been good for you," she said, motioning to Carpentier, and Dougherty realized she thought he was a detective now. He let that go and then she said, "Anyway, haven't you heard? We're getting kicked out."

77

Dougherty said, "Yeah, I've heard something." He'd been to a few of their demonstrations protesting against the high-rises some big developer was trying to build, arrested a few people, but not this woman. He said, "What's your name?"

"You can look it up in your files."

Carpentier stepped up then and said, "Look, miss, we're not here about any of that, or any of your other issues, we need to talk to you about David Murray."

"Never heard of him."

Dougherty was surprised — it was such an obvious lie, he wondered why she'd even bothered — but before he could say anything Carpentier said, "We're just trying to find out who killed him, perhaps you can help."

"No, sorry."

"We're trying to find out where he was on Saturday, who he was with."

"I don't know."

"He lived here?" Carpentier said, looking up the stairs to the second floor. "May we see his room?"

"No, I don't think so." She looked from Carpentier to Dougherty and then back to the detective and said, "You can talk to our lawyer. They have all the information at the Council office."

Carpentier said, "Is that really necessary?"

"I think it is, yes."

Dougherty was about to leave but Carpentier said, "Mr. Murray's parents will be here later today. Their son has been murdered, and we'd like to be able to tell them we're doing everything we can and that his friends are cooperating."

The woman considered it and then nodded a little and said, "All right, come in."

They followed her up the stairs and into the building and waited while she walked down the hall and put the bag of groceries in the kitchen. Dougherty looked into the living room while they were waiting and saw the usual things he saw in student apartments: old couches, mismatched chairs, posters on the walls. Here, though, there were a few posters of impressionist paintings mixed in with Che and Jimi and notices about rallies and demonstrations.

She came back from the kitchen and said, "This way," and they all went up the narrow stairs to the third floor.

"David hasn't been spending much time here."

She opened the door at the end of the hall but didn't go into the room.

Carpentier said, "Was this unusual?" and she said, "What's usual these days?"

Dougherty walked into the room and thought it was true, it didn't look like anyone had been spending much time in it recently. There was a single bed with a pillow and a blanket in a heap on the middle of the mattress and a dresser against the wall. Dougherty took a step to the window and didn't think it could be opened, there were so many coats of paint on the trim and the frame.

Carpentier, still in the hall, said, "When was the last time you saw David?" but before the woman could answer a man's voice said, "Don't say anything."

Dougherty couldn't see the guy coming up the stairs but he knew what he'd look like: young, long hair, beard, jeans, jean jacket — maybe leather jacket.

The woman said, "They're homicide detectives."

"They're pigs, they shouldn't be in here — they don't have the right."

Now Dougherty could see it was actually a corduroy jacket, but otherwise the guy looked just like he'd expected. Maybe a little older.

Carpentier said, "Did you know Mr. Murray?"

"Get out. You have no right to be in here." Then the guy looked at the woman and said, "Why did you let them in? What's wrong with you?"

She was already walking away, saying, "Oh for Christ's sake."

The guy turned to Carpentier and said, "You have to leave, right now."

Dougherty said, "Answer the question: how well did you know David Murray?"

"I don't have to answer any of your questions."

"You don't have to," Carpentier said, "but it might help."

"I don't help cops."

Dougherty turned back to the dresser and started looking through the stack of books, mostly paperbacks, and the guy said, "Stop that, you can't do that."

Carpentier said, "We understand David was expected for dinner on Sunday but he didn't arrive. When was the last time you saw him?"

"I'm not answering any of your questions. I'm calling my lawyer."

Dougherty said, "You all have lawyers?"

The guy said, "Clearly we need them," and he turned and walked down the stairs.

Carpentier said, "Anything?"

"Maybe he was homesick." Dougherty held up a photograph that had been under the stack of paperbacks that showed a slightly younger, clean-shaven

David Murray standing beside a woman who was probably his mother in front of a small house.

"Maybe."

Dougherty took a last look around the small room and said, "Nothing else, but he must have had somewhere else he was living."

"Yes." Carpentier started down the hall and Dougherty followed him.

As they came down the stairs Dougherty heard some shouting and banging of dishes, so he pushed past Carpentier and headed towards the kitchen yelling, "Hey!"

The woman was backed up against the sink, the guy right in her face.

Dougherty said, "All right, back off," and the guy turned, wild eyed and red in the face, and he said, "You get out."

Now Dougherty was a constable again, feeling familiar territory and he easily took charge, saying, "That's enough," and moving between the man and the woman.

She said, "I don't need your help," and Dougherty was staring at the guy, looking him right in the eyes and the guy said, "Yeah, you get out."

Dougherty was still moving and the guy didn't even seem to realize he was backing up himself, moving down the hall towards the front door where Carpentier was waiting. Dougherty said, "Talk to Detective Carpentier."

Then Dougherty went back to the kitchen and the woman said, "You do need to get out of here."

"If that guy thinks he's a peace activist, he's still got a few things to learn."

"And you're going to teach him?"

"If I have to."

"You need to get out."

They were looking at each other and Dougherty started to feel there wasn't anything he could tell her she didn't already know, so after a moment he nodded and started to walk away but he turned back and said, "You know, asshole trumps everything. No matter what people believe in or anything like that, an asshole is always an asshole."

"I'll remember that."

The tension was letting up, no doubt, and Dougherty stopped by the doorway to the hall and wanted to say something else but he couldn't think of what to say, so he just nodded again and turned and walked down the hall.

Outside, Carpentier was standing by himself on the sidewalk and Dougherty said, "What did you do to him?"

"He remembered a more pressing engagement he needed to attend."

"Just like that, he remembered?"

"Just like that. But he was right, we should talk to the lawyer. Come on, the office is on the next block."

Dougherty said okay, and they started walking. Carpentier said, "You're single, aren't you?" and Dougherty said, "What do you mean?"

"You two," Carpentier said, "flirting, talking about old times."

"I don't even know her name."

"No," Carpentier said, "but like she said, you can look it up."

"At least you admitted you're cops."

Carpentier said, "Of course."

The bearded man was coming around the desk in the small office, saying, "We're never sure who we're dealing with here."

"As I said, we're homicide detectives."

Dougherty liked Carpentier saying that, even though he knew it was just to make talking to this guy easier.

They were in the office of the Montreal Council to Aid War Resisters on the main floor of a three-storey walk-up at 3625 Aylmer, a block over from Hutchison. Down a few steps from street level was the Yellow Door Coffeehouse and the top floor was still an apartment. There were a few other offices in what used to be bedrooms and the living room of the main floor: Planned Parenthood, Legal Aid and the Milton Park Defence Council, where Carpentier and Dougherty had stopped first, but there was no one there, just a note taped to the door saying deliveries should go to the War Resisters office.

"It's still such a shock to think that David was murdered."

Carpentier said, "Yes, of course." He and Dougherty had stepped into the small office and Carpentier had done all the talking, saying they were trying to find out who killed David Murray. The bearded man looked suspicious, but Dougherty thought Carpentier was doing a good job of putting him at ease.

Then Carpentier said, "But he was among the underground?"

The guy smiled and shook his head a little and said, "It's not like that."

"No? What's it like, Mr. . . . ?"

The guy looked at Carpentier for a moment and then said, "Gardiner, my name's Bill Gardiner."

Carpentier shook his hand, and then Gardiner said, "Come on, why don't we get some coffee downstairs?"

Lunch service was finished but there were still a few people in the coffeehouse playing cards and a couple of guys playing chess. Gardiner went to the counter by the door to the kitchen and got himself a mug and picked up the coffee pot, holding it up to Carpentier and Dougherty who both said, "No, thanks," at the same time.

Gardiner poured himself a cup and said, "They have hot apple cider if you want," and this time Dougherty kept his mouth shut while Carpentier said no thanks.

They sat down and Carpentier said, "What can you tell us about David Murray?"

"Maybe you can tell me what you know first."

Dougherty said, "We know someone caved in his skull."

"That's what happened?" Gardiner said. "I don't know any of the details."

"We're trying to find out who would do that, why they would do it. If Mr. Murray was in the underground he may have dealt with," Carpentier paused and then said, "unsavoury people."

Gardiner laughed a little and said, "That's a good word, very French, I like that," and then looked at Dougherty and didn't say anything else.

"We know that Mr. Murray was denied landed

immigrant status and wasn't able to get a job legally," Carpentier said. "Do you know how he was making his living?"

"I know he wasn't making much of a living. I told him, like I tell so many of the others who come in here, you can't speak French, you should go to Toronto or Calgary."

"But he didn't take your advice?"

Gardiner looked at Carpentier and said, "No. He hung around. He works for us, he volunteers, he does some work for our sponsors and they slip him a little cash. Slipped him, I guess."

"What do you mean," Carpentier said, "sponsors?"

"People who support us financially. We get a little from the United Church, from some Quakers, the QFL and from individual donors. And we raise money ourselves putting on concerts here at the Yellow Door, Jesse Winchester, the McGarrigles, Louise Forestier and sometimes bigger places. We had Pete Seeger at Place des Arts, did you see that one?"

"No," Carpentier said, "I didn't see that one."

"It was good. We tried to get Joan Baez but she said the men should go to jail rather than come here."

Dougherty said, "That's easy for her to say."

Gardiner said, "Yes, well, anyway, David did work for us and for some of the private donors, work in their houses, that sort of thing."

"It's quite a network," Carpentier said.

"Built up over years. As the war in Vietnam gets bigger, so does the fight against it."

Dougherty said, "And the number of guys running away from it?"

"They aren't — we aren't, I'm one of them — running away, Detective. All due respect to Joan Baez, but we feel we can do more to protest the war from here than we could from jail cells."

"So you saw Mr. Murray frequently?"

Gardiner looked at Carpentier for a moment and then said, "Not really. The thing is, Detective, when American men first started coming to Canada in '67, '68, they were — we were — mostly of a type." He drank some coffee and got a pack of cigarettes out of his jacket pocket.

Dougherty watched him light up, wanting one himself and wanting to jump in with more questions, but he could feel Carpentier beside him waiting, giving Gardiner all the time he needed to say too much or the wrong thing.

Blowing out smoke, Gardiner said, "I'm not saying we were better or anything like that, but we were mostly better educated, college graduates, from good families, and we were political, we were making the best choice out of what was available. We were refusing to fight an unjust war."

A man at a table in the corner said, "That's check and mate," and laughed. Another man said, "Again," and the sound of the chess pieces banging on the board bounced around the room.

86

Carpentier waited, and after a moment Gardiner said, "At first when the deserters started to come to Canada we didn't know what to do with them and they formed their own group. They were different, you see — some had been to Vietnam, done a tour and were supposed to go back and do another and some had deserted during basic training. They were generally . . . not all, of course, but most, were more what you might call working class."

You might, Dougherty thought, and he almost said, Or you might call them guys like me.

"Good men," Gardiner said, "but they often had different issues. Some had barely made it through high school."

Dougherty said, "So?" with more of an edge than he wanted.

"It just made it difficult to find work for them, Detective." Gardiner drank more coffee, smoked and then said, "And a lot of our volunteers who let young men stay in their homes until they get settled here are professors and other professionals and it could some- times be . . . difficult with some of the deserters. And, of course, it's harder for deserters to get landed immi- grant status — it's a point system, you know, and being a college graduate gets you quite a few points."

Dougherty nodded and hoped Carpentier wasn't too upset with him for jumping in, but then Gardiner said, "Canada and the United States have a special agreement to return men who desert from ships or units stationed in each other's country, but it doesn't apply to men who enter the country in normal civilian ways."

A man came into the coffeehouse then and looked at Gardiner, looked like he wanted to come over to the table but stayed by the door.

Gardiner said, "I'll be with you in a minute," and then looked at Carpentier. "I have a meeting. But look, David was very helpful when the two groups, the deserters and the resisters, merged into the Council. He was in some ways the ideal liaison: he had a couple of years of college and he'd been through basic training. He could talk to people, you know?"

"Yes," Carpentier said, "it can be valuable."

"But after the merger, and after the trip to Toronto where we met with the other groups and issued our statement, after all the press, David started to keep more to himself and we didn't see him as much."

Carpentier said, "Do you know who he was associating with the most?"

Gardiner stood up and said, "I'm sorry, I really don't. Colleen knew him best. If she doesn't know then I don't think anyone else involved with the Council will know."

"And what about," Carpentier said, "some of the donors whose houses David worked in? Can you give me their names?"

"No, of course not. Look, Detective, you may very well be sincere in looking for whoever murdered David, but our experience with the police hasn't been . . . well, it hasn't been very good."

"I can get a court order."

"You can try," Gardiner said.

"All right, well, thank you for your time." Carpentier stood up and shook Gardiner's hand and watched him go back upstairs, followed by the guy who'd come into the coffeehouse and had been waiting by the door.

Outside, as they were walking back to the car, Carpentier said, "It seems your theory may be correct," and Dougherty was happy to hear it but he didn't know what to say so he just said, "Oh?"

"Mr. Murray may have been involved in criminal activity, possibly something to do with drugs. Smuggling, perhaps."

"It doesn't look like he was killed over territory," Dougherty said. "He wasn't dumped anywhere, just left where he was killed."

"That may not mean anything."

"Right. So what now?"

"Keep asking questions."

"Who do we ask?"

Carpentier stopped beside his car and lit a cigarette. "Back to Colleen Whitehead, I suppose."

"Back to her?"

"Yes. What's the problem, you think we're going in circles?"

"I don't know."

"You want to be a detective," Carpentier said, "this is it. Boring, isn't it?"

Dougherty wanted to say no, it's not, it's a lot better than wrestling with drunks in bars and fighting with drug dealers in parks in the middle of the night and shoving your face between raging pimps and their whores, but he just said, "It's okay."

"Okay," Carpentier said. "Yes, it's okay. If we find the murderer."

89

CHAPTER
SEVEN

Her name was Judy MacIntyre.

Dougherty had worked another shift doing surveillance on Mullins from the museum — watching him go home and fall asleep in front of the TV again — and then in the morning it was back to Station Ten for a day shift that he started by going through the files.

Judy MacIntyre had been picked up as part of the St. Henri Workers' Collective twice, once by Dougherty in an early morning raid looking for a couple of Americans who'd set off a bomb at the University of Wisconsin and once as part of a sit-in strike at a shoe factory. She'd also been picked up once as part of the Milton Park Defence Committee.

The first two charges had been dropped before they

got to court but the Milton Park charges were still pending and Dougherty noted the court date was set for October 2nd, a few weeks away.

He also noticed her date of birth was November 2, 1948, so she was twenty-four, just a couple of years younger than he was, and she was born in the Reddy Memorial Hospital in Montreal. The address on the first two arrest reports was the house in St. Henri where Dougherty had picked her up in 1970 and for the third arrest it was the house he'd just been to on Hutchison, but he had a feeling Judy MacIntyre had grown up on the West Island: Dorval or Pierrefonds or farther out in the suburbs.

Delisle came up behind him then and said, "'*Eille, as-tu une minute?*"

"For you," Dougherty closed the file, a little surprised that Delisle wasn't even looking over his shoulder to see what it was, and said, "anytime."

"Ha ha."

Then Delisle stood there for a moment not saying anything and Dougherty said, "So, what is it? *Un seau d'marde?*"

"Yeah, yeah, lots of problems I have, but that's not it. Look, Dougherty, it pains me to say this." He paused and Dougherty was thinking, Okay, so don't say it.

"The thing is," Delisle said, "you're good at this."

"What?"

"I know, I know," Delisle said, "I didn't think you would be, either, but here we are, you're one of the best patrolmen I have."

Dougherty nodded a little, still surprised, and didn't say anything.

"I send you out on a call you always stay with it till it's finished."

"Yeah."

"You never call, say there's nothing you can do, you never ask for help when you don't need it."

Dougherty said, "Yeah," still having no idea where Delisle was going with this.

"So, the thing is, you have a future here."

"I do?"

"Don't give me that shit, you know you're one of the best."

Dougherty started to say, Best of a bad bunch, but he stopped himself. He still didn't know where Delisle was going, but now he wanted to find out.

"Why you want to go running around playing detective?"

So that was it. Dougherty said, "I'm not missing any shifts. I'm never late."

"*Exactement*," Delisle said. "You're good at this."

Dougherty said thanks, and Delisle shook his head and said, "As much as I hate to say it."

Dougherty thought he really did hate to say it. Well, not really, Delisle seemed to like the idea that one of the patrolmen in his station was good, he just wasn't thrilled that it was Dougherty. Or maybe Delisle was okay with that, too — Dougherty couldn't always tell when he was joking and when his hang-dog, put-upon look was serious.

But Dougherty knew this wasn't the time to say how every patrolman wanted to be a detective and how every detective wanted to work in homicide. It was the top of the heap, wasn't it?

No, this was the time to just shut up and listen. Maybe Dougherty was learning.

"You keep working like you do," Delisle said, "and it will go well for you."

Dougherty said, "Okay, thanks."

"*Bien*, now here's a call for you, apartment building on Tupper, a car in the parking garage broken into."

"Again?"

"She's in the lobby."

Dougherty checked out a squad car and drove the few blocks to Tupper, just below St. Catherine. The street was only a few blocks long and lined with mostly old two-storey stone walk-ups but a few tall steel and glass apartment buildings had gone up in the last couple of years and Dougherty found Debra Rankin in the lobby of the one at 2121.

She was sitting on a couch smoking a cigarette and she stood up when he walked in and said, "Officer."

He held out his hand and said, "Dougherty."

"I guess you want to see the car?"

Dougherty said sure and followed her through the lobby and past the elevators to a stairwell thinking it had been a couple years since he'd been disciplined for asking out a woman while he was on duty and if he was going to get written up for it again this Debra Rankin might be the one.

And then he was thinking, Why did I look up the file on Judy MacIntyre? Some hippie in torn jeans and a peasant blouse, that wasn't his type. Debra Rankin in her miniskirt and tight sweater, she was his type.

"I thought it was safe down here: it's always locked and you need a key to get in."

93

They came out of the stairwell into the underground parking, all concrete pillars and fluorescent lights.

"No," Dougherty said, "what happens is a guy waits outside the garage door and comes in after one of the building tenants drives in."

"But you need the key to get out, too."

"Same thing. After they get everything they can out of the cars they wait for someone to leave."

She stopped walking and said, "You mean they might have been down here while I was here?"

"It's possible."

"Oh my God, well, now I'm really glad I'm moving." She started walking again and Dougherty was right beside her but he didn't say anything.

"Here it is, this is mine." She stopped.

Dougherty said, "What is it?"

"It's a Datsun, B210. It's Japanese."

"Do you pedal it?"

She twisted her red lips in a half-smirk, half-smile and raised an eyebrow. "These cars are all over Japan, they're going to be big."

"They're not big now."

"It's brand new," she said, "I just bought it."

It was the smallest, most orange car Dougherty had ever seen. A two-door sedan, it was practically square. "So," he said, "what was stolen?"

94

"A couple of boxes, all kinds of things. I'm moving."

"It's not May move."

"I don't have a lease," she said. "I have roommates. I'm a stewardess with the Montreal-Vancouver-Tokyo run, that's where I saw these cars." She glanced at her little orange car and then looked back at Dougherty.

"Now you're getting your own place?" Dougherty thought they might have started flirting when he asked her about pedalling the car and now the way she was looking at him, blue eyes under blue eyeshadow, he was feeling pretty sure of it.

"Now I'm getting different roommates. In the Swingles building."

"The what?"

"'When you get married, we'll ask you to leave.'" She laughed a little, but Dougherty didn't think she was nervous. "Have you seen their ads in the *Gazette*?"

"No, I must have missed those."

"The Royal Dixie," she said. "In Dorval. 'The building where you must be single and like to swing.'"

"Sounds like quite the place."

"So," she said, "could you live there?"

Dougherty said he could and wrote down the address and phone number, and then she said, "But I work odd hours," and he said, "So do I."

She didn't say anything and Dougherty said, "So we should probably pick a time for dinner right now, to avoid all those missed phone calls."

"You move pretty fast."

"Well, you know," Dougherty said, "this is dangerous work, you never know what could happen."

"Taking reports about cars getting broken into?"

"I just started this shift. You wait till tonight."

She was smiling a little. "Okay."

"I've got a rare Saturday night off this weekend."

"I don't fly out till noon on Sunday."

95

"There's a steakhouse out on the Metropolitain, isn't there?" Dougherty said. "Past the airport in Pointe Claire?"

She said, "There sure is."

———

The man was about the same age as Dougherty's father, around the same age as Detective Carpentier.

Dougherty watched them, both men looking up at the twin spires of Notre-Dame Basilica, and Chuck Murray said, "It looks just like the one in France."

Carpentier said, "Have you been?" and Murray said, "In the war."

Dougherty wondered if he went inside that time. They were standing across the street in Place D'Armes waiting for Murray's wife to come out of the big church, and Dougherty was keeping quiet and watching Carpentier talk to the father of a murdered son.

"I never made it overseas," Carpentier said.

Murray nodded a little and Dougherty got the feeling this guy didn't talk much about his war years. Like Dougherty's father, it was a big part of him but too personal. And then Dougherty wondered how the guy felt about his son running off to Canada.

"You know," Carpentier said, "the only man buried here in Notre-Dame is English. A protestant named O'Donnell, the architect who designed the building. He did convert on his deathbed."

Dougherty couldn't tell if Carpentier was just making conversation or if brought up the idea of burial to get Murray talking about a funeral and then talking about his son. One thing Dougherty had noticed with

Carpentier was that the line between what was work and what was personal was vague at best. The detective always seemed to be gathering information but he rarely made it seem that way, and now Dougherty was wondering if that was something he could learn just by watching. He didn't like the idea of trial and error, that kind of error with a grieving relative seemed like too much.

Chuck Murray said, "It's a beautiful building, real workmanship."

"Are you a builder?"

"Not really," Murray said. "I'm a machinist, but I've done a little building, enough to appreciate it."

A few tourists were going in and out of the church but it was the middle of September and the summer crowds had thinned out.

After taking the report from Debra Rankin, and making the date, Dougherty had gone back to Station Ten and got the call from Carpentier telling him that the parents of David Murray were in town. Carpentier asked Dougherty to come to Bonsecours Street and meet them, and by the time he'd got there they'd already arrived and walked the few blocks to Notre-Dame.

Now Chuck Murray was saying "Here she is," as a woman came out of the church and crossed the street.

Carpentier said, "Mrs. Murray, this is Constable Dougherty," catching him by surprise and Dougherty held out his hand.

Mrs. Murray took Dougherty's hand in both of hers and held on. She looked him in the eyes and said, "You found David."

Dougherty said, "I was first on the scene, yes."

"It must have been difficult for a young man like you — had that happened before? Had you been first on the scene before?"

Dougherty said, "Yes." He didn't know what else to say. Mrs. Murray was still holding his hand, still looking at him. "The night before there was a fire," Dougherty said. "Quite a few people were killed."

She grimaced. "We heard." Then she glanced back at Notre-Dame and said, "People are lighting candles." She still had kind of a dreamy look on her face but it started to fade as she said, "Oh my, were you on the scene there, Constable?"

"Yes."

"Such a terrible time."

"Yes."

No one said anything for a moment and then Carpentier cleared his throat and said, "Would you like to have some lunch?"

Chuck Murray said, "Might as well," at the same time his wife said, "Oh no, that's all right," and then they looked at each other and she said, "Maybe a little something."

Carpentier took them around the corner to a small restaurant that was almost empty now that the lunch hour was over.

When they sat down Mrs. Murray looked at the menu and said, "What's *pâté Chinois*?"

Carpentier said, "It's a kind of casserole with mash potato," his French accent coming out just as his voice trailed off a little and Dougherty said, "It's shepherd's pie."

After they ordered, roast beef sandwiches for Chuck

Murray and Dougherty, shepherd's pie for Carpentier and Mrs. Murray, Murray said, "This fire, it was arson, wasn't it?"

"Yes," Carpentier said, "I'm afraid it was."

"And you caught them?"

"One of them," Carpentier said, "and we have identified two more."

"And you're still looking for them?"

"That's right."

"So," Murray said, "is anyone looking for the guy who killed my son?"

Carpentier said, "Of course," and Murray looked at Dougherty and then back to the detective and said, "Just you and a constable?"

"We've interviewed your son's roommates and a lawyer with the War Resisters Council," Carpentier said. "Do you know anyone else he had been associating with?"

Mrs. Murray said, "We didn't talk much lately."

Murray said, "You talked to him." He looked at his wife and she nodded a little.

"I did. He phoned sometimes."

"And you phoned him."

Dougherty got the feeling this was something the Murrays fought about and he glanced at Carpentier to see if he was going to push it, maybe get them fighting now so they'd say more than they wanted to but it didn't look like it.

Mrs. Murray said, "I did, it's true." She looked at her husband and said, "I phoned my son."

Now Murray was nodding a little himself and Dougherty couldn't tell if he was angry or not.

When the silence at the table started to get awkward, Carpentier said, "When was the last time you spoke to David?"

"A few weeks ago. There wasn't anything unusual."

Carpentier said, "The lawyer we spoke to said that David became a little withdrawn after the trip to Toronto and the statement."

Murray looked at his wife and said, "What statement?"

"About the amnesty."

"Oh, for Christ's sake."

Something else they fought about, Dougherty figured.

Carpentier said, "I don't know about this amnesty."

"A few resister groups from all over Canada got together in Toronto," Mrs. Murray said. "Back in January. They issued a statement saying they rejected the amnesty proposals that are being talked about."

"They don't want amnesty?" Carpentier said.

"I'm not sure of the details. They said something about the amnesty, the way it was worded still had them guilty."

"They are guilty," Murray said.

Mrs. Murray looked at Carpentier and said, "They claim they're the ones who refused to commit the crime — they say the whole Vietnam War is a crime."

Murray was shaking his head but he didn't say anything.

"And they say the amnesty offered doesn't have the same provisions for deserters as it does for draft dodgers."

Dougherty was looking at Murray when his wife said the word deserter and he saw him wince but it looked like it might have been more pain than anger.

Carpentier said, "This amnesty, it is happening soon?"

"Oh, it's just election talk," Mrs. Murray said.

"And do you think David became more withdrawn after the trip to Toronto?"

She took a moment and then said, "Maybe. It's been very hard on him. On all of us. People think . . ." She stopped and took a breath and then said, "People think he was just afraid to stay in the army, to go to Vietnam, they think he just ran away. It's not like that."

Dougherty watched Chuck Murray staring at his coffee mug and he really couldn't get a read on the guy.

Mrs. Murray said, "David is very patriotic. Was. I remember when he was in third grade he drew a big map of the United States for a project. He was so sweet, writing in all the capitals. Do you remember that, Chuck? It was on his wall for years."

Murray nodded but didn't say anything.

"I think when David first came to Canada," Mrs. Murray said, "he thought people would understand that he wasn't running away, he wanted to continue his work, his protesting of the war. He always hated the idea of war. I remember when they had to do that duck and cover in school, he was just a little boy but he said to me, 'Hiding under our desks won't save us from the bomb.' He had nightmares about the bomb. We heard so much about it, the bomb, the bomb, the bomb."

She paused and Dougherty was thinking about the stuff he saw on TV when he was a kid, the explosions at the Bikini Atoll and others he couldn't remember the names of, how powerful and huge the blasts were and, of course, the two in Japan during the war. And the bomb had only gotten more powerful.

"But since he's been in Canada?" Carpentier said.

"The longer it's gone on the harder it gets. David didn't expect . . . No one expected it to go on this long, to be this . . . deadly."

Carpentier nodded and Dougherty watched him, couldn't tell if he was considering it, thinking about it, or just waiting a moment to get back to the questions at hand. For a moment Dougherty wondered if this stuff would be taught in some detective classes but then realized this was the class. On-the-job training.

Talking to a mother whose son has been murdered.

"He didn't mention anyone he was working for?" Carpentier said.

Mrs. Murray shook her head. Then she said, "But maybe he was different lately. The last couple of times he called we didn't talk about what he was doing. Usually he told me about an article he'd written, promised to mail it to me but he almost never did." She smiled. "But this spring and through the summer, he didn't talk so much about that kind of thing." She shrugged. "He was getting nostalgic, I think."

Carpentier looked at Chuck Murray and said, "Did you talk to him?"

Murray shook his head. "I haven't spoken to him since he came to Canada."

Carpentier nodded and Dougherty felt he would leave it at that, but Murray said, "Even before that, we didn't talk. We just fought."

"Not always," Mrs. Murray said. She was giving her husband an out, a way to think about better times but he didn't take it.

He said, "Since he got mixed up with the hippies,

the demonstrations and the protests, all we did was fight." He paused and Mrs. Murray put her hand over his, held it and he said, "I thought he was throwing his life away. He was supposed to go to college and have a good life. Better one than mine."

Mrs. Murray said, "Chuck."

"Him and his dirty friends, those college kids. Ruining the country."

Carpentier said, "So, you haven't spoken to David in a few years?"

Murray shook his head and Dougherty thought it was like the guy couldn't believe it himself. Murray didn't look at anyone at the table, not even his wife, and he said, "The last time we talked was after the riot in New York, just after Kent State."

Mrs. Murray said, "Chuck," again but her husband didn't look like he was getting mad. He said, "David was so mad about Kent State, but then he was just crazy about what happened in New York. He had pictures, some of them had been in newspapers, the hard hats going after the students." He looked at his wife and said, "You remember?"

She nodded and glanced at Dougherty and at Carpentier and said, "There was a protest in New York, an anti-war rally. They were marching through the streets and some construction workers confronted them."

Murray smirked at the word, but his wife continued, talking to Carpentier, "They beat the students." She paused and then she said, "The police just watched them."

Dougherty thought, Well, sometimes that's riot

strategy: let it run out of gas on its own.

"David was so mad," Chuck Murray said, "he was yelling about how they used pipes with the flag wrapped around them as clubs."

Carpentier said, "I don't remember that."

"It was the last time we talked," Murray said. He looked at his wife for a moment and then looked away.

Dougherty was watching Carpentier, seeing if he'd steer the conversation back to what Mrs. Murray and David had talked about but he was thinking about all the fights he'd had with his own father and how they still fought sometimes. Dougherty's father was still trying to get him to go to university, now talking about law school of all things, but Dougherty couldn't imagine not talking to him for two years.

After that it was awkward small talk till they finished their lunch and Carpentier paid the bill. Then they stood on the sidewalk on St. Jacques Street, and Carpentier asked if they needed any help making arrangements.

Mrs. Murray said, "Oh, thank you, but that's all right. Father Denison — he's our priest at St. Bernard's in Middleton, just outside Madison — he's talking to the church here. They're arranging to have David sent home."

"How long will you be staying in Montreal?"

"Just one more night," Mrs. Murray said.

"In that case," Carpentier said, shaking Murray's hand, "I'll phone you as soon as I have any information." He shook Mrs. Murray's hand and held out a business card saying, "And if you have any questions for me, or if you think of anything that might help, please call me."

Mrs. Murray took the card and shrugged her shoulders. Then she looked at Dougherty and said, "Thank you, Constable."

Dougherty had no idea what to say so he didn't say anything. He tried to look as earnest as he could, but he couldn't hold it when Mrs. Murray smiled at him and gave him a quick, awkward hug.

Then Chuck Murray said, "You know, I always thought I was right and David was wrong."

It was quiet for a moment and then Murray said, "I'd like to argue with him one more time."

Carpentier said, "*Oui*, of course."

Murray gave a quick nod and then Dougherty and Carpentier watched the American couple walk away towards the parking lot behind police headquarters.

"*Bon*," Carpentier said after a moment, "have you spoken to any of your contacts?"

"What?"

"Drug dealers? Did any of them know David Murray?"

Dougherty said, "I don't know, I haven't talked to anyone."

"Why not?"

Dougherty was going to say because he was still working a regular shift and doing the surveillance on the museum robbery and no one told him to talk to drug dealers but he just said, "I will tonight."

"Good. Okay, *au travais*."

Before he walked away Dougherty said, "Why did you bring me to this lunch, Detective?"

Carpentier said, "I thought with you being the same age as the son they might see something in you, *quelque chose de semblable*, some similarity."

"Something the same between me and that kid with the long hair and the beard?"

"Maybe, yes, for the mother. I thought maybe it would help her if she had something to say and she wasn't sure if she should."

Now Dougherty was thinking that it wasn't a terrible strategy and he said, "Too bad it didn't work."

"We don't know that," Carpentier said. "She took the card."

CHAPTER
EIGHT

"Penalties are killing us," Duclos said. "Two in the first ten minutes and they scored on both power plays."

There was a twenty-inch colour TV on the counter beside the coffee maker in the break room, a couple cops watching but most of the squad had gone back out on patrol. Friday night, it could get lively.

Dougherty said, "Where'd you get the TV?"

"Evidence room."

It was just after nine, Dougherty finally finishing his day shift, so just after six in Vancouver where the game was being played, and he was wondering how the cops there would do with crowds that had started drinking in the middle of the afternoon.

Dougherty took a quick shower, changed into jeans and a leather jacket and was looking through some files when the second period ended with the Soviets up 4–1 and Duclos saying, "These *maudits épais* should go to Russia and not come back."

Dougherty said, "You don't think they'll win all four games in Moscow?"

"*Tabarnak*, Dog-eh-dee, aren't you going home already?"

"I'm off till Monday, see you then."

As he was leaving, Dougherty looked at the other cops. Like Duclos, most of the other guys in the room were going from resigned to angry. Mad.

Dougherty was in the Rymark Tavern on Peel when the game ended, 5–3 for the Soviets, and the place was silent, most of the drinkers still just stunned, but it came alive when Phil Esposito was interviewed on the ice and he told Johnny Esaw how hard they were trying, how they were giving their hundred and fifty percent, and he couldn't believe the booing they were getting in their own buildings.

There was booing in the Rymark then.

On the TV, Esposito looking pissed off, kept talking, saying that he was really disappointed in the fans, and someone yelled at the TV, "You're disappointed?" and there was a little laughter but not much. There was anger. Esposito said, "Every one of us guys, thirty-five guys who came out to play for Team Canada, we did it because we love our country and not for any other reason. They can throw the money for the pension fund out the window, they can throw anything they want out the window — we came because we love Canada."

Dougherty finished his beer and started for the door then. A few guys were yelling at the TV, saying, "Yeah, now you're fucking patriotic, go back to Boston," and someone else was saying, "Maybe if you weren't so fucking arrogant, playing golf all summer, you wouldn't be making a fool of yourself."

If he'd been on duty, Dougherty would've been getting ready for the fights he knew would be starting when the drunks got tired of shouting at the TV and started shouting at each other but he wasn't, he was just looking for one guy. He'd been to a couple of bars before the Rymark, and heard the same kind of anger building, but he hadn't seen Danny Buckley.

Buck-Buck was a guy Dougherty had known since they were both kids in Point St. Charles. Dougherty's parents had moved across the river into a nice duplex with a front lawn and a backyard when Dougherty was in his last year of high school but he still thought of the Point as home. A couple of years back when he first worked with Detective Carpentier and they were looking for a guy who was killing young women and a girl disappeared in the Point after buying some dope, Dougherty had looked up his old friend Danny Buckley.

His old tormentor, really. Buck-Buck was one of the gang of English kids who beat him up because Dougherty went to the French school. Or because his mother was French. Or because he was a loner. Or because they could. Then Buck-Buck grew up and got into a real gang, the Point Boys, Irish guys who started out unloading ships in the port of Montreal, slipping heroin from Marseille and hash from the Middle East to the Mafia, and then went into business for themselves, getting dealers out onto the streets.

And a rising tide lifts all boats. A couple years back, when Dougherty needed information he ran his own undercover operation, buying grass from him, but Buckley had moved up to wholesaler and now there was a layer or two of insulation between him and the street.

Still, Dougherty spent the night looking in bars where Buckley was known to spend time and he got lucky in George's across the street from the Playboy Club on Aylmer.

"Look at you," Dougherty said, "finally put on a jacket and a tie and you don't need one anymore."

Buckley was standing at the bar, looking out over the red and black room, the low ceiling curving around the stage, the place intimate even though there were probably a hundred and fifty people looking to have a good time, and he said, "Too bad, you wouldn't have gotten in."

"I would've," Dougherty said. He leaned back against the bar and looked out over the room, too, and said, "They used to have a rock band in here."

"Still Life," Buckley said. "They were good."

"They must be at the Laugh-In now."

Buckley took a drink from the highball glass he was holding and said, "They broke up, nobody has a house band anymore."

"Or an orchestra."

"Jesus, Dougherty, how old are you?"

Dougherty didn't say anything, but he was thinking that he felt old. That was funny, a guy in his twenties, but like George's he felt in between — too old for the

Laugh-In or the Yellow Door, filled with long-haired guys and rock bands that were way too loud, but too young for the Playboy Club or the Stork or Altitheque on the fiftieth floor of Place Ville Marie. He said, "The clubs are dying."

"What, because the Playboy Club closed?"

"What?"

Buckley smirked. "Last week, why do you think all these girls are here?"

Dougherty looked at the waitresses, saw them for the first time really, in their miniskirts and boots and tight white blouses and realized they did look like bunnies without the ears and tails.

"The Hawaiian closed, too."

"That dump? About time." Buckley said, "Something else will open. This is Montreal — it's all about the nightlife." He smiled, but he looked like a shark. Then he said, "What're you doing here, Dougherty, why aren't you out looking for O'Brien and that other moron?"

For a moment Dougherty didn't recognize the name and then he said, "Boutin, Jean-Marc Boutin." The other two guys who'd started the fire at the Wagon Wheel. "We're looking. You know where they are? O'Brien's from Verdun, maybe he was a customer?"

Buckley shook his head.

Dougherty felt out of his depth, like he was playing a game he was no good at. But Buckley, man, he looked right at home leaning against the bar, looking over the club, not worried at all about the cop.

Screw it. He had to keep trying, so Dougherty asked Buckley about working at the port and were they on strike again and Buck-Buck told him yeah, and Thunder Bay and Sarnia, too, and they shot the shit for a while, Buck-Buck saying how they were going to get a raise, all the way from $3.50 an hour to $4.70, and Dougherty said, "Someday you'll be up to five bucks an hour," and Buckley said, "That what they pay you?"

Dougherty nodded and drank some of his beer, thinking that if he got paid for this shit he was doing on his own time it'd be over two hundred a week.

Then Buckley said, "What do you want, Dougherty? I can't help you, I'm not in that business anymore."

"Sure you are, and I still don't care," Dougherty said. "I'm looking for someone you might know."

"Do I look like I know any bikers?"

"Of course you do," Dougherty said. "To me." He'd almost forgotten the dead biker on Atwater, the other murder Carpentier was working on, and it drove him nuts that Buckley was on top of everything. He tried to look casual, looked around the club and said, "These people don't know you like I do, Buck-Buck. They don't go way back with you."

Using the nickname helped — Buckley was finally getting mad and that's what Dougherty wanted. But not too mad, so he said, "I don't care about that murder, I want to know if you know a guy named David Murray. An American, draft dodger."

As much as Dougherty could tell Buckley wanted to say fuck you and walk away, he knew he wouldn't. Just the chance of having something on a cop, especially Dougherty, was too much for an ambitious guy like Buck-Buck to let pass, so he said, "How much is it worth to you?"

Dougherty said, "It could be worth something."

"You can't afford me, Dougherty," Buckley said. "Not anymore."

"Somebody killed him on Mount Royal, last Saturday night."

"Saturday? I was at the hockey game. Assholes."

"He was probably bringing in dope from the States, maybe he was a little competition for you."

"Shit, Dougherty, you don't have any idea what's going on, do you?"

"Why don't you tell me?"

"Mount Royal in the middle of the night? Probably a fag."

"You'd know all the hangouts," Dougherty said, and he expected Buckley to get mad but he didn't.

"And you don't know shit."

He pushed off the bar and put his highball glass down. "See you around."

Dougherty said, "Yeah, you will."

He watched Buckley walk through the club, stopping to say hi to people and people stopping him all the way to the door — handshakes, backslaps, eye contact. Buck-Buck knew almost everyone.

And Dougherty realized there wasn't a single person in the club he recognized.

"She called," Carpentier said and Dougherty said, "Who?"

"The mother, Mrs. Murray. She remembered the name of someone David was working with."

Dougherty rolled over in bed and picked up his

watch from the nightstand. Eight fifteen. He said, "She just called?"

"They're leaving now, driving back to Wisconsin," Carpentier said. "I think her husband was out, getting breakfast or something, I'm not sure, but she called. I'll meet you at Station Ten in half an hour."

Dougherty said okay and hung up. He was showered and dressed and walking the two blocks to the station when he thought for the first time that it was his day off, a rare Saturday off, and he wouldn't be able to put in for overtime unless Carpentier officially requested it, something Dougherty doubted would happen.

The detective was waiting in his Bonneville, idling on de Maisonneuve outside the station house, and he rolled down the window and said, "*Va chercher deux cafés.*"

"*Et des beignes?*"

Dougherty didn't wait for an answer and went into the greasy spoon on the corner and ordered two large coffees to go.

In the car, Carpentier took his paper cup and bent back the plastic tab on the cover and then folded out the two handles. Dougherty had never seen anyone actually use those little handles, but Carpentier held the cup and drank as he put the car in gear and pulled away from the curb.

Dougherty said, "Where are we going?"

"Just across the border."

"Into the U.S.?"

"No, the Ontario border, a place called Vankleek Hill." Carpentier motioned to a map on the seat and Dougherty picked it up.

"Oh, Vankleek Hill. Why are we going there?"

"Mrs. Murray said that David was staying with some people, some Americans, who have a farm near there."

"A commune?"

"A what?"

"Is it a hippie commune?"

"Why, you're not wearing the beads and the poncho?"

"Did she say David was living there?"

"She wasn't sure. She didn't have an address or anything, she just knew it was a farm in Ontario and she had a name, Scott Parker. I did a property search."

"Do you know anything about this guy?"

"Just that he bought the property a few years ago."

They were on the 2-20 then, heading west out of town, passing through the suburbs, Baie-D'Urfé and Beaconsfield and then over the bridge and off the island of Montreal into Vaudreuil.

Carpentier finished off his coffee and got out his cigarettes so Dougherty reached in his coat pocket and got out his own pack and his lighter, which he flicked on and held for Carpentier.

"Did you see that game?" Carpentier said. *"Incroyable."*

"And now Savard is coming home with a broken ankle, how much of the season will he miss?"

"That speech Esposito gave," Carpentier said shaking his head. "Well, it doesn't matter now. The Russian amateurs are as good as our professionals. We knew it was coming."

Dougherty said, "We did?" and Carpentier said,

"Yes, do you remember a few years ago when the Russian team played the Junior Canadiens?"

"No."

"They lost, the Russians, by a lot, nine to two or three," Carpentier said. "After the game the coach said, 'We learned a lot.'"

"They were playing patsy?"

Carpentier looked sideways at Dougherty and said, "They were learning, like he said. This is the same team, the only difference is the goalie."

"Did you hear what Plante did?"

"Jacques Plante? No, what?"

Dougherty rolled the window down a little and exhaled smoke. "Before the first game in Montreal — seems like a long time ago now, doesn't it?"

"Yes."

"Anyway, before the game Plante took a translator and went into the Russian dressing room and talked to their goalie, went over all the Canadian players — what to expect, how they play, everything."

Carpentier nodded and didn't say anything for a moment and then said, "Well, that's Plante, eh? Cares more about the goalie than anything. And he's a sportsman. And this series, it's supposed to be about bringing us closer, no? Détente, or whatever the Americans are calling it."

"That was when we thought we'd win all eight games."

Carpentier laughed. "Anyway, this Russian goalie, Tretiak, he's a teenager and he'd never seen professional hockey players in his life. *C'est bien*, what Plante did."

"Goalies have to stick together?"

"Like cops," Carpentier said.

Dougherty thought he saw him wink but he wasn't sure.

"And the Olympics are over in Munich and we're next," Carpentier said. "We'll have to be ready."

"You think something will happen? More kidnappings, assassinations?"

Carpentier shrugged and said, "Anything's possible, non?"

"I was at the ceremony at Mackenzie King Park."

"Why did you go to that?"

"Undercover assignment," Dougherty said. "One of the museum workers went."

"You're really working," Carpentier said.

"Yeah."

Carpentier smoked and flicked ash out the window. "Israel has already bombed some places in Lebanon and Syria."

"What?"

"They say guerrilla bases."

"So this could still be going on in four years," Dougherty said and Carpentier said, "This or something else."

Half an hour later they saw the sign on the Trans-Canada saying *Welcome to Ontario* and Carpentier slowed down. Dougherty thought he was reluctant to leave Quebec, but then Carpentier said, "Should we pick her up?"

Dougherty said, "She looks like my sister."

The car ahead of them had also slowed down and pulled onto the shoulder and as they passed it Dougherty saw the girl was older than Cheryl, probably in her mid-twenties. She tossed a bag into the back seat and hopped into the front. It looked like a middle-aged woman was driving the car.

"Did you see the warning," Carpentier said, "that the QPF issued? Did you know that in May and June there were over one hundred sexual assaults on hitchhikers?"

"No, I didn't."

"That's just what got reported."

For a second Dougherty could easily imagine his sister, Cheryl, jumping into a car with anyone who stopped but then he had to admit to himself that maybe that was a couple of years ago, maybe now she wouldn't do something like that. Or maybe he just wanted to think that about Cheryl because now he couldn't remember the last time he'd actually had a conversation with her.

A few minutes later, they were in the small town of Vankleek Hill and needed directions to find Dunvegan Road, passing through rolling hills and farms, past Aberdeen Road, Lochnivar Road, Fraser Road — Carpentier saying it was so Irish and Dougherty saying, "Scottish," and then, "We passed D'Aoust, that's French."

A few miles along Dunvegan Road, Carpentier slowed down, looking at the farm houses all set back off the road and the mailboxes with names on them and little flags, all down.

Then Carpentier turned onto a tree-lined driveway and as they passed the mailbox Dougherty didn't see a name. He said, "Are you sure this is it?" and Carpentier pointed behind the red-brick farmhouse to an old school bus painted bright red and blue and orange and green and said, "Yes, I think so."

He stopped the Bonneville beside the house and a woman came out of the kitchen and stood by the door.

Carpentier got out of the car and said, "*Bonjour*, hello."

The woman said, "Who are you? What do you want?"

Dougherty was out of the passenger side then and looking over the roof of the car towards the woman, and now he realized she wasn't much older than he was, between twenty-five and thirty for sure, her hair in a loose ponytail, wearing a plaid work shirt and jeans. She didn't smile.

"You're police?"

Carpentier said, "Yes."

"You can't come here."

"We only want to ask you about David Murray."

"We don't have to say anything. You have to leave."

A man came out of the house then and said, "What's going on, Penny?"

"They're police."

"From Montreal," Carpentier said. "We want to talk to you about David Murray."

"What about David?"

"Scott, don't."

She was looking at Scott, but he was looking at Carpentier. "Why do you want to talk to us?"

"David's mother told me that he had been spending time here."

The man, Scott Parker, looked doubtful. "She told you that?"

"To be honest," Carpentier said, "she was somewhat reluctant."

Dougherty noticed that Carpentier was working hard to speak English with as little accent as possible and doing a pretty good job.

Parker said, "No one likes to talk to cops."

Dougherty was going to say something about how only guilty people didn't like talking to cops, but he saw Carpentier nod a little and look serious and maybe even a little understanding, and he figured the detective was playing them.

"We're trying to find out who killed David," Carpentier said. "We're homicide detectives."

Parker looked at Dougherty and said, "The Mod Squad needs to let his hair grow," and Dougherty was thinking there was no way he'd ever have long hair and a beard like this loser. But he kept his mouth shut.

"Perhaps there is somewhere we can sit," Carpentier said, motioning towards the house.

Parker looked at Penny and said, "What do you think? A cup of tea with the Gestapo?"

She said, "We don't have to."

"No, that's true. It's up to us, isn't it?"

He stared at Carpentier and Carpentier nodded, agreeing it was up to them, and that seemed to be good enough.

"All right then, come on in."

Parker stepped aside and Penny gave him one more angry look, though now it was more resignation, and then she went inside. Carpentier followed and Dougherty and Parker had a little stare-down before they went in.

"The tea isn't necessary," Carpentier said but Penny was already putting a kettle on the stove.

There was a big wooden table in the kitchen with almost a dozen chairs around it, and Dougherty got the feeling the place was often full of people. There was a big pot on the stove that he figured was probably always there — add more water to the soup more people are coming, that kind of place.

But today it was quiet and felt empty.

Parker had come in and sat down in a chair near the head of the table, across from the big stove. Dougherty thought it was likely the guy's usual spot where no one else ever sat, not that anyone would say that. Probably the spot where the guy ran all the discussions without really acting like a guy in charge.

Carpentier sat at the table, but Dougherty was still standing by the door and now he was wondering if he was reading too much into everything, trying too hard to be a detective.

Parker said, "So, David's mother told you about us?"

"Not really," Carpentier said. "She mentioned your name," nodding towards Parker, "and said you had a farm where David had been working."

At the stove, Penny made a dismissive sound, and Dougherty looked at her. She wasn't looking at Carpentier, she was looking at Parker, and Dougherty could tell there was something going on there, he just couldn't tell what.

"That's right," Parker said, "David was helping out."

"How long had he been doing that?"

Parker looked at Penny. "What would you say, six months?"

She stared back at Parker for a moment before she said, "On and off."

"We have some greenhouses, mostly tomatoes. We've got strawberries and some corn. There's always a lot to do."

And marijuana, Dougherty figured, but he didn't say anything.

"When was the last time you saw David?"

The whistle went off on the kettle and Penny turned away from them and turned off the heat.

Parker looked at Carpentier and said, "I'm not sure exactly . . . a couple of weeks ago?"

"David was killed last Saturday," Carpentier said, "a week ago today."

"He wasn't on any kind of a schedule — he came and went."

Penny came to the table with mugs in one hand and a teapot in the other. She looked at Dougherty and said, "Are you going to sit?"

He said, "Thank you," and took the mug as he sat down across from Parker.

Carpentier said, "It could be very important — can you remember anything more specific about the last time you saw David? Anything else going on at that time?"

Parker looked at Penny again and said, "Was David here for the get-out-the-vote meeting? When was that, the weekend before?"

Penny shrugged and Dougherty saw Parker almost smile and then say, "We're really trying to get the students out to vote for McGovern. Since the Twenty-Sixth passed, it'll be the difference."

"I'm sorry," Carpentier said, "the Twenty-Six?"

"Lowered the voting age from twenty-one to eighteen," Parker said. "Twenty-Sixth amendment. We get out the vote, McGovern will win."

Penny said, "Nixon stole this election a long time ago."

"She has no faith," Parker said. "She's a red-diaper baby." He was smiling, amused with himself. "Her parents were communists."

She stood up and walked to the stove. "Not communists."

Parker looked at Carpentier and said, "She went on freedom rides in her stroller. She was a student activist, she gave speeches about desegregation and civil rights, tried to organize the other students — in her grade school."

Dougherty couldn't see Penny without turning around and making it obvious, but he knew what look was on her face — he was getting good enough at being a detective for that.

"She can't stop working," Parker said, "even when she thinks all is lost."

Carpentier said, "Like a homicide investigation. We have to keep working, keep trying." He was looking past Dougherty at Penny, but she didn't say anything so after a moment Carpentier looked at Parker and said, "David was at this meeting, about the vote?"

"Yeah, him and about twenty other people. I'm not going to give you their names so don't bother asking."

Dougherty had a feeling that was to placate Penny.

"We're only interested in David," Carpentier said, "and who he was with. Did he leave here with someone? Someone must have given him a ride back to Montreal?"

"Sometimes he went to Toronto," Parker said.

"Why did he go to Toronto?"

"David worked with deserters," Parker said. "It's not easy. After My Lai we started getting a lot more, a lot more who had been in Vietnam. They're lost when they get here."

Carpentier said, "What do you mean?"

"They usually come here from Europe. They leave the jungle in Vietnam and manage to get to Amsterdam, something like that. Then they get here with nothing, the clothes on their backs, in terrible shape."

Dougherty was thinking maybe they shouldn't run away but Parker said, "We really have no idea what they've been through so it's not up to us to judge." He looked at Penny as he said that and kept looking at her, saying, "These guys, usually they don't have any family support. Not support, I mean they're usually working-class guys, or poor, it's not that their families don't want to help them, they just don't have the means. A lot of these guys, they'd never been outside the USA before they got sent to Vietnam. Never been outside their home states."

Dougherty wanted to turn around and see how Penny was taking this, it was so clearly directed at her, but he kept looking at Parker.

"And they're scared, they think the CIA is after them or the FBI."

"Or," Penny said, "they're working for the CIA, we don't know."

"When we put together the manual we didn't really think there'd be these kinds of guys, we thought it'd be all college students, guys like . . . me."

Carpentier said, "What manual is this?"

"The *Manual for Draft-Age Immigrants to Canada.*"

Parker stood up and walked into a kind of enclosed back porch and came out and dropped a book on the table. Mimeographed pages stapled together, really, with a yellow cover that had a map of Canada on it that looked like it was drawn by a kid. Along the bottom it said, *Summer 1970 — Fifth Edition*. Dougherty recognized the book: he'd seen a few when he'd been involved in apartment raids over the years, mostly looking for Black Panthers and other American radicals.

"Sold a hundred thousand of these," Parker said.

Dougherty wondered if that's what bought this farm but he didn't say anything, he just kept watching Carpentier being understanding and developing a relationship, as the detective manual said. Dougherty smirked a little then, thinking, We've all got our manuals.

Carpentier said, "And David helped the deserters?"

"He helped everyone," Penny said. "But he was good with the deserters."

"Can you think of anyone who might have known where David was last Saturday?"

"I really can't," Parker said. "I'm sorry."

Carpentier stood up then and took a step towards the stove, holding out an empty mug and saying, "Thank you for the tea." Dougherty hadn't even touched his and he hadn't noticed Carpentier drink his.

Penny took the mug and said, "We didn't have to talk to you."

Carpentier said, "*Bien sûr.*"

Parker and Penny both came out of the farmhouse and stood by the door and as Dougherty walked around the Bonneville to get into the passenger seat he looked at them — at Penny — and she was staring at him.

Parker said, "Give my regards to David's mother, will you?" and Carpentier said, "Yes, of course."

But something about the way Penny was looking at him made Dougherty uncomfortable.

He got into the car, and they drove in silence for a while, and then Dougherty said, "So, what now?"

Carpentier said, "I don't know, that's about all we had."

"His mother didn't know anyone else?"

"Who?"

Dougherty said, "Mrs. Murray, David's mother."

"Oh," Carpentier said, "no, this was all she had, the farm."

"And this guy's name, Scott Parker."

"Yes, that's right."

Dougherty said okay, and silence hung in the car for a moment. Then Carpentier said, "I'm sorry to drag you out here on your day off," and Dougherty said, "No problem."

Carpentier said, "Saturday night coming up, you have plans?"

"I have a date," Dougherty said.

"With that woman from Milton Park?"

"No, with a stewardess."

"Oh," Carpentier said, "that's good, a stewardess."

But as they turned off Dunvegan Road and onto the Trans-Canada Highway Dougherty couldn't help but think that Carpentier was being too chatty, too upbeat. Too quick to want to move on and talk about something else.

And that look Penny had given him, Dougherty could still feel it.

Now he was thinking it could have been the RCMP who tipped them about the farm. It could have been the CIA.

Anything seemed possible.

———

The restaurant was called The Place for Steak on highway 20 in Pointe Claire. It was just as expensive as a place downtown would've been and it had Linton Garner on the piano in the lounge, but it was suburban all the way. Dougherty and Debbie Rankin were the youngest people in the place by ten years, it was all guys still in their suits from the office and housewives in dresses worrying about the babysitter back home.

When they'd ordered their steaks and fried mushrooms and mashed potatoes and house salads with French dressing, Dougherty said, "So, did you grow up on the west island?"

"Oh, no, I'm from Toronto."

"What are you doing here?"

She looked at him over the top of her highball glass, rye and ginger, and said, "It's exciting, Montreal. It's where the action is."

"You like the action?"

"Don't you?"

Dougherty said, "Yeah, I do." It was why he'd joined the police, to get in on the action.

"I was sixteen when we came here for Expo. It was just a great party."

"It was," Dougherty said, quickly figuring out this meant Debbie was twenty-one, a couple of years younger than he'd thought. Then he said, "I worked there."

"At the Canadian pavilion or Quebec?"

"Not during the fair, before. I worked construction. The American pavilion, the dome."

"I remember going through that on the monorail, what was it called?"

"Minirail."

"That's it. It was so fun."

"The Minirail?"

She smiled and almost winked at him, saying, "There was fun everywhere."

"So you moved to Montreal."

"I couldn't wait to get out of the house. Tell the truth, I ran away a couple of times when I was still in high school."

Dougherty made an exaggerated surprised face and Debbie laughed.

"I know? Hard to believe, eh? A real wild child."

"But you're all grown up now?"

"I don't know about that."

They ate their steaks, skipped dessert and went back to Debbie's new apartment in Dorval. As Dougherty pulled his Mustang into the parking lot behind the building someone yelled from a balcony, "Cool car," and when he got out a woman yelled, "It's Steve McQueen."

Dougherty looked over the roof of the car to Debbie and said, "Well, it's his car, anyway." and she said, "What do you mean?"

"Bullitt."

As they walked towards the building, there was more yelling from the balcony and Dougherty said, "There's a party going on," and Debbie said, "There's always a party going on," and she didn't seem unhappy about it.

The Swingles building, as the newspaper ad called it, was actually two four-storey buildings side-by-side with an outdoor pool between them. It was a warm evening for the middle of September and there were a few people standing around the pool with drinks in their hands but no one was in the water.

Debbie took Dougherty's hand and led him into one of the buildings through the back door, which was propped open with a brick, and up a flight of stairs to the second floor. Music was coming out of at least two apartments they passed — not the same music, but the same kind of music, anyway, lots of guitars and harmonies — and when Debbie opened an apartment door further down the hall, music was blasting there, too.

As soon as they were inside Debbie disappeared into the crowd.

For a moment Dougherty stood by the kitchen looking over the apartment and thinking how different everybody was from the people he'd talked to at the farm earlier. They were all in their twenties, but these people were dressed up — the women had their hair done in salons; they were wearing makeup and bright nail polish.

Really, Dougherty was thinking how different they all were from Judy MacIntyre in her workboots back in Milton Park.

Then Dougherty was wondering how he could be feeling so out of place in both places, both extremes. A woman came up to him with a drink in one hand and an unlit cigarette in the other and he got out his lighter. She smiled and said, "I'm Karen," and he said, "I'm Eddie."

Karen leaned in to get her cigarette lit and then tilted her head back and blew smoke at the ceiling saying, "Do you fly for United?"

Dougherty said, "No."

"There's some kind of layover, a lot of people here are from United. Hey, you don't have a drink!" She took his hand and pulled him into the crowded kitchen, and a minute later Dougherty was drinking a rum and Coke and talking to a different woman.

After a little while, he went looking for Debbie and saw her sitting on the arm of the couch, waving her cigarette as she talked but somehow as he was making his way through the crowd he ended up on the balcony with a few other people.

One of the guys was saying, "Vegas is great: all the lights coming in, terrific airport."

"Better than L.A., that's for sure."

"Do you fly for United?"

Dougherty said, "No, I'm not a pilot." The guy

who'd asked the question was a little older, probably in his late thirties, and then he realized that most of the men at the party looked to be in their thirties. They could be young executives.

The guy said, "What're you doing here then?" and the other people on the balcony laughed and Dougherty said, "I came with Debbie. This is her apartment, isn't it?"

A woman said, "She moves fast," and one of the other guys said, "You're telling me," and everyone laughed again.

"I'm Frank." He held out his hand and Dougherty shook it.

"Eddie Dougherty."

"Which airline?"

Dougherty said, "I don't work for an airline," and now he was enjoying the fact none of these people could tell he was a cop, he was starting to see the benefit of not feeling like he fit in with any single group of people, maybe he could fit in a little with all of them.

"So," Frank said, "what do you do?"

A woman screamed inside the apartment, and Dougherty stepped forward towards the sliding door: a woman he'd seen dancing on the coffee table earlier looked like she'd slipped, but a guy caught her and was twirling her around, and now everyone was laughing.

Dougherty didn't see Debbie in the living room.

Frank said, "That was fast, you a fireman?"

Dougherty said, "Cop."

"Oh, the boys in blue. Dorval?"

"No," Dougherty said, "Montreal."

"The big time."

Dougherty shrugged and one of the other guys on the balcony said, "You carry a gun?"

"When I'm working."

One of the women said, "Are you working now?"

There was some giggling and a couple of women were looking at Dougherty and he felt the place tense up a bit, like when he was squaring off against some drunk in a bar.

Frank made a kind of dismissive smirk and said, "You ever use it?"

Dougherty looked at him, feeling it was a challenge but not wanting to get into anything, and said, "Not yet."

"Yeah, of course."

As much as he didn't want to get into anything, Dougherty also didn't want to let it go. If Debbie had been on the balcony he would have said something for sure but as it was he just kept looking at Frank, daring him to say something more.

But then Frank laughed and said, "Jerry didn't need a gun, just an axe," and turned a little and raised his glass to the guy, Jerry, who raised his own back.

Dougherty figured there was a story coming, something to show all these women how Frank and Jerry were the toughest guys, but he didn't feel any need to ask for it, thinking he may not be a detective yet, but he could tell when a perp wanted to talk.

A woman next to Dougherty said to Jerry, "You were on eight-one-two, weren't you?"

Frank said, "He sure was."

It was crowded on the balcony and the woman was leaning on Dougherty's arm, so he turned a little to let her more into the conversation and she leaned a little more into him.

"Calgary to Toronto," Frank said. He looked at Dougherty and said, "This was last year, November — you probably heard about it."

"I don't remember."

"Hijacking." Frank said it seriously, gravely, nodding and looking into his drink and Dougherty said, "Seems like there's one every week."

Frank looked up quickly, eyes narrowed, but then he broke into a smile and said, "Yeah there is. This one, Jerry was the captain." He motioned a little towards Jerry but kept looking at Dougherty. "About a half hour out of Calgary a young guy, about your age, comes up to the cockpit, he's got a sawed off shotgun and ten sticks of dynamite. You ever see a stick of dynamite up close?"

"Yeah," Dougherty said, "I have."

Frank looked at him for a second, but Dougherty knew he wouldn't ask about it.

"Guy said he was with the IRA," Frank said. "Wanted to go to Belfast and be a freedom fighter. Oh, and he wanted a million and a half dollars."

Dougherty said, "Figures," thinking about the time he saw all the dynamite a couple years earlier when the freedom fighters in Montreal wanted a half a million dollars in gold and a trip to Cuba. "They always want money."

"They do," Frank said. Then he turned around and looked at Jerry and said, "And what did good old Air Canada manage to put together, a hundred grand?"

"Fifty."

"Fifty grand," Frank said. "But that was good enough for this kid, so they land in Great Falls, Montana, and pick up the money and a navigator to get them to Ireland."

"The kid," Jerry said, "tells me to go down to three thousand feet. He's got a package, brown paper wrapped up with twine."

Frank said, "He's got a plan. He tells Annabelle," he looked around and said, "I thought she was here?"

"She will be," one of the women said, "she lands later."

"Okay," Frank said. "So, this kid, he takes Annabelle to the emergency exit and says, 'open it.' Jerry goes to see what's going on. The kid tells him he's taking the money and he's jumping. He starts to unwrap the package he's got."

"But it's tied too tight."

Jerry and Frank were both starting to laugh, and Dougherty was getting the feeling that he was the only one who hadn't heard the story but no one was going to interrupt.

"The twine around the package, it's tied too tight," Frank said, "he can't get it off. So Jerry here says to the kid, 'how about this?' and holds up the fire axe. And the kid looks at him and thinks he's helping, so he puts down the shotgun, and when he looks up again . . . pow, right in the head with axe."

And everyone on the balcony laughed.

Then the woman leaning on Dougherty said, "Did you kill him?"

Jerry said, "Naw, but there was a lot of blood, wow, I didn't expect so much."

"You should've killed him," Frank said. "He's probably out now." He looked at Dougherty and said, "Right? All these left-wing judges."

"I don't know," Dougherty said. "But I guess that's where D.B. Cooper got the idea."

Frank laughed and said, "There's no way that guy survived the jump."

A woman said, "But they haven't found him," and Frank said, "They'll find his body someday."

The tension was gone on the balcony then and Dougherty went back into the apartment looking for Debbie. He asked a couple of people if they knew where she was but no one did.

He felt like he could stay, he might even get lucky with one of these women in the Swingles building, but Dougherty slipped out without anyone noticing.

Driving back into Montreal he was thinking that being able to blend in with lots of different groups would sure help with the surveillance and undercover and lots of other police work but it might not be the best way to live his life.

Not that he had much say in the matter.

CHAPTER
NINE

A woman leaned a sign, cardboard nailed to a hockey stick, against the wall. The hand-painted letters said, *No More Craters in Vietnam and No More Demolition in Milton Park.*

Dougherty said, "What's the connection?" and the woman said, "No connection, just all part of the same thinking."

She held the door, the yellow door, but Dougherty put his hand on it and said, "After you."

The woman smiled and said, "You cops are so polite," and Dougherty started to say, How do you know, but he stopped when she said, "Oh, come on in."

He followed her into the club.

Sunday night, just after eight, and the place was starting to fill up. Carpentier had called Dougherty a few hours earlier and told him that David Murray's friends were going to have a wake for him and Dougherty should attend.

Now he was standing by the back wall of the Yellow Door Coffee House looking at all the people, probably fifty of them, all about Dougherty's age but seeming so different from him. They didn't all have long hair and they weren't all young but they were comfortable in the surroundings and Dougherty wasn't.

He was hoping it didn't show when the woman he'd held the door for came up and stood beside him and said, "If you're going to stand here like this you might as well have worn your uniform."

"I have to put it in the laundry sometime."

"You don't have more than one?"

There was a microphone set up at one end of the room. There wasn't really a stage, but there was a piano and a little open space and now a couple of guys were trying to get everyone's attention. One guy had a guitar and he started to strum and then both guys leaned up to the mike and sang, "In this dirty old part of the city," and the whole place cheered and sang along with the next line, "Where the sun refused to shine."

Dougherty hadn't recognize the song without the bass line intro but he was almost singing along when they got to, "We gotta get out of this place, if it's the last thing we ever do."

He'd never heard it as a folk song. But every bar band he'd ever heard had mangled it. This was the first time that Dougherty really heard the words about watching his father's hair turn grey, working and slaving his life away and how I've been working, too, babe, every night and every day. On the job almost ten years and now those words meant more than the part about the girl being so young and pretty.

When they finished the two guys started another song right away, singing about being on a plane, "On your way up north," and how Canada is so far from where you want to be. A couple of people sang along, not many. Dougherty didn't know the song, but a few more people joined in with the words about what you always wanted to be, always wanted to be was just a man and then the whole place was singing, "Fulfilled but a little more free, a little more free."

Dougherty noticed a couple of guys on the far side of the room who might've been Black Panthers, they had the sunglasses and leather jackets and the serious looks on their faces. And they were weren't singing along or mingling.

This time when the song finished one of the two guys at the mike said, "We're here for David." Then he gave a good speech, short and not very personal, Dougherty thought, and he drifted into, "what we all have in common," and then he seemed to talk about himself more than about David Murray.

Then the guy said, "Colleen, would you like to say a few words?" and Colleen Whitehead stepped up to the mike.

She stood there for a moment and then it stretched into a long moment, and Dougherty thought someone else was going to have to say something and help her out but finally she said, "I don't think any of us really knew David. Not really." She paused and looked at all the faces looking back at her and then she said, "But we all knew his struggle, his battle. The battle that was going on inside of him."

Then there was a lot of murmuring and agreeing.

Dougherty looked at the woman beside him, the one he'd held the door for, and she was nodding, looking at Colleen.

"It's different for each of us, of course," Colleen Whitehead said into the mike, "and we never really know what anyone else goes through, how they arrive at their decisions. I know that for David the decision to come to Canada instead of going to Vietnam consumed him. It tore him apart."

It was the kind of thing Dougherty was hearing a lot lately, but he wasn't sure he was buying it. Americans and war, he wasn't so sure. His own father had joined the navy in 1938 when everyone in the world knew what was coming but, of course, the Americans didn't get into it for years, not until it actually came to them. So now, for once, they were getting involved up front, keeping the communists on the other side of the world, and it's tearing them apart.

Then Colleen said, "From the moment we arrived we found so many people going through what we were going through." She paused and then she said, "We found so many people willing to understand . . . to try and understand . . . us."

Dougherty looked around the room as she continued, talking about what David was like in high school and how she felt he'd always been looking for a community he could be a part of and how the closest he'd ever come was here, "with all of you." Dougherty noticed she didn't say "all of us," but he wasn't sure if that meant anything, and then he wondered if anyone in the room had seen David the day he was killed. The day before? Did these people have any idea what he was really doing?

Colleen finished, "I hope David has found his peace now."

And then Dougherty finally saw the tears on her face, saw how they had been streaming down her cheeks the whole time she was talking and now she put her hands over her face and started to sob. One of the folk singers put his arm around her shoulders and helped her away from the mike and the other guy started to play the guitar.

"What are you doing here?"

Dougherty turned and saw Judy MacIntyre and he said, "I didn't recognize you without the workboots."

"I recognize you without the uniform."

The woman Dougherty had held the door for was still standing beside him and she said, "Hey, now I recognize you."

Judy said, "Did he arrest you, too?"

"No, he didn't, that's why I remember."

"You come back looking for another chance?"

The other woman said, "I'm Corky King, what's your name, Officer?"

Dougherty could tell the two women knew each other but he didn't think they were close. He looked at Corky and said, "Édouard," as French as possible.

Corky was holding out her hand and Dougherty shook it, and Judy MacIntyre said, "Edoo-ard

Dougherty, he's an English oppressor."

"Only on my father's side, on my mother's I'm under the boot of the capitalist pigs."

Corky said, "Yeah, I thought you were conflicted." She looked at Judy and said, "You remember, just before the evictions on Park Avenue? We had that demonstration."

"Yes, I remember, Concordia called the cops." She looked at Dougherty and said, "And you rushed right over."

He still wasn't sure what they were talking about so he didn't say anything.

"Concordia is the development company," Judy said, "that's throwing everyone out."

"There was a big demonstration on the street in front of the building, a big crowd, and the police came and they were talking to us, remember?"

Judy said, "I don't remember any talking."

"Yeah, they were kind of mingling for a while. I remember because I had Noah with me. It was just after his birthday — he'd just turned two. I was holding him," she looked at Dougherty and said, "and you let him wear your hat."

Dougherty said, "Oh yeah."

"Yeah," Corky said, "you were there for about an hour, just talking and walking around and then you came up to me and you said, you whispered to me, that you were getting orders to arrest everyone so if I wanted to, I could step behind you, you said."

She looked at Judy MacIntyre then and said, "I felt bad, I felt disloyal, but I had Noah with me and I didn't know what would happen so I did it." She looked at

Dougherty. "I stepped behind you. Lots of people got arrested that day, but Noah slept in his own bed that night."

No one said anything for a moment and then Dougherty said, "You're American."

Corky laughed a little. She said, "People keep telling me that's okay," and he said, "Well, you know, the news and all."

She shook her head and said, "Canadians," and Dougherty said, "We're not Canadians, we're Montrealers." Dougherty looked at Judy MacIntyre when he said it and saw her nod a little.

Then Dougherty said, "Did you know David well?"

"Be careful," Judy said, "he's working."

Corky said, "Not really. I met him working with the deserters. I'm a nurse. I was in Vietnam for a while. I don't mean I was in the jungle but I saw enough."

"But you didn't know David very well?"

"I'm not sure anyone did."

"That's the feeling I'm getting," Dougherty said. "A real man of mystery."

"I can't believe someone killed him. His whole life was about peace."

"Are you sure?" Dougherty said. "I mean, if you didn't know him that well?"

Corky turned to face Dougherty and said, "I saw David help people. I saw men, boys really, come here scared and alone, no idea what to do, and I saw David help them. Sometimes he would drive them back across the border so they could enter Canada legally and get the help they needed. Do you know how much of a risk that was for him?"

"Yes, I do," Dougherty said.

"So, I guess I knew him that well," Corky said. "For whatever that's worth."

Dougherty said, "Thank you."

Corky said, "Right, well . . ." and she nodded a little and walked away into the crowd.

Dougherty watched her and looked the place over, looked at all the people and didn't see anything to make a note of really. The Black Panthers were standing pretty much exactly where they'd been all night, but now a few people were talking to them, a couple of women and one guy. The rest of the place was just people standing around drinking out of beer bottles and paper cups.

The folk singers were finished and recorded music was playing, Bob Dylan, singing about the times a-changing, and Dougherty could certainly agree with that.

"You're not going to find anything here," Judy MacIntyre said.

"It sounds like you don't want me to." He looked at her and said, "You don't want somebody to get away with murder, do you?"

"Of course not. You're just wasting your time here."

"Because none of these peaceniks could kill anyone?"

"No one's going to talk to you."

"I don't get that," Dougherty said. "These people are supposed to be his friends, why don't they want to find out who killed him?"

"They don't have any idea who killed him."

"Do you?"

"Of course not."

Dougherty said, "You know, we don't even know what might be important. Right now we're just trying to find out where he was the day he was killed, or where he spent the night before that, the days before. No one seems to know."

"It's true," Judy said, "he wasn't around much."

"So look around," Dougherty said, "who here did he spend time with?"

She looked around and Dougherty thought he saw her pause over a couple of guys, older guys, maybe in their late thirties, but he couldn't be sure.

"What did Gardiner tell you?"

"The lawyer?" Dougherty said. "The same as everyone else: David Murray was a man of mystery."

"I'm still getting used to that."

"Man of mystery?"

"No, that he was. That he isn't anymore. I walk past his room and I'm used to seeing it empty but there were usually signs he'd been there."

"Like what?"

Judy shrugged and as Dougherty looked past her he saw Corky King on the other side of the room talking to the older guys. She was laughing and doing most of the talking but Dougherty couldn't tell if she was nervous or not.

144

"Oh, you know, dirty clothes, clean clothes, maybe, in a laundry bag. Just some sign of life."

Dougherty said, "I'm sorry for your loss."

Judy looked at Dougherty and said, "Well, I didn't really know him."

"No, but you had some things in common."

She said, "Don't try and be my friend."

Dougherty said okay, and they stood next to one another in silence for a moment. People were drifting out of the club, the evening was winding down.

He said, "Look, if you do remember something, anything, give me a call, would you?"

"There's nothing for me to remember."

"All right," Dougherty said. "But if you do."

He watched her nod a little and he couldn't tell at all what she was thinking. He figured she was probably right, there probably wasn't anything for her to remember, but if she did . . . would she tell him? If he was going to be a detective, a homicide detective, he'd have to be able to get a read on people better than this, he'd have to be able to work informants better than this.

Then he was wondering if that's what he was doing, if he was trying to work her like an informant or if it was something else.

She said, "Well, see you around," and wandered into the thinning crowd and Dougherty stood by himself for a while. No one called him pig, but it was clear no one was going to talk to him. After another fifteen minutes or so he left.

Outside the Yellow Door, Dougherty was walking along Aylmer heading back to where he'd parked his car when he heard a voice call, "Officer, Edoo-ard, hey," and he turned around to see Corky King.

She said, "I just wanted to say . . ." and she paused until she was standing right beside him, "Maybe there's someone you should talk to."

"Who?"

She looked around as if they were in a movie and then she said, "A guy named Smith," and Dougherty said, "You're kidding, right?"

"That's his name, Kenny or Kevin or something. David called him Two Fingers."

Now Dougherty was thinking they really were in an old movie and he said, "Are you serious?"

"Yes, but I don't want to be involved."

And she walked away without looking back.

CHAPTER TEN

Dougherty walked into Station Ten at five o'clock Monday afternoon, an hour before his shift ended and the desk sergeant, Delisle, said, "*Eh, qu'est-ce que tu fais?*"

"I'm doing that surveillance, the museum thing."

"Still, you're doing that? Nice to get the overtime."

Dougherty walked towards the locker room saying, "As long as they tell me," and Delisle said, "They don't tell me anything."

He changed into jeans and a blue shirt that looked a lot like his uniform shirt without the markings and a leather jacket.

He was window-shopping on Sherbrooke Street across from the museum fifteen minutes before Mullins came out of the building.

147

Dougherty was walking towards Côte-des-Neiges, where Mullins would catch the bus heading north to his apartment, but this time the guy crossed Sherbrooke and walked down Guy, almost bumping into Dougherty as he passed him.

At de Maisonneuve, Dougherty thought he was going into the Métro but Mullins stopped in front of the Guy Cinema, and Dougherty thought he'd have to spend a couple hours watching a porno. Mullins read the poster — a double feature, *Her Private Life* and *Suburban Housewives* — but then he started walking again, south towards St. Catherine.

Dougherty felt exposed on the wide sidewalk of St. Catherine Street — even in the crowd he thought he was standing out as a cop and tried to stay far back from Mullins, but then he felt he was too far back.

Then he thought, screw it, he was just thinking that way because of the draft dodgers and the hippies, they thought everybody looked like a cop. None of these people going home from work or going out for a meal gave Dougherty a second look.

And Mullins never looked back. He stopped in front of the Seville and looked at the poster for *Billy Jack*, and Dougherty thought that would be okay, he hadn't seen it, but then Mullins started walking again.

At Atwater, Mullins got in line waiting for the 107 bus, and Dougherty realized he was going to Verdun. They were going to Verdun. Dougherty got on the bus, too, and they rode down the hill to Verdun Avenue.

Mullins got off at 6th Street and Dougherty crossed the street and stayed back as far as he could as Mullins walked along the line of three-storey walk-ups, exactly the same kind of building Dougherty had grown up in on Fortune Street in the Point, wrought-iron stairs on the outside up to the second- and third-floor apartments and just like Dougherty's old place, Mullins went into the apartment on the ground floor.

The street was lined on both sides for blocks with row houses so Dougherty couldn't just stand around. He made a note of the address, 485, and then walked back to Verdun Avenue.

A few minutes later, Mullins came down the street with an older woman Dougherty figured was his mother. They turned onto Verdun Avenue and walked a block to a restaurant, the New Verdun, and went inside.

It looked like something Mullins and his mother did often. Dougherty figured it was probably a weekly event. He watched them take a seat in one of the booths by the window and figured he had an hour while they ate their spaghetti and garlic bread and rice pudding and had a cup of tea but he couldn't take the chance of wandering off in case someone came by and spoke to Mullins.

Someone said, "Eddie Dougherty?"

It was a guy about Dougherty's age standing on the sidewalk beside him. The guy was smiling and he said, "From Verdun High."

"Yeah."

"Scott Leary."

"Oh yeah, Scotty. How you doing?"

"Good, good, you? I heard you were a cop." He paused and then said, "That shit with Arlene Webber's sister."

Dougherty said, "Yeah, that's right," and then he said, "You still hanging out with Danny Buckley and the Higgins brothers?"

"No, I was working at Northern Electric."

"The big factory on St. Patrick?"

"Yeah."

"What do you mean," Dougherty said, "you were?"

"You didn't hear? They're shutting it down."

"No, I didn't."

"Yeah," Leary said, "the whole thing. Everybody getting laid off."

Dougherty said, "Holy shit." Growing up half the kids in his class had parents working in that factory making telephones. "That's gotta be a couple hundred people."

"Three-sixty."

"Wow."

"On top of the seven hundred at SOMA."

Dougherty was looking past Leary at the New Verdun — he thought he saw Mullins leaving, but he was still sitting in the booth across from his mother.

"SOMA," Dougherty said, "I thought that was staying open? That's the car plant, right?"

"On the South Shore, yeah." Leary shrugged. "One shift still working, couple hundred guys, supposed to be till Christmas anyway, but they lost the contract with Renault so they'll be shutting down."

"That's tough."

"Yeah, and fifteen hundred guys laid off from GM."

"In Sainte-Thérèse?"

"Yeah, over the last year."

"Laid off," Dougherty said, "maybe they get called back."

Leary shook his head. "No way. So, there any open-ings on the police force?"

"I don't know," Dougherty said. "*Tu parles Français?*"

"Oh yeah," Leary said, "I forgot your mom was French."

"She still is."

"Yeah, well, name like Dougherty, you just got in under the wire."

"I guess."

"You better keep your head down."

Dougherty said, "It's not that bad."

Leary nodded but didn't look convinced. He didn't say anything for a moment and then he said, "Hey, you remember Alice Bedard?"

"Yeah, sure," Dougherty said. "You're not going out with her? She's out of your league."

"No," Leary said, smiling a little but then getting serious. "She was at the Blue Bird. She died in the fire."

Dougherty said, "Shit." He remembered Alice Bedard as another one of the French kids, or half-French kids, from the neighbourhood. Unlike Dougherty, she didn't go to a French elementary school, though. He said, "They had the funeral I guess?"

"Last week."

"That's too bad."

"They're still looking for those guys," Leary said. "You're still looking, I guess."

Dougherty said, "Yeah. We got one of them — he gave up the others. We just haven't found them yet."

"I hope you do."

"We will," Dougherty said.

"Okay, good, well, I gotta go."

"It was good to see you," Dougherty said and Leary said, "Yeah," as he crossed Verdun Avenue. "Good luck."

Dougherty was thinking, Yeah, of all the things I should be working on, and he looked back at Mullins in the window booth of the New Verdun listening to his mother talk. Dougherty thought he probably knew what she was saying, telling Mullins about all the people who were still in the neighbourhood, telling him about the people who had moved away. He figured Mullins probably didn't even know half of the people his mother was talking about.

A half hour later, Mullins walked his mother back home, got back on the bus and went to his own apartment. He never noticed Dougherty following him, even though by the time they got to Côte-des-Neiges, Dougherty wasn't doing much to stay out of sight.

It was still early, barely ten o'clock, so Dougherty decided to hit a couple of bars downtown and see if he could find Danny Buckley.

He didn't find him, but he found Kevin "Two Fingers" Smith.

Dougherty checked out George's again and a couple other bars near Place Ville Marie but they were all dead on Monday night, even the after-work office crowd gone back home to the suburbs. Same with the Rymark and the Peel Pub, even the workingmen home early. Things were a little more lively on Crescent, a bit of a crowd in the Winston Churchill and the Cock 'n' Bull, but no sign of Danny Buckley.

Just before midnight Dougherty thought maybe he'd take a run down the hill to the Point and see what was doing at the Arawana or the One and Two, but first he stopped in at the Royal on Guy. As he was walking to the bar, he saw a couple guys at a table in the corner and something about them made him take a closer look. One of them had only two fingers on his right hand, but it was the other guy at the table Dougherty recognized as he walked up and said, "Tucks, what are you doing on this side of the river?"

"Free country."

"You guys on the South Shore are sure behind the times."

There was a bit of a crowd in the Royal, students from Sir George from what Dougherty could tell, taking up a couple of tables on the other side of the room. They were talking loud and laughing and didn't seem to care if there was anyone else in the place.

Tucker said, "What do you want, Dougherty?"

"Who's your friend?"

"Sorry, can't help you, he's not a fag."

Dougherty took his beer from the bartender and sat down across the table from Matty Tucker and the guy with the bent fingers.

"Kevin Smith, right?"

The guy shrugged an admission — what was the big deal? He said, "What's it to you?"

Dougherty was feeling comfortable now, easing into the conversation. These two guys could just get up and walk away but Dougherty knew they wouldn't, he knew they were all comfortable with the way it worked — he was the cop and he asked the questions and they were the perps and they put up a fight but then they gave the answers.

"You from the Park, too, Kevin?"

"So?"

"I lived in Greenfield Park, for a while."

"You want a fucking medal?"

"My little brother has those patches they give out for playing on the hockey teams and the football team, shaped like a tree, you know them? League champs, playoff champs? They're like medals."

Yeah, Dougherty was comfortable as the cop now, screwing with these guys, taking his time. He drank from the beer bottle, leaned in a little closer and said, "You selling nickel bags to the smart kids?"

They were tense, Tucker and Two Fingers, but they were trying not to show it. Then Dougherty thought maybe Two Fingers wasn't that tense. The guy didn't look worried. Dougherty said, "Oh, I get it, you don't sell on the island, you're not my problem."

"We're not anybody's problem," Tucker said.

Dougherty was looking at the other guy while Tucker was talking, though, and now he was sure the guy wasn't worried. It could mean he had nothing to hide, but Dougherty figured it was more likely because he had some connections.

"I need to ask you about a guy," Dougherty said, and Tucker said, "Shit, I told you, you want to suck a dick, go to Bud's."

Dougherty said, "The grown-ups are talking here, Tucker," never taking his eyes off Two Fingers, saying, "American guy named David Murray," and he could see the recognition right away.

But Two Fingers shrugged and said, "Never heard of him," and Dougherty knew the game so he said, "I'm only going to give you one chance," and Two Fingers said, "Give me as many chances as you want, pig, I don't know the man."

Dougherty looked around the Royal, saw the students still deep in some important argument, life-changing no doubt, and the bartender watching a little black-and-white TV on a wall mount and then back to Tucker and Two Fingers.

But before Dougherty said anything, a man came into the bar and started towards the table. He saw Dougherty and walked to the bar, pretending that was where he was headed all along.

Two Fingers glanced down at a canvas bag on the floor by his feet, and Dougherty saw a brown paper bag the size of a record album sticking out of it.

"Okay," Dougherty said, "if that's the way you want it to be." He stood up and finished off his beer and put the empty bottle on the table. "Stay clean."

He walked out feeling good. Inside the paper bag was a record album and in the corner was a small square sticker with the words Cheap Thrills stenciled on it. Two Fingers had made sure he'd seen it.

The next day, Dougherty clocked out early, changed out of his uniform and walked a few blocks from Station Ten to Bishop Street and up the stairs of an old three-storey building to a store called Cheap Thrills.

The place was smaller than Dougherty expected, really only what would have been the living room and dining room when the building had been a home. A couple of people were browsing through the bins of records and there were a couple of bookshelves of used paperbacks and some textbooks.

A girl was working the cash, putting the square stickers on the corners of album covers.

Dougherty flipped through a few bins, flicking the albums and looking at the covers but he barely recognized anything, all skinny bare-chested guys with long hair and weird-looking paintings. He wandered over to the bookshelves and saw a few copies of *Immigration for Draft-Age Americans* and something called *Handbook for Conscientious Objectors*.

A man's voice said, "That's a good one," and Dougherty turned to see Two Fingers standing beside him pointing at the handbook. "It'll blow your mind."

"Really, I'm looking for a record," Dougherty said. "For my kid brother."

"Oh yeah, what's he like?"

"I'm not sure. He was disappointed he didn't get to the Alice Cooper concert."

"He like Jethro Tull?"

"Yeah, I think so."

"Get him a bootleg."

Two Fingers walked to a bin and pulled out an album with a couple of black-and-white pictures on the cover that looked like a cheap photostat. "It's got both of them."

Dougherty took the record. Across the top it said *Alice & Ian 9-71*, so he figured the guy on the left under the word Alice must be Alice Cooper. In the picture he was bare chested, of course, and holding a beer, a stubby. Dougherty said, "Is this from Montreal?"

"Recorded at Hofstra University in New York. The

Tull side has 'Aqualung,' the Cooper has 'School's Out' and 'I'm Eighteen.' He'll love it. You can be the cool brother for once."

Dougherty said okay and they went to the cash, and Two Fingers rang it up and then said to the girl, "I'm taking a break."

Outside on the sidewalk, Dougherty said, "You want a coffee?"

"Let's get away from here." He motioned along de Maisonneuve and said, "And from there." The big Sir George building.

They walked a block up Bishop to Sherbrooke, and Two Fingers said, "I hope you do a better job than he does when you go undercover."

"What're you talking about?"

"The cop on the corner there, see him, pretending to be reading the newspaper. He's watching the museum."

"You think so?"

Two Fingers got a pack of smokes out of his pocket. "Because of the robbery. Please tell me you know about that."

"Yeah," Dougherty said, "I was on that call."

"You guys are so stupid, looking at janitors and art students."

"Oh yeah?" Dougherty got out a cigarette himself and lit it. Then he handed his lighter to Two Fingers and said, "Who should we be looking at?"

Two Fingers blew smoke in Dougherty's face and said, "Gee, I don't know, Officer, but maybe Montreal isn't big enough for two mobsters."

"Mobsters?"

"You heard of Cotroni, right? And Rizutto?"

"I've heard of them," Dougherty said, but he didn't think he could come up with either guy's first name.

"Well, maybe they're stepping on each other's toes and maybe the guys in New York don't want a war here."

"What do they care?"

"Are you a rookie?"

"Mobsters aren't my department."

Two Fingers shrugged and said, "Okay, so, maybe one of the guys here was asked about getting out of town and maybe he said he'd think about it if the price was right."

"The price?"

"Maybe a couple of million dollars' worth of paintings."

Dougherty said, "How many times have you seen *The Godfather*?"

"Fine, don't believe me."

Sherbrooke Street was lined with office buildings on the south side where they were standing and the wide sidewalk was filling up with people leaving work for the day.

Dougherty said, "I want to know about David Murray."

Two Fingers slipped a book out of his pocket. *Choosing Peace.* Dougherty hadn't even noticed him take it from the shelf in Cheap Thrills.

"How much is it worth to you?"

Dougherty looked at him and Two Fingers said, "The museum stuff was a free sample. This you have to pay for."

"I had a date this weekend," Dougherty said, getting out his wallet. He handed Two Fingers a couple of fives, and the guy waved his odd fingers and said, "I hope you got laid." Dougherty gave him his last five and said, "You want the deuce, too?"

"We'll call this a down payment."

"Let's hear what you've got."

Dougherty noticed the money was gone as smoothly as Two Fingers had picked up the paperback.

"David Murray had some friends up the hill." He motioned towards the side of Mount Royal. Westmount.

"Bullshit."

"Who loves these draft dodgers the most? Who invites them to parties to talk about how evil America is?"

"But Murray wasn't a dodger, he was a deserter."

Dougherty saw Two Fingers react and then try to pretend he hadn't. He didn't know.

"Same dif."

"Not to everybody."

"Well, he had friends. And he did favours for them."

"Drug smuggling?"

"He knew his way across the border."

"I need a name."

"Richard Burnside."

Dougherty said, "You think I'm going to believe that? One of the richest guys in the city?"

"I don't care what you believe."

Dougherty was thinking it was a waste of time, working informants not as easy as he thought, and then Two Fingers said, "You've got nothing else."

"You sure about that?"

Two Fingers started walking back down the hill and said, "You're talking to me, aren't you?"

Dougherty watched him go thinking, Yeah. He already felt like the last guy interested in David Murray's murder and his interest was slipping away, too.

CHAPTER
ELEVEN

Dougherty was getting a coffee in the break room when Delisle yelled, "Hey, Dog-eh-dee, phone call," and when Dougherty got to the desk he held the receiver and said, "No personal calls, you know that."

Dougherty said, "How do you know it's personal?" thinking it might be a woman, but maybe it was work. He said, "Hello," and his brother, Tommy, said, "Hey, Eddie."

"What's going on?"

"Yeah, we're at the hospital. It's Dad."

"What? Are you at the General? What happened?"

"The Butcher Shop, the Charlie. He had a heart attack or something."

Dougherty said, "Shit, okay, I'll be right there," and

handed the receiver back to Delisle saying, "My dad's in the hospital, I gotta go," and for a second he thought about taking a cop car, but he ran the couple of blocks to where his Mustang was parked and took off in that, over the Champlain Bridge and along Taschereau, swearing at every red light until he saw the ten-storey Charles Lemoyne Hospital rising up above every other building around it.

In the crowded waiting room, Dougherty took a minute to find Tommy sitting by himself and then he rushed over to him, saying, "Tommy, hi."

The kid stood up looking stunned. "Hey, Eddie."

"Where's Dad?"

Tommy pointed. "In there." Dougherty followed his look and then said, "Is Mom with him?"

"No, she's . . ." Tommy looked down and Dougherty realized the woman sitting there was his mother.

"Ma, hi."

She turned her head slowly and looked up at Dougherty and didn't recognize him for a moment, and then she stood up and said, "*Oh, Édouard, il était comme un fantôme.*"

Dougherty hadn't recognized her, she looked a hundred years old. And scared.

"*Qu'est-ce qui s'est passé?*"

"*Il était un fantôme.*"

"Yeah, Ma, I heard — a ghost, he looked like a ghost. But how is he now?"

"*Je ne sais pas, ils l'ont . . .*"

Dougherty said, "Okay," and then looked at Tommy and said, "I'm going to talk to someone," and went to the admissions desk and found a nurse who told him to talk to a different nurse and eventually he found that his father was in the ICU, but he was going to be moved to a room in a little while, and the doctor would talk to them there.

Dougherty said, "When will that be?" and the nurse said, "Soon."

"How many minutes is soon?"

The nurse motioned at Dougherty's uniform and said, "*C'est comme ça,*" and Dougherty said, "Yeah, I know how it is."

He went back and sat down beside his mother, still having trouble believing it was her — he'd never seen her look so frail. "They said they'd be moving him into a room soon and we can see him then."

She nodded, or Dougherty thought he saw her nod. The adrenalin pump of driving across the bridge and bursting into the hospital was wearing off and Dougherty was starting to feel anxious. He fumbled in his pocket for his smokes and got one out and got it lit. He let out a long breath and then took another quick drag and tried to settle back in the chair, but he was still fidgety and tense.

There was an ashtray on a stand across the room, so Dougherty got up and went over to it and stood there flicking his cigarette until he finished it and butted it out.

Tommy and his mother hadn't moved. The seat beside his mother was still empty but Dougherty couldn't go back to it.

Shit, he was thinking, his father was only fifty-three, too young for a heart attack, but then he thought of Detective Marcotte at Station Four a few years earlier, dropped dead in the break room. Marcotte wasn't much over fifty at the time.

But Dougherty's father hadn't dropped dead. He was going to be moved to a regular room; he was going to be fine.

The nurse Dougherty had spoken to came into the waiting room then and said, "Madame Doe-er-dee?"

Dougherty stepped up to her and said, "Can we see him now?"

"He has been moved," she said, "but he is resting. *Peut-être juste madame pour l'instant?*"

"I better go with her."

Dougherty crossed the room to where his mother was sitting and said, "Ma, come on." He helped her up and Tommy stood up, too, and Dougherty said, "Why don't you wait here."

"I want to see him."

"Wait here for now."

Dougherty took his mother's arm and led her, as if he was leading his grandmother, down the hall, past the nursing station and to a big room with half a dozen beds.

His father was in the far bed by the window.

Dougherty's mother stopped as soon as they got into the room.

"Come on, Ma, *viens avec moi.*"

He had to pull her a little.

There was one chair beside the bed and Dougherty helped his mother into it. His father opened his eyes and said something but it just came out as a mumble and then his eyes closed.

A few minutes later a doctor came into the room

and spoke to Dougherty in French, saying he'd spoken to his father's doctor at the Royal Victoria and they'd be transferring him later in the day. Dougherty said, *"Quel médecin au Royal Vic?"*

"Dr. MacIsaac."

Dougherty had completely forgotten. "Oh right, the high blood-pressure pills."

The doctor said he'd be back later and left.

Dougherty said, "Dr. MacIsaac is the specialist, right?"

"Oui, le spécialiste du cœur."

"I forgot about the last time."

"La dernière fois était pas un arrêt cardiaque."

Dougherty watched his mother close her eyes and then he said, "No, what was it?"

"Au travail, l'année dernière . . ." She waved her hands a little. *"Il avait, une constriction. Des douleurs à la poitrine."*

"Shortness of breath, that's all?"

His mother didn't say anything and Dougherty said, "How many . . . incidents have there been?"

She shook her head a little and said, *"Quelques."*

"How many is some? Never mind." Dougherty had nothing else to say. He was mad now, angry that this was going on and he didn't even know. But then he realized he was angry because he hadn't remembered about the high blood pressure and the previous visits to the heart specialist and he hadn't taken it seriously enough.

His mother said, "He will need surgery."

"Heart surgery?"

She nodded.

Now Dougherty just wanted to get out of the room, out of the hospital. He said, "I've got to get back to work."

"What about Tommy?"

"What about him?"

"He can't go home by himself."

Dougherty thought, Sure he can — the hospital was next to the Dairy Queen he went to by himself all the time — but then he realized what his mother meant, and he said, "Where's Cheryl?"

"I don't know."

Dougherty looked at his watch, nearly noon, and said, "Okay, I'll take Tommy to lunch and I'll find Cheryl. You're going to go with Dad to the Royal Vic?"

She nodded and Dougherty walked to the door and stopped and looked back and all the anger drained away. His parents, both of them, looked so old and weak and it seemed to him it had happened overnight.

In the waiting room Dougherty said, "Okay, he's going to be fine, he's just going to get some sleep. You want to get some lunch?"

"Can I see him?"

"Let's get some lunch first. He'll be awake when we get back. You can talk to him then."

Dougherty drove a few blocks on Taschereau until they came to the A&W drive-in and he pulled into one of the angled parking spaces and rolled down the window. "You want a teen burger?"

Tommy said, "Sure," the first thing he'd said since they left the hospital.

Dougherty pushed the button on the box and

ordered a couple of teen burgers and fries and a root beer and a coffee.

Tommy said, "Is he really going to be okay?"

"Yeah, he's going to be fine."

"He's going to come home today, is he?"

Dougherty looked at his little brother and wanted to tell him everything would be fine. He said, "Everything will be back to normal soon," and Tommy said, "Yeah, normal," and Dougherty figured the kid knew a lot more about what was going on than anybody realized.

"He's going to be transferred to the Royal Vic."

"For heart surgery," Tommy said. "I knew it."

Dougherty didn't say anything.

"He was on the kitchen floor," Tommy said. "When I came home from delivering my *Gazette*s, he was on the floor. Mom . . . she was just sitting on a chair at the table. They're usually gone to work when I get back."

Dougherty waited a moment and then Tommy said, "I said we have to call an ambulance, we have to call, and she was just staring."

"In shock, I see it at work."

Tommy looked like he didn't believe it was shock. "I called them."

"You called?"

"The police. 671-1931. The number's on the back of every stop sign, I stare at it waiting for the bus."

"It's good you knew it."

"They came to the front door, and I told them to come around the back. The ambulance guys, they couldn't get the stretcher into the kitchen so they left it on the balcony and carried Dad out." Tommy paused. "I knew about the last one, that time at work. Mom came home by herself and he didn't come home till the next day and they didn't want to tell me. They never want to tell me anything."

"I know how you feel."

Tommy didn't say anything, and Dougherty said, "They don't want you to worry."

"They think that's better?"

It was quiet for a minute and then the waitress came up to the car, and Dougherty rolled the window down so she could set the tray on it.

She said, "Out for lunch, Officer?"

"Yeah." He gave her a five and she gave him his change and he said, "Thanks." He handed Tommy his burger and fries and said, "Don't spill anything in my car."

"You should have brought a police car."

"I thought about it. You can spill anything in that —" he put the glass mug on the dashboard and said, "but not in here."

"I heard you, jeez."

They ate their burgers and didn't say anything for a while and then Dougherty said, "You think we'll win all four games in Moscow?"

"You think we'll win one?"

"We better."

They finished their burgers, and Dougherty said, "That was okay. Too bad the Burger Ranch closed."

"Scott MacKenzie has about ten gallons of cherry milkshake stuff at his house."

"That's right," Dougherty said, "his father owned it, didn't he?"

"Him and that guy on the Alouettes."

"Mr. MacKenzie is friends with Dad, isn't he?"

Tommy said, "I don't know."

Dougherty said, "Yeah, I think he is."

The waitress came then and took away the tray, and Dougherty drove back to the hospital. A couple hours later, Dougherty's father was put into a St. John's Ambulance and taken to the Royal Victoria Hospital. At first the driver said Dougherty's mother couldn't travel in the ambulance, but Dougherty asked for a personal favour. The guy looked at his uniform and said, "I don't work on the island," and Dougherty said, "You never know, I'm at Station Ten, you might go to the Forum," and the guy nodded okay.

Dougherty drove Tommy home to Patricia Street and went inside with him. Tommy went down to the basement to watch TV and Dougherty got on the phone looking for Cheryl. He called a couple of her friends and found out that Frannie Massey had an apartment downtown and that's where he found Cheryl. He said, "Dad's in the hospital," and she said, "Again?" and Dougherty thought everyone else knew but him. Or everyone else remembered.

"Can you come home and stay with Tommy?"

"How bad is it?"

"They're taking him to the Royal Vic — they're talking about surgery."

"Shit."

"Can you come home now?"

"No, I have a class tonight and an early class tomorrow, I'm staying here tonight."

"A class tonight?"

"Sir George has a lot of night classes."

Dougherty said, "Sure," trying for sarcastic but then he was thinking about the fights he'd had with his father when Dougherty finished high school and didn't want to go to university, his father talking up McGill until Dougherty joined the police force and then talking up Sir George and the night classes. Now Dougherty was thinking it had been a while since his father had mentioned university.

He said, "I'm going to go get Mom and bring her home tonight, but I don't know how late it'll be." And then, to try and make his case better he said, "She's having a really hard time with this, she's in shock."

"She's not in shock," Cheryl said, "she's suffering from depression."

"Jesus, Cheryl, you take one psychology class and you know everything," Dougherty said before he could catch himself.

"I didn't even need the class," Cheryl said. "I can't believe you don't see it." Then she said, "Yes, I do, you don't see anything — how can you be a cop?"

"How long will it take you to get here?"

"I told you, I can't."

"Can you go to the Royal Vic and pick up Mom?"

"Why did she even go, what can she do?"

"Look, just come home. I have to get back to work and then I'll go get Mom."

There was a pause and then Cheryl said, "How's Tommy?"

"He's okay."

"All right, I'm coming home."

"Thanks."

He hung up and sat in the kitchen for a few minutes. He looked at the ashtray full of butts and saw his father sitting at the table with a smoke and a rum and Coke after everyone else had gone to bed, reading every page of the newspaper.

Then he saw Tommy's canvas newspaper bag on the floor by the stove and he picked it up and called down to the basement, "I'm going to go see Mom and Dad at the hospital. Cheryl's coming home, she'll make dinner." Then he got a few bucks out of his wallet and said, "She'll order a pizza from Miss Italia."

For a moment the only sound from the basement was *Gilligan's Island* and then Tommy said, "Okay."

Dougherty felt shitty leaving the house. He felt shitty all the way to the hospital and when he got there the first thing his mother said was, "*C'est tout en anglais, ici,*" and Dougherty said, "Yeah, Ma, it's the Royal Vic." He was thinking that she didn't have any problem understanding English so what was she talking about now, but he looked at her and she took his hand and looked helpless.

Dougherty looked at the doctor, figuring he must be MacIsaac, and then back to his mother and translated, "*C'est une procédure simple, c'est commun,*" he said. "*Ils vont prendre un bout de la veine de sa jambe et l'utiliser pour contourner les artères endommagées.*"

MacIsaac clearly didn't understand any French but nodded in agreement and said, "That's right, Mrs. Dougherty, bypass surgery is a very common procedure."

"But this is emergency bypass," Dougherty said. "That's different, isn't it?"

"Not really," MacIsaac said. "It's exactly the same

procedure." He shrugged. "I've spoken to your father about this. We've been monitoring him, as you know," and he looked accusingly at Dougherty who said, "Right, yeah," and then the doctor said, "And with his smoking and drinking and stress levels we knew this would be a possibility."

"Heart surgery?"

"Bypass surgery, yes."

"So, you're going to do it now?"

"He's being prepped now, yes."

Dougherty said, "Okay, thanks."

MacIsaac looked at Dougherty's mother and said, "You might as well have your son take you home and you can get some sleep. Your husband will be in surgery most of the night and in recovery most of the day tomorrow."

Then he nodded quickly at Dougherty and turned and walked away.

"Dormir? Comment je peut dormir?"

"Come on," Dougherty said. "He's right, there's no point in staying here."

Dougherty felt shitty all the way back home with his mother and even though he knew he should have felt better when Cheryl met them at the door and talked gently and reassuringly and had things in order in the house and was clearly handling it better than anyone else he still felt shitty.

172

Carpentier said, "That's funny, he was in court yesterday. He won."

"Cotroni?"

"That's right."

Dougherty said, "I thought that wasn't till tomorrow?"

"That's the other one, Frank," Detective Robert Ste. Marie said. "The extortion on the restaurant."

Dougherty said, "Yeah, the Greek."

Ste. Marie drained his coffee and said, "You making sure he gets to court?"

"Someone is."

"This was Vincenzo. That thing with the magazine." Carpentier picked up his smoked meat sandwich. "He asked for a million dollars in damages."

Ste. Marie said, "*Un million deux cent cinquante.*"

"He won a million and a quarter?" Dougherty said but saw Carpentier smiling already.

"He won the case, the judge lowered the claim a little."

Ste. Marie was laughing. "*Deux dollars.*"

"Two dollars?"

"That's right. It was St. Germain," Carpentier said. "He said one dollar for the English article and one for the French. He was feeling generous, I guess."

"It was ten years ago, the article," Ste. Marie said. "Called Cotroni the most powerful mafioso in Canada."

Dougherty said, "Is he?"

The waitress was at the table then with the coffee pot but Ste. Marie said, "*Non, merci.*" She held up the pot for Carpentier and Dougherty but they both waved her off and she walked away.

"*Comme ton stooler dit,*" Ste. Marie said, "*il y a une fight, maintenant.*"

"Between him and this Rizutto guy?"

Ste. Marie shook his head and looked at Carpentier, making a "this guy" motion towards Dougherty. Then Ste. Marie spoke English, saying, "At this libel trial with *Maclean's* magazine, that went on for a fucking year, Cotroni's lawyers were trying to get us to show them everything we have on him. The judge wanted us to show everything. I testified ten fucking times, I told them these investigations are ongoing, we can't tell them anything now."

"But it is possible he's right," Dougherty said, "that the paintings really were stolen to give to this Rizutto guy?"

"It's not so crazy," Ste. Marie agreed. "Paintings are easy to get out of the country and the value will only go up."

"And they can make him feel sophisticated," Carpentier said. "Like a big shot. There were other robberies?"

Dougherty said, "Yeah, in Italy and in the USA and England, I think."

"And this woman from the museum, she said they could make a collection?"

"Yeah, she said people don't have just a bunch of paintings on the walls," Dougherty said, "they have collections. I don't really get it."

174 Ste. Marie shrugged and said, "Who knows. But it's true, there were guys here from New York staying at expensive hotels. They had meetings."

"I didn't see anything about that in the papers," Dougherty said, and Carpentier shook his head a little at the sarcasm.

"They don't want the Italians going to war with each other — they have to watch these bikers getting stronger all the time."

"And killing each other," Carpentier said. "But they're getting better at it. This body dumped on Atwater," he looked at Dougherty and said, "we've got nothing."

"And the English," Ste. Marie said, "coming out of the Point now, working the whole west end."

Dougherty said, "Irish," but he knew the French cops wouldn't see any difference.

Carpentier said to Ste. Marie, "You talking to Boisjoli?"

"*Oui*." Ste. Marie was standing up then and he said, "We'll see if this is true, with the paintings," and Dougherty said, "How?"

Ste. Marie said, "If Rizutto leaves town," and walked out of the restaurant.

Carpentier lit a cigarette and said to Dougherty, "You're not still on the museum surveillance?"

"We're rotating guys," Dougherty said, "so it's not the same faces all the time." And then he said, "And I missed a shift, my father's in the hospital."

"Is it serious?"

"Looks like heart surgery."

Carpentier nodded. "The Royal Vic?"

"Yeah."

175

"That's good."

Dougherty said, "Yeah."

Carpentier waited a moment and then said, "The coroner's inquest starts tomorrow. Did they call you as a witness?"

"No."

"Maybe they will. It's going to be bad, *câlisse*."

Dougherty said yeah. The final count was thirty-seven people killed in the fire, what everyone was calling the Blue Bird fire even though the club upstairs where all the people died was called the Wagon Wheel. "It would be good if we had the other two."

"We'll get them," Carpentier said.

Dougherty lit a cigarette himself and leaned back in his chair. He was in his uniform, on lunch and he was thinking he should get back to Station Ten but he stayed in his seat.

Then Carpentier said, "This *stooler*, he knew David Murray?"

"He did. He said he did. I don't know, what he gave me sounds useless, he said Murray was hanging out with Richard Burnside."

"It's possible, why not? Like the lawyer said, lots of people with money are helping the Americans, giving them jobs, places to stay."

"I guess."

"Isn't Burnside in the rock 'n' roll business?"

"Oh," Dougherty said, "you mean the son."

"Not the old man." Carpentier shrugged and took a drag on his smoke. "But I would like to look into him, too, someday."

"Maybe he'll kill someone and you'll get your chance."

"I don't think he'd ever do it himself," Carpentier said. "He has people for that."

"Should I talk to the son?"

Carpentier said, "You'll need more than the word

of a *stooler*, to talk to such a rich guy, so connected, so many lawyers."

Dougherty said okay. But he did want to do something. He was feeling how a homicide investigation could get under his skin, how the idea that someone who beat a man to death could be walking around the city like nothing happened and he wanted to do everything he could to find the guy.

He was starting to understand how little it had to do with being his job.

———

Dougherty called the *Gazette* reporter, Keith Logan, and asked him what he knew about Richard Burnside and the rock 'n' roll business.

Logan said, "Are you working narcotics now?"

"Maybe, depends what you can tell me."

"Nothing, really, just rumours."

"Good place to start."

"I'm pretty busy," Logan said. "Why don't you buy me lunch."

"Sure, we'll grab a couple hot dogs."

"When you're a real detective, you'll have an expense account." There was a pause and then Logan said, "You know the Star of India?"

"Yeah, but I've never eaten there."

"Neither have I, but I need some quotes, I'll be there in an hour."

———

Dougherty sat across from Logan and said, "You a restaurant critic now?"

"Local spin on the big story."

A waiter came to the table and Logan said, "Have the butter chicken — he says it's just like St. Hubert."

"All right."

The waiter did a quick bow and was gone.

Dougherty said, "What's the big story?"

"Idi Amin is kicking all the Asians out of Uganda."

"The Chinese?"

"No," Logan said, "Asian." He waved his hand motioning around the restaurant and said, "Indians."

"India Indians, not native Indians."

"Right. Sixty thousand people. They have a month to get out."

"Or what?"

Logan shrugged. "What do you think? I might call the story 'None Is Too Many.'"

The waiter was back at the table then, and he put down a plate with a large, thick piece of bread on it. Logan said, "Naan." He thanked the waiter and the guy backed away.

"What's that mean, none is too many?"

"In the war, in the lead-up to it, when the Jews were trying to get out of Europe, trying to get anywhere else and someone asked Canada how many refugees we'd take, that was the answer, none is too many."

"I didn't know that."

Logan tore a piece off the naan and motioned for Dougherty to do the same. "I doubt the editors will let me say that — doesn't fit with our current image of ourselves."

"Why are they getting kicked out?"

"Amin says he had a dream." Logan shrugged. "But

there's been tension for a while, the Asians are pretty good businessmen, they came in with the British, built the railways and all that."

"And now they've got to go?"

"Expelled. Like the Acadians."

"*Le Grand Dérangement*," Dougherty said. "My mother's family."

"So, I'm trying to get some quotes but no one wants to say anything."

"Not even off the record?"

"No one knows what's going to happen. Amin used the word 'camps,' people are scared. I talked to the owner here, the waiters, everyone's worried they might say the wrong thing."

The waiter was back at the table then, smiling as he put down a little silver dish filled with pieces of chicken in a kind of yellow sauce and a bowl of rice.

Logan said, "My friend here is a policeman, he's here to protect you."

The waiter said, "Yes, of course," still smiling as he walked away.

"I did answer a call here once," Dougherty said. "Some drunk wouldn't leave. He was telling war stories, the time he spent in India."

"I bet he said it was hot."

Dougherty laughed a little and said, "I don't remember."

"So," Logan said, "what's this about rock 'n' roll."

"This is off the record," Dougherty said.

"It always is. Until it isn't."

"Fair enough." Dougherty took a bite of the chicken and said, "This is good."

"They have a dish here with eggplant. I didn't think it was possible to make eggplant taste good."

"So, what do you know about Richard Burnside?"

"He's a dilettante."

"His rock 'n' roll business looks real."

"With his father bankrolling it. But yeah, he's booked some big concerts, he might be doing okay."

"But there are rumours about him?"

Logan scraped the last of the butter chicken onto the rice on his plate. "It's not so much that there are rumours, it's just that's all there are — rumours."

"What do you mean?"

"No one really seems to know much about the guy."

"He's kind of famous."

"That's just it," Logan said. "He's famous but he's not. Outside of publicity stuff, getting his picture taken with Marc Bolan, no one ever sees him."

"No one you know."

"I know everyone."

Dougherty said, "Sorry, I forgot." He used some of the naan to wipe up the last of the butter chicken sauce. "He must hang around with someone."

"He spends money. He invests."

"In what?"

"Clubs."

"Which ones?"

"I heard some guys who worked at Winston Churchill's opened their own place and they got the money from friends, artists mostly but artists don't have any money."

"So it was Burnside? Why wouldn't they say that?"

"Who knows, but he doesn't want his name tossed around."

Dougherty said, "Okay," and he was thinking that it would be impossible to get a meeting with the guy but he might be able to just run into him. Then he said, "So, are we going to take in any of these Asian refugees?"

"I think so," Logan said. "If we can be quiet about it."

***

The Rainbow Bar and Grill was only a block from the Playboy Club but a world away inside.

The new world, Dougherty figured, now that the Playboy Club was closed and the Rainbow was going strong, Tuesday night, just after eight, and the place was crowded. The music was canned, no sign of a band, but it was rock 'n' roll and the customers were all in their twenties. A thick cloud of smoke filled the room and Dougherty noticed more packs of Gauloises on the tables than Export As.

He sat at the end of the bar, and a waitress passing by said, "You want to eat, or just a beer?" without slowing down. Dougherty watched while she loaded her tray and came back around the bar and he said, "What's good?"

"Lamb curry."

Dougherty was thinking everyone was getting in on the Indian food. After he'd left Logan he'd asked around and found out that the guys from Winston Churchill's had opened the Rainbow. He said, "Just a beer, a Fifty."

A minute later, the waitress put a beer bottle on the bar in front of Dougherty without stopping as she headed off towards the tables in the back. The lights were low, of course, and Dougherty couldn't make out many faces. They all looked the same, anyway, the men with beards and long hair, the women with even longer hair hanging straight down. From what he could see there was more wine being drunk than beer.

And then he saw someone he knew. She was sitting at a table with a few other people but she was looking at Dougherty.

He nodded a little and she looked away.

Still wearing the workboots.

Dougherty saw a back door open then and a couple of people come out into the bar, a man and woman who both looked to be in their early thirties, and he figured they were the owners he'd heard about. He watched them circulate a little, stopping at a couple of tables and moving on until the guy sat down at a table and the woman disappeared into the back room.

Judy MacIntyre was getting up then and putting on her coat. Dougherty left a dollar bill tucked under his beer bottle on the bar, and he followed her outside.

She was walking up the hill towards Sherbrooke and didn't seem surprised when Dougherty caught up to her.

"Don't tell me," he said, "you've got work to do."

She didn't slow down. "So what if I do?"

"It just seems," Dougherty said, "that in all your groups, you're the only one doing any work."

"What do you want?"

"I want to find out who killed David Murray."

"Well then," she said, "it seems that in your group you're the only one doing any work."

"Oh, there's lots of work being done," Dougherty said and he hoped it sounded more convincing to Judy MacIntyre than it did to himself. "I'm just the only one you see."

"You don't make much of an undercover cop."

"I was looking for Richard Burnside, he owns that place. Do you know him?"

She didn't slow down. "A lot of people invested."

"I heard. I wonder how many put up as much money as Burnside? Do you think if we looked we could find a connection between his family and the building the bar is in?"

"Why don't you go do that."

"Why didn't you tell me that David Murray was hanging out with Richard Burnside?"

They were at Sherbrooke then and she stopped. "They weren't hanging out."

"Are you sure?"

"You don't know anything, do you?"

The light changed and she started across Sherbrooke.

"Why don't you tell me?"

"It's true, Burnside's family owns a lot of buildings," she said, walking quickly through the Roddick Gates onto the McGill campus. "So Richard is helping us fight this development."

"What development?"

She stopped walking then and looked at Dougherty and said, "Every time I think you can't possibly know any less you surprise me."

"With so many people keeping secrets," Dougherty said, "how can I know anything?"

"It's no secret what's going on in Milton Park: they're throwing people out of their homes to build a monstrosity that will —"

"Okay," Dougherty cut her off. "There's a lot going on, it's tough to keep up. And you're right, I guess I'm not very good at it yet. But doesn't it seem odd to you that no one knows where David Murray was for a week before he was killed, and then someone caved in his skull with a rock? Don't you want to know what happened?"

She was still looking at Dougherty but her anger was fading. She said, "I guess I didn't think about how he was killed. It sounds awful."

"I don't think there's a good way for it to happen but, yeah, it was awful." Dougherty shrugged a little and said, "And the detectives think it was probably someone he knew."

"Why do they say that?"

Dougherty hesitated and then said, "The blows hit him from the front, he would've been looking at his attacker. There was no struggle, no sign that he tried to run. It looks like he was face to face with someone and they beat him. To death."

"My God, I didn't . . ." Judy started walking through the dark, quiet campus. "I feel bad I don't have any idea what he was doing lately."

"But he did know Richard Burnside?"

"I don't know. They were at some of the same meetings."

"But you don't really know where David was spending his time."

"But Richard, he's just —" she paused then and Dougherty waited and she said, "Well, you know."

"I thought we already figured out," Dougherty said, "that I don't know anything."

For a moment he thought he saw her smile.

"Richard Burnside is a rich kid who likes to hang out with the people, you know? Maybe he feels guilty his father is bulldozing all these houses, maybe he wants to be in the bar business or the rock 'n' roll business, maybe he just wants to meet girls, I don't know."

Dougherty had a feeling not many people involved in her causes lived up to Judy MacIntyre's expectations. He said, "But he did know David Murray."

"He knows lots of people."

They were walking off campus and onto Milton Street, past the McConnell Engineering building and Dougherty was thinking the last time he was here was probably a couple of years ago when a bomb had gone off in the basement. Seemed like a long time ago now.

"Well, look, if you think of anything, call me, okay?"

"I've told you everything."

"Have you?"

She glanced over her shoulder but didn't slow down, and Dougherty thought about stopping and watching her walk but he had the feeling that there was something going on here, something she wanted to say, so he kept pace with her, and they both turned onto Hutchison.

It was a cool September evening and with the school semester only recently started up, there were a few students on the street and they seemed to be in a good mood.

Judy MacIntyre slowed down as she got closer to her house, and Dougherty said, "Would you like to get a drink somewhere?"

She laughed and said, "With you?"

"Yeah, with me."

"Aren't you working?"

They were stopped in front of the house then and a couple of students pushed past them on the sidewalk.

Dougherty said, "Aren't you?"

Judy was watching the students as they joined a group of friends and continued up the street, and Dougherty was about to say something about how young they were or maybe how old he felt, and then he realized Judy was looking at him.

She said, "You probably know places where there aren't any students."

"And even some where there aren't any cops."

He took her to a little bar on St. Laurent just below St. Catherine that was almost all men, gay men, and Judy thought that was funny. They had a good time.

Such a good time they ended up back at Dougherty's apartment.

CHAPTER
TWELVE

Dougherty was the first cop on the scene, and a middle-aged man in a suit and tie met him at the door saying, "This way."

"Is everyone out of the building?"

"Yes."

The building was on McGregor, a couple blocks above Sherbrooke, in with a few other consulates in big old stone buildings that were once houses in the Golden Mile. Dougherty followed the man into the reception area and saw the letter in the middle of the desk. The envelope was about three by six inches and maybe an inch thick, white, and addressed to a man personally.

Dougherty said, "Are you Pinchas Shaanan?"

"Yes, I'm the consul-general here."

"What kind of stamps are they?"

"They are Dutch," Shaanan said. "It was mailed from Amsterdam. Like the one in London."

"Which one in London?"

"Yesterday, a letter bomb exploded at our embassy in London, a man was killed."

"The ambassador?"

"No," Shaanan said, "but the letter was addressed to him personally. The man killed was named Sachori, the agricultural attaché. The bomb was like this one — it was among the letters of condolence. For Munich."

Dougherty said, "All right, you better get out, too."

The rest of the consulate staff were standing around on the sidewalk on McGregor as the black station wagon pulled up and Sergeant Vachon got out and said, "Good to see you, Constable."

Dougherty said, "Just like old times."

"But we have different procedures now," Vachon said, following Dougherty into the building.

"There, it's a letter bomb."

Vachon put his hand on Dougherty's shoulder and said, "Just like in Ireland."

"The guy said the other one was in London."

"Oh no," Vachon said, "I just meant there have been many from Ireland to England. This is something new, from Amsterdam." He leaned over and looked closely at the envelope and then looked around the office and said, "*Bien*, we should take it away from here. Which is the nearest park?"

"Jeanne-Mance, I guess."

"All right, we'll take it there."

Vachon had a canvas bag over his shoulder and he put it on the desk next to the envelope. Then he looked at Dougherty and said, "Perhaps you should wait outside, Constable, just in case."

Dougherty didn't want to leave the room, but he understood and walked down the hall to the front door. Standing on the front steps he saw an old car pull up and the newspaper reporter, Logan, get out.

A minute later Vachon came up behind Dougherty saying, "Let's go," and Dougherty said, "Follow me."

He got into his squad car and drove along Pine Avenue, no siren or light, and then up Park Avenue. Vachon was following in his station wagon and behind him was a black truck with no markings on it at all.

Dougherty drove a couple hundred feet up Park Avenue and then pulled up onto the sidewalk and drove into the middle of the grass. Jeanne-Mance Park was a flat, open space between the wide Park Avenue and the base of Mount Royal and although there were very few people around when the convoy of police vehicles pulled in, there was a small crowd by the time Vachon and a couple of technicians had removed their portable x-ray machine from the truck.

"This is your new procedure?" Dougherty said.

"Yes." Vachon stood back with Dougherty and watched the technicians work.

Logan came up beside them and said, "Were the stamps Dutch?"

Vachon said, "You know we can't comment," and Logan looked past him to Dougherty who shrugged.

"All right," Logan said, "the police do not deny that the envelope was mailed from Amsterdam."

One of the technicians by the x-ray machine waved Vachon over, and as he walked away he looked back at Dougherty and said, "Don't tell him anything."

Dougherty nodded, and Logan waited a moment and said, "Was it addressed to the consulate or to a man personally?"

"Didn't you hear what Vachon just said?"

"Police do not deny that the envelope was addressed to the consul-general personally."

"I'm sure there'll be a full statement this afternoon," Dougherty said, "if it is a bomb."

"Oh, it's a bomb," Logan said. "They've been delivered all over the world."

"What?"

"At least twenty," Logan said. "The one in London is the only one to have gone off."

A couple more cop cars had arrived in the park, and the small crowd was keeping back on their own.

Dougherty said to Logan, "They have a portable x-ray machine."

"It's the first time they've used it."

A minute later, Vachon was walking back towards them with a piece of paper in his hand saying, "Plastic explosive."

"That's it?" Dougherty said.

"No, the technicians are taking it," Vachon said. "It was moulded to be flat in the envelope and there was a small detonator. Quite sophisticated."

"So what's that?"

"I can't read it," Vachon said, "I don't know."

Logan said, "'Remember Black September.'"

"You can read Arabic?"

"It's what all the others said."

Vachon looked surprised and said, "Others? Here?"

"No," Dougherty said, "all around the world, at least twenty of them."

Vachon looked impressed that Dougherty knew this, and Dougherty shrugged a little and said, "Or so I heard."

"Good, Constable, that's good," Vachon said. Then, "*Bien*, we'll take this back, start the investigation, see if it's the same as the others."

As Vachon was getting in his station wagon and driving away Dougherty said, "That'll keep him busy for weeks. Maybe he'll get a trip to London out of it."

"If there's no more here," Logan said. "We got a letter at the *Gazette*, from the other side I guess, someone calling themselves the International Anti-Terrorist Organization, said they're planning on bombing Arab airlines and embassies around the world."

"So they're not totally anti-terrorist," Dougherty said.

"They say after the deaths at the Tel Aviv airport, the murders in Munich and more attacks on airplanes flying into Israel, they have no option."

"These Remember Black September guys," Dougherty said, "they have no options either."

"No one does, they say."

The other cop cars were pulling out and the small crowd was dispersing but Dougherty leaned back against his car and watched.

Logan said, "Hey, they arrested an IRA leader in Belfast yesterday and found a rocket launcher."

"Great," Dougherty said.

"You don't sound happy about it."

"Neither do you."

"No," Logan said, "I guess not. The newsroom always gets excited, it sounds like a good story, but it never ends well."

"For anybody."

"Yeah."

"Does it seem like a coincidence to you," Dougherty said, "that all these guys have no other choice but to act like James Bond? I wonder if they'd work so hard at it if it was boring work and didn't make the papers but helped people."

Logan did a little double-take looking at Dougherty and said, "Where did that come from?"

"Someone said it to me yesterday."

"Woman?"

"What makes you say that?"

"Because it sounds like you actually listened to it. Watch it," Logan said. "If we're going to play cops and robbers we need the cops in the game."

"Oh, we're in the game," Dougherty said, "don't worry."

Logan was walking back to his car then, saying, "You better be."

Dougherty didn't move for a moment, and then he got out his pack of smokes and lit one, still leaning back against his car. Of course it was a woman who'd talked to him about all these guys acting like James Bond instead of doing the boring work — it was Judy MacIntyre. After they'd got back to Dougherty's apartment and made out and were lying in bed, they talked. And talked and talked.

Judy asked him how he knew about the gay bar, and Dougherty said he worked downtown, he had to know all the bars. But she was easy to talk to and waited for more and then he got serious and said of all the bars downtown they were the least of his problems, almost never called the cops, but he was being asked to check them out a lot more often. "There's a rumour," he said, "that the mayor wants to clean up downtown for the Olympics."

"But you said those bars aren't a problem."

"Remember what happened before Expo," Dougherty said, "they bulldozed Goose Village so you wouldn't see it coming in off the bridge. The mayor has his own ideas about what's a problem."

That got them talking about all the neighbourhoods being knocked down, people kicked out so shiny new buildings could go in, and Judy had quite a bit to say about Milton Park, how much was going on behind the scenes, who was getting paid off, who could be trusted, who couldn't, and Dougherty said, "You mean there are spies?"

"It's just word travels fast, people always seem to know exactly what we're going to do."

"And this is a big development?"

"Huge, haven't you seen the plans?"

"No."

Judy was looking up at the ceiling then, taking a drag on her cigarette and blowing out a stream of smoke, and she said, "It'll completely change downtown — the whole area from McGill past Park Avenue, from Pine to Sherbrooke. They're planning half a dozen forty-storey apartment towers, shopping malls, hotels. It's huge."

"But you guys are fighting it?"

"Every step of the way."

"And there are spies?"

"Yes."

"So it's dangerous?"

She turned her head on the pillow then and looked at Dougherty and smiled a little and said, "Do you think I need police protection?" and he said, "Oh, I'm sure of that, but that's not what I was thinking."

"What were you . . . oh no, couldn't be."

"Why not?"

"You think someone killed David Murray because of this development?"

"All I know for sure," Dougherty said, "is that someone killed David Murray."

"But it couldn't have been because of this."

"What could it have been because of?"

"Well, I don't know, but . . ." and that's what got Judy talking about the boring work that needed to be done for change. Whether it was anti-war movements in the U.S. or pro-democracy in South America, or Middle East peace, or housing issues in Montreal, the real work was always slow and boring and was all about meetings and talking to people and finding common ground and making compromises and baby steps. She said that a few times, how the progress was in the small steps, but then she said, "But boys will be boys — they love to hijack airplanes and kidnap people and set off bombs."

Dougherty said, "There are usually women with them."

"I know, I know. I just hate it, all the violence. It just leads to more."

Dougherty didn't say anything for a minute and then Judy said, "They always say they have no choice but they always seem to enjoy it *sooo* much, all the sneaking around, the secret codes, everything's *sooo* dramatic, like a big game of cops and robbers."

"Except people really get hurt."

"Yes, they do."

Dougherty said, "They really don't want to put on the workboots."

"No fun in that."

Dougherty wanted to say the workboots were what he'd remembered about her, what he liked about her, but he didn't think that was what she wanted to hear.

Then she said, "Democracy's hard and it's boring. And slow. These guys are all in a hurry."

"Our democracy is a terribly flawed system," Dougherty said. "It's just the best one we've come up with so far."

"Who said that?"

"I don't know — I heard it from my father."

Then they talked about their fathers a little. Dougherty didn't want to, but Judy asked and he couldn't see a way to avoid it, so he told her about the heart attack and his father going in for surgery, and she told him it wouldn't be so bad, saying, "My father had a double bypass last year."

"How old is he?"

"Old," Judy said. "Really old, fifties." Then she smiled a little and said, "Anyone over thirty . . ." and Dougherty said yeah.

"Can you talk to him?" Judy said. "To your father?"

"More now."

"I can't talk to mine. He doesn't want to listen."

Dougherty said, "Do you listen to him?"

"I guess not. All my talk about finding common ground, and I can't find any with him. Or with my mother."

"Baby steps," Dougherty said.

"Yeah, baby steps." She curled up to him then and closed her eyes.

Now Dougherty was looking around Jeanne-Mance Park, he could see the McGill athletic building on Pine and some old apartment buildings beyond that and he wondered if they were part of the development, if they were going to be demolished, and he thought he could understand why people would fight that.

But he didn't have any idea how far anyone would take it. The longer he was a cop the more he realized he had no idea what people were capable of.

CHAPTER
THIRTEEN

That night Dougherty caught a break.

But he couldn't help but wonder who really arranged it.

He got an overtime shift with the Morality Squad raiding a couple of bars. Captain Boisvert had forgiven Dougherty for his testimony in the strippers' indecency trial, even though the women were acquitted. The squad hit two bars just before closing, one in the Iroquois Hotel on Place Jacques-Cartier in Old Montreal and the one Dougherty was in on, Le Chat Noir on Sherbrooke East, at the corner of Ste. Famille — between Jeanne-Mance and St. Urbain.

They arrested thirteen people in all, taking them to Bonsecours Street to process them and Dougherty figured they probably brought him along to the Chat because the seven people they picked up there were English, students mostly.

But when he'd filled out the arrest reports and started processing them, Detective Carpentier showed up and told Dougherty to pull three guys out and put them in a separate cell while the others were sent to Parthenais.

It was almost four in the morning by then and Dougherty said, "They only had a few joints."

"A few each?"

"Yes," Dougherty said, "but it was one of the other guys who had the LSD, forty-four capsules. And some hash, almost a dozen grams, I think, each one rolled up in tin foil."

Carpentier was looking at the arrest reports and he said, "These three are deserters. They're wanted by the U.S. Army. We should talk to them."

"That was lucky," Dougherty said, "that they happened to be in Le Chat Noir."

Carpentier said, "Yes, lucky." And then he said, "Why don't you talk to this one, Brian Lindenmuth." Carpentier handed the arrest report to Dougherty and said, "He's the youngest — was he the most nervous?"

"None of them were very nervous," Dougherty said. Now he was nervous himself.

"*C'est bon,*" Carpentier said, getting it right away. "You're already dressed like a detective, he won't know. Treat him like a drug dealer. Try and find out who he buys from or if he smuggles it himself."

"He probably won't say."

"But you can lean on him," Carpentier said. "You

can threaten to turn him over to the American army."

"I thought we didn't do that."

"We can if we want to. And then when he gets nervous," Carpentier said, "and don't worry, he'll get nervous, ask him about David Murray."

"Will you be interrogating him, too?"

"Not yet, let him think he has a friend in you. But not too much of a friend."

Dougherty said okay and took the report, a single piece of paper, and went down to the cells, wondering how Carpentier knew the three men were deserters and how he'd known they'd been in the bar that was picked to be raided.

Walking down the stairs of police headquarters Dougherty figured there was a lot going on in the building he didn't know about. Probably a lot of stuff he'd never know about.

The three men were all in the same cell, and Dougherty told the constable on duty he was taking one of them upstairs to Interrogation. Then he said, "Lindenmuth, let's go."

None of the men moved. Dougherty looked them over. They all looked the same to him: unshaven, hair too long, jeans, jean jackets, workboots — but unlike Judy MacIntyre they didn't look like they'd ever done much work — and that smug look that was getting to be more than just annoying.

He said it again, "Lindenmuth."

One of the guys said, "We haven't called our lawyer yet."

"Gardiner?"

The guy looked surprised and Dougherty said, "If

you want we can just give you to the army, they have an office in the consulate here."

"You can't do that."

"They might even send someone over to pick you up, take you straight to Fort Drum."

Now all three were looking surprised, and Dougherty said, "Or you can talk to me for a few minutes. Who knows, maybe there won't even be any charges and the army will never know you were here. Which one's Lindenmuth?"

In the interrogation room, Lindenmuth took a cigarette from Dougherty and lit and said, "Playing good cop won't help."

Dougherty said, "I'm not the one who needs help."

Lindenmuth shrugged and tapped his cigarette on the ashtray.

Dougherty could see how nervous the guy was — his hand was shaking and he was looking anywhere but at Dougherty.

"So, you don't have landed immigrant status, and you can't get a job here. What do you do for money?"

Another shrug.

"You sell drugs, of course. The question is, who do you get them from? Do you get them here in Montreal or do you smuggle them in?"

"A couple of joints," Lindenmuth said. "I'm not a dealer."

200

"Whichever one of you three talks first will get the best deal," Dougherty said. "And the other two will get handed over to the army."

Lindenmuth was starting to look worried. "Why

aren't you talking to the real dealers? The guys who had real drugs?"

"Who do you buy from?"

"You think I'm going to tell you anything? You think I'm afraid to go back to the army?"

"Yes."

The guy was squirming, and Dougherty was thinking this being a detective was good. But then he realized that most of the drug dealers they were picking up these days were connected to something — bikers or mobsters or the Point Boys — and it was probably a lot tougher to get them squirming.

"Well, I'm not afraid," Lindenmuth said. "Come on, let's go."

Dougherty said okay and stood up.

But Lindenmuth stayed sitting on the wooden chair.

Dougherty said, "I'll help you out. When was the last time you saw David Murray?"

"Murray?" It caught him off guard. "I haven't seen him in weeks."

"How long before he was killed?"

Lindenmuth shrugged, took a drag on his smoke and said, "Couple weeks at least."

"When you were slipping across the border with the drugs?"

"I told you, I'm not a dealer."

"But David Murray was."

Another shrug.

Dougherty sat back down and said, "Maybe you would prefer to go back to the army. Who are you scared of here?"

"I'm not scared of anyone."

"Don't worry," Dougherty said, "it's okay. You're a pacifist, right? You chose peace. But you're backed into a corner: you need money to live but you can't get a job." He watched Lindenmuth thinking, and he felt the guy wanted to talk. A more experienced detective could probably make the right move and get everything out of this guy, but Dougherty wasn't sure what to say.

"And these guys," Dougherty said, "these guys are criminals, real criminals. You deal with the bikers or the Point Boys? Either way, they don't choose peace, do they?"

"I don't know anything about that."

"No one needs to know where I found out. I just need to know who David Murray was working with."

Lindenmuth made a slight, dismissive snort and tapped his cigarette on the edge of the ashtray. "No one needs to, but they could."

Dougherty was thinking the guy was really in a bind: he could tell Dougherty the names of the dealers and they probably would find out and go after him or he could get sent back to the army. Exactly the position Dougherty wanted him in, but he wasn't sure how to play it and the guy, this Lindenmuth, didn't look smug now, he looked like a scared kid. And Dougherty felt a little like a bully.

"Here's what we can do," Dougherty said. "You tell me who David Murray was working with, and I'll process you for the possession but it'll get dropped before it gets to trial."

"You can do that?"

Dougherty wasn't sure if he could or not but this guy would never know.

"I saw him with some guys, English guys from the Point."

"Names?"

"I don't know their names."

Dougherty could tell that was true, he was feeling it now, the difference between a lie and the truth. Lindenmuth was nowhere near the liar the real criminals were, but Dougherty was feeling like he could do this. He said, "Tell me what you do know about them."

"One guy was called Goose, another guy was called Ronnie."

"Okay," Dougherty said, "that's good."

He took Lindenmuth back to the cells, and then found Carpentier in the squad room and said, "I think I got something."

Carpentier said, "*C'est quoi?*"

"Couple of names. Well, not full names but I can work with them."

"Very good," Carpentier said. "The other two didn't give anything up."

"I guess you were right, this guy was the youngest, the most nervous."

"Did you make him an offer?"

"I said we'd charge him with the possession so no one would think he gave anything up but we'd drop that before it gets to court."

"That might not work," Carpentier said. "The lawyers talk to each other. These bikers, they have the same lawyers as the mobsters now — they're getting

203

more professional. If it gets dropped for no reason word will get around."

"It's not bikers," Dougherty said, "it's Point Boys."

"*La même chose,*" Carpentier said. "It's the same lawyers. What we can do, there can be some problem with the evidence, you can lose it or not record it properly."

"It has to be my fault?"

Carpentier smiled a little and said, "You are getting too far along for rookie mistakes."

"It's okay," Dougherty said, "I'm still making plenty."

"*Bon*, you can talk to the guys he gave up?"

"Yeah," Dougherty said, "I can find them."

On his way back up the hill the sun was coming up and Dougherty was feeling good, feeling like he could be a detective.

But first he had a day shift to work in uniform.

———

"We got them, we got them both, bastards."

Dougherty was in the break room.

Sergeant Delisle slammed down the phone and said, "In Vancouver, *les maudits* pricks, in a drug raid."

One of the other cops asked who, but Dougherty knew. And he was seeing how useful these drug raids could be.

"*Les boys* didn't even know who they had," Delisle said. "One of them gave a fake ID, couldn't even spell the name on it."

Jimmy O'Brien and Jean-Marc Boutin. Started the fire at the Wagon Wheel. Killed thirty-seven people.

Delisle was walking around the station, restless, full of energy. "One of them tried to kill himself — too bad he didn't do it."

The other cop said, "Who?" and Delisle said, "I'd like to take him over to Phillips Square and set *him* on fire."

"Shit," the other cop said, "from the Wagon Wheel?"

Dougherty closed the file he was looking at, arrests from a summer rock concert at the Forum, and stood up.

Delisle said, "We gonna go get them in Vancouver, you gonna go?"

"I doubt it," Dougherty said. "They'll send detectives."

Delisle said, "You been playing detective."

"Well, I'm a patrolman now," Dougherty said, walking towards the door. "So I should be on my beat."

"You should . . ." Delisle said and left it hanging.

In the small parking lot behind the station house, Dougherty checked out a patrol car and drove up to Sherbrooke and headed east. He was pretty sure Goose was Greg Herridge, little brother of Imelda who'd been in some of Dougherty's classes at Verdun High. From what he could remember, Goose wasn't the sharpest knife the drawer, but he was always trying to hang around with Imelda and her friends. Which would have included Danny Buckley, so now Dougherty was thinking the old gang's all here and they're all involved in the drug business and somehow connected to David Murray. Then he wondered which one killed him.

He pulled into the parking lot at the Royal Vic, and the guy in the booth looked annoyed when Dougherty motioned at him to raise the gate, making it clear he was going to pay the eighty cents. He parked and got out of the police car, looking up at the building, thinking it must have been a hundred years old and looked like a castle, Scottish baronial, the way it had been described to Dougherty, built by Scottish money, for sure. It was on the slope of Mount Royal, felt like it was under the brow, on the edge of the old Golden Square Mile on the McGill campus.

Dougherty was used to bringing people to the hospital and, if they were calmed down enough, leaving them in Admitting, but this time he went to the elevators and rode up to the fifth floor.

As he walked by the nurse's station one of the women said, "Officer, I don't think anyone here called the police," and Dougherty stopped and said, "No, I'm here to see my father."

"Do you know which room?"

"Yes."

He was still having trouble with it, with the idea of his father in the hospital, but now Dougherty felt he was ready. They could talk, make a few jokes about the hospital food and Dougherty could say he had to get back to work.

But his father was sleeping.

Dougherty hadn't expected that, and he stood in the doorway. He stared at the body on the bed and didn't see his father. He saw a pale, weak, thin body under a sheet. He saw a tube going into a nose and a needle in an arm. He saw black hair with streaks of grey.

Weak. Fragile. Vulnerable.

A nurse came by, and Dougherty was scared she was going to tell him to go into the room and wake up his father but she said, "He just fell asleep."

Dougherty said, "I shouldn't wake him," and then felt he'd said it too fast, sounded too anxious, but the nurse said, "If that's okay. Maybe you could come back later?"

"Sure," Dougherty said, "I'm working, I can stop in anytime."

"Thanks."

And he walked away without looking back.

CHAPTER
FOURTEEN

Judy rolled over the edge of Doughtery's bed and lifted her purse up from the floor saying, "So, you can't be seen with me in public?" and Dougherty said, "I thought it was you couldn't be seen with me?"

She got out a cigarette. "It would look bad."

"I could make it look like I'm arresting you,"

"Again."

She lit her cigarette and held the match.

"So, how's your father?"

"In good hands." He blew smoke at the ceiling. "That's what they tell me."

After he'd visited his father and finished his shift Dougherty called Judy and asked if she wanted to go out somewhere for dinner and she'd asked if he knew any out-of-the-way places. He said plenty.

"How did the surgery go?"

"Complete success, they say."

Judy stood up and walked naked to the little bathroom, the red tip of her cigarette glowing in the dark. "My father's was a double bypass and there were some complications — he was in the hospital for months."

"I didn't even ask how long he'd be in for."

Dougherty heard the toilet flush but he hadn't heard Judy going so he realized the flush was to drown the sound. Sure enough after the tank filled she flushed again and came back to the bed.

She said, "A few weeks, at least."

"Shit."

"They had to put him under anesthesia, cut him open, break his ribs, put him on a heart-lung machine." She sat on the edge of the bed with her back to Dougherty. "It's a big deal."

"Well, there's no choice, right?"

"They never mentioned one." She slid back under the sheet. "My father wears it like a badge of honour. Did you know if an airline pilot has a heart attack he has to retire?"

"No, I didn't."

"My father likes to say that if everyone who had a heart attack had to retire there wouldn't be anybody left at the top levels of government or industry or the professions."

"Well now it looks like it's spreading to the lower levels," Dougherty said.

"Don't tell my father. He loves his status symbols, his executive perks."

Dougherty didn't say anything and then Judy said, "Anyone still at home?"

"Little brother, but he's fourteen, he can take care of himself."

"Can he?"

Dougherty said, "Sure. And my sister, Cheryl, she's going to Sir George, she can help out."

"My sisters are younger, but not much and they all had a tough time when my dad was in the hospital. And my mom, I practically had to move back home."

"You're the oldest?"

"Yeah, you?"

"Yeah."

"Look at us," Judy said, turning on her side and snuggling up to Dougherty, "getting to know each other and everything."

"Fraternizing," Dougherty said.

"Do they warn you against that?"

"They don't think they have to."

"Yeah," Judy said, "it's so unlikely."

She was pressed up against him and her hand was on his chest, the smoke rising from the cigarette.

"These days," Dougherty said, "I'm not sure who I'm supposed to fraternize with."

He could feel her react to that a little, tense up a bit and he wanted to ask her about that, but he didn't want to push it. He was on his back, one arm around Judy, and he just held on and didn't say anything.

It was quiet for a minute and then she took a drag on her smoke and exhaled and said, "So, what're you interested in? Politics?"

"Not really."

"Big election coming up."

"We're not supposed to take sides."

"Who's we?"

"Good question."

"Well, anyway," she said, "Nixon's going to win big, it looks like."

"There's an election here, too, isn't there?"

"Oh, right, well here it's still Trudeaumania."

"You don't like him?"

"He's a politician."

"So, it's all politics all the time," Dougherty said.

"No, it's just . . . Well, I guess it is, pretty much," Judy said. "Now, anyway. Everybody's going crazy about the indictment, the Watergate thing."

"What's that?"

"Gordon Liddy and the others, indicted by the Grand Jury." She looked at Dougherty and said, "For breaking into the Democrats' headquarters and planting bugs?"

"Oh right, I heard something about that."

"So, everybody's going crazy: who are they working for, how high up does it go? At least all the Americans in town are going crazy."

Dougherty said, "It might go pretty high."

"Wow, I expected more resistance."

"Yeah?"

"Maybe even a little defensiveness."

Dougherty shrugged a little and Judy said, "What's going on?"

He said, "Nothing," and Judy said, "No, it's okay, you can tell me."

Dougherty pulled away from her and stood up,

walked around, barely enough room to pace. "No, it's nothing."

"Come on, it's not nothing, what is it?"

Dougherty stopped and looked at Judy and he expected her to say something, to push him to talk about it or to say, Never mind, forget it, something like that, but she was just waiting. It was giving him the feeling that she really wanted to talk about it, that she really wanted him to tell her what he was thinking.

He said, "I don't know, it's just . . . Sometimes it's easy, I'm just trying to keep the peace, you know? Go into a bar and people are trying to beat each other to death and all you have to do is get them separated and calmed down. It's not complicated. They're drunk, whatever, you just want to make sure no one gets hurt, no permanent damage."

Judy said, "Yeah, that's good."

"But then, it's just . . ." he paused and turned around and then turned back, "It's just, you know, all I'm trying to do here is find out who killed your friend."

"We weren't that close."

"And it feels like there's a lot more going on."

She was sitting up in the bed then. "What do you mean?"

"I don't know, I guess I mean that the official story, you know, is that we don't track draft dodgers, we don't share information with the FBI or the CIA or anything like that."

Judy said, "Yeah."

"Well, I don't know, but it just seems like every time we need something, a little information or something, we get it." He was going to say something about the farm, the way Carpentier just happened to know about it or the way they just happened to pick up the deserters in the drug raid but he didn't want to go into specifics, he didn't want to give examples.

Or really, he didn't want to give evidence.

He was naked but he also felt exposed.

Judy said, "We know there are FBI agents in town. We know half the guys who try to join the committees are RCMP."

"I guess I knew that, too."

He sat on the edge of the bed and smoked and didn't say anything.

Judy moved a little closer and put a hand on his arm and said, "You having trouble figuring out whose side you're on?"

"I didn't think I had to pick."

"You joined the police."

"I thought that was everybody's side. I thought the police were who you called when you were in trouble."

"And now?"

Dougherty turned and looked at Judy. "I don't know."

Judy squeezed his arm and then slid around and sat next to him on the edge of the bed, wrapping herself in the sheet. "Okay, I've been thinking about this, too."

"About being a cop?"

She laughed and said, "No." She took another drag on her cigarette and looked around for an ashtray.

Dougherty took the cigarette and stood up, saying, "Thinking about what then?" as he walked to the kitchen and stubbed out both smokes on a plate beside the sink.

213

"Well, I haven't been talking about it, just thinking about it, so it might not make sense."

Dougherty said, "I'm used to that."

She smiled and shook her head a little. "Okay, well, here's the thing, I've been in a few groups."

"No kidding."

"Just listen, okay?"

"Okay." He sat down on the bed and waited.

"Okay, so you know about the St. Henri Workers' Coalition. That was part of the Company of Young Canadians, have you heard of them?"

"Yeah, they still around?"

"No, they splintered. There's the Company of Young Québécois now, but they don't really have any English members. So, then I got involved with the Milton Park Defence Committee and there were some anti-war activists there already."

"Draft dodgers. And deserters."

"Peace activists."

"Oh yeah." Dougherty reached over to his dresser, almost pressed up against the bed, and picked up a book and said, "'Choose Peace.'" He handed it to Judy.

"Yes, like this." She looked at him and raised an eyebrow. He knew it would be wrong to say how cute it looked.

"But now that's splintering," she said.

"People joining other groups?"

"Or just dropping out."

"And turning on?"

"You think you're funny," she said, "but you're not."

"Are you sure?"

"Okay, here's the thing, people are dropping out of these committees and these movements. Stop the development of Milton Park, stop the war in Vietnam, that kind of thing."

"Yeah, so what's the next movement?"

"That's just it — there isn't a next movement. People are dropping out of these but not doing anything else. I'm not sure what it is exactly, it's more personal."

"I don't get it."

"I don't really, either, it's just —" she trailed off a little and then nodded and said, "Have you heard of self-actualization?"

"Are you serious?"

"It's a psychology thing, a humanistic approach."

"Of course it is."

She said, "Okay, be sarcastic," and started to get up.

"No, wait."

"Look, all I'm saying is, people are talking about themselves more, about what they want for themselves."

"I don't really understand."

"Like I said, I don't really, either. It's just that . . . It's that, I guess I'm not as sure about things as I used to be. I guess, you know, we went from all these big ideas, peace in the world and worker solidarity and then housing right here in Milton Park and it all seems so . . . I don't know, abstract?"

"I think I do," Dougherty said. This was really unusual territory for him, talking about how he felt about these personal things, but after seeing his father in the hospital bed, after seeing the way higher-ups in the police force acted, after so much, he was feeling very close to Judy. He said, "I always felt in between, you know? I grew up in the Point and I'm Irish but I'm also French. I joined the police but most of the guys I grew up with are joining gangs."

Judy nodded.

"And all this separation stuff, it's starting to feel so, I don't know, us and them."

"Two solitudes — did you read that book?"

"No, but I think I get it now."

"So that's it," Judy said, "things feel like they're falling apart."

"And you're still trying to hold them together?"

She scowled at him but it turned into a kind of a smile and she said, "You're the one breaking up the fights," and she threw a pillow at him.

He jumped on the bed and got his hands up under the sheet and tickled her, and she pushed him off and rolled over and got on top, one knee on each side of his chest, a hand holding each of his wrists and she said, "I can keep you in line," and he said, "Oh yeah?"

She said, "Yeah," and leaned forward and kissed him.

When she pulled her lips away from his, she kissed his cheek and then his ear and she whispered, "I think you need to do more undercover work."

The next morning when they were getting dressed, Dougherty said he was going back to his old neighbourhood to find a guy who might have been smuggling dope with David Murray, a guy named Greg Herridge that everybody called Goose. He said to Judy, "Have you ever heard of him?"

She said no, and Dougherty said, "Well, it's all I've got. The only other name anybody gave me was

Richard Burnside, and I can't imagine him hanging out with David Murray."

"He did," Judy said. "They hung out a little."

"Do you know Burnside?"

"Yeah, why?" Then she said, "Oh, come on, you don't think he killed David?"

"No," Dougherty said, thinking about what Carpentier had said, about how he'd have people for that kind of thing. "But he might have some idea who else David was hanging around with."

"I guess he could. Do you want to meet him?"

"Yes."

"I don't know," Judy said, "it does feel like taking sides."

"Yes, but we're the good guys."

"Are we?"

Dougherty said, "I don't know about any of the big issues, the politics or anything like that. I just know that someone killed David Murray and we have to find out who it was."

"Okay," Judy said. "That's right."

CHAPTER
FIFTEEN

Dougherty spent Friday morning at the coroner's inquest into the Blue Bird fire. The fire inspector said he was at the club ten days before the fire but he didn't go upstairs to the Wagon Wheel — it was a re-inspection he said, to check three things on the ground floor and they had all been addressed. Then there was a lot of reports presented saying things like the rear fire exit was one and a half inches too narrow and that there hadn't been a full inspection in over two years.

By the lunch break, Dougherty had had all he could take, and he went back to Station Ten.

A Volkswagen Beetle was parked in front. Dougherty recognized it as one of the delivery cars from King of the Pizza on St. Catherine, and he walked into the building saying, "I hope you got all dressed."

Delisle was paying for the four extra-large pizzas and he said, "You suppose to be at the inquest."

"I was."

The first game from Moscow, with the time difference, was starting in Montreal at one. And it started with a laugh, Phil Esposito slipped during the opening ceremonies, landed on his ass.

Delisle said, "*Tabarnak.*"

Esposito got up and took an exaggerated bow.

Gagnon said, "*Bon, c'est la vraie série qui commence maintenant.*"

Dougherty was taking a bite of pizza and thinking, Now it's real?

It was better, anyway, Canada scoring early and heading into the third period up 3–1. By that time Delisle had started answering the phone again and sending guys out on calls.

"This is more like it, now we win the four games in Russia."

One of the cops in the room said, "Soviet Union," and Delisle said, "What?"

"Not Russians, Soviets."

Five minutes into the third period Paul Henderson scored and it was 4–1.

Delisle said, "*Bon, tu retournement à l'enquête?*" and Dougherty said, "No, they're not going to call me, they have dozens of expert witnesses to get through."

"Then you better get on patrol, *les drunks vont célébrer.*"

Dougherty said yeah and started towards the door but then he heard the groan in the break room and stopped.

"4–2, no big deal."

"*Tabarnak!*"

Delisle said, "Right between the legs. Why is Esposito playing, you can drive a truck through his legs, shit. Why isn't Dryden playing?"

Dougherty came back into the room and picked up another slice of pizza. "Was it even ten seconds to score that one?"

"Why are they playing defence?" Delisle said. He was whining now. "This team was built to score, why don't they score?"

Dougherty didn't say anything but he watched the team running around, panicking in their own end. This whole series nothing like they'd expected.

Gagnon said, "We could use Martin and Hadfield now."

Another cop asked him what he meant and Gagnon said that Vic Hadfield, Rick Martin and Jocelyn Guevremont had left the team and come back to Canada.

"*C'est vrai? Ils ont déserté?*"

"They weren't playing," Gagnon said.

Dougherty was thinking the people he'd been talk-
ing to lately probably wouldn't call a guy who left a hockey team a deserter, but it seemed strange. Still, he couldn't blame them, take them all the way to Russia and then not play them.

"*Qu'en est-Perrault?*"

"*Ne joue pas.*"

"*Tabarnak.*"

And then the Soviets scored again, tied it up.

"Why don't they play, Perrault and Martin?" Delisle said.

"Sinden doesn't play the young guys," Gagnon said.

A young cop sitting near the TV said, "*Les amis d'Eagleson,*" and Delisle said, "*Quoi?*"

The young guy looked back over his shoulder and started talking about how Alan Eagleson, the player agent who seemed to be running the tournament, got all his clients on the team to raise their profile so he could get more money out of their NHL teams, how they treated it like a vacation, they had forty guys at the training camp, took thirty-five to Russia. "*Qu'est-ce que une équipe fait avec trente-cinq joueurs, si il y en seulement vingt qui jouent?*"

"Holy fuck!"

Delisle was standing up then, pointing at the TV. "Fuck! *C'est ca*, that's it, *tabarnak.*"

The Soviets had scored, they were up 5–4 and the Canadians hadn't touched the puck in five minutes.

Dougherty stood by the door and watched the end of the game, the Soviets pressing the whole time, moving as a five-man unit, every one of them touching the puck as they moved it around and totally controlled the play.

Every cop in the room, probably fifteen guys, all disgusted. There was a lot of swearing.

And Dougherty was thinking about how the Soviets were still a group but the Canadians were all going their own way. He was hearing it in Judy's voice and he wanted to talk to her, hear what she had to say about it, and that surprised him but then he was snapped out of it by Delisle saying, "What the fuck you smiling at?"

"Nothing."

The game ended 5–4.

"Three more games," Delisle said. "We win them all we win the series."

"We were supposed to win all eight games," Gagnon said.

Delisle looked like he was in pain. "We weren't ready. We're ready now."

Gagnon shrugged and turned off the TV. "It's too late now."

"We can still win the series," Delisle said. "It's not over."

Dougherty didn't say anything, but he was feeling the same way Gagnon was, a little ashamed they'd taken the Russians so lightly and mad at the way they were scrambling all over the place.

And again that made him think of Judy and what she was saying about the groups breaking down and people talking more and more about themselves, personally. Dougherty knew he'd never use a word like "self-actualized" but he could feel the same fraying everywhere he went these days.

"*Bon*," Delisle said and slapped his hand on his desk. "Let's get out there, the drunks are going to be in a bad mood."

Yeah, Dougherty was thinking, Let's get out there, but it was just the constables moving out of the room, heading for patrols.

It was only three thirty in the afternoon, and Dougherty figured most of the drunks would have time to sober up before heading home and it wouldn't be too bad, so he checked out a radio car and drove a few blocks west to Westmount.

He parked in front of a hydrant on Greene, and as he was crossing the street he looked up at the three black towers that made up Westmount Square a block away. Dougherty'd never been inside, Westmount had their own police force, and he'd never been invited into any of the apartments. Two of the towers were offices, and he'd never been in there, either. It had only been up a few years and already the twenty-some-storey black cubes, designed by a famous architect Dougherty couldn't remember, looked dated. They were supposed to be modern, Dougherty knew that much, but he thought they just looked out of place.

Most of Greene Avenue was old three-storey brick buildings: banks, clothing stores, restaurants, a couple of coffee shops. Dougherty walked into the only office building on the street and stopped in the lobby.

A couple of girls who looked like Dougherty's sister, Cheryl, in their torn jeans and plaid shirts and leather vests were standing by the building directory and one of them was saying, "Let's just go up to CKGM — it must be there, it used to be CKGM AM, didn't it?"

Dougherty found the listing for the Burnside Music Group, third floor, just as a guy who looked to be close to thirty but trying hard to look hip in his turtleneck and sports jacket stopped and said to the girls, "Are you looking for CHOM?"

"Yeah."

"Moved across the street in the summer. Come on, I'll show you."

Dougherty watched them leave the lobby together and didn't think the guy had a chance with either girl, but then, you never know, Dougherty was getting used to being surprised.

The receptionist, a young woman who looked very businesslike in her skirt and jacket, got up from behind her desk as soon as Dougherty walked in and said, "May I help you, Officer?"

"I'd like to talk to Mr. Burnside."

"I'll see if he's available."

She walked into the office and closed the door but a moment later she was back saying, "Right this way. Would you like a cup of coffee?"

"No thanks."

"If you need anything, just let me know." She stood by the door, and when Dougherty walked past her into the office, she closed it behind him. Richard Burnside was in his late twenties, about the same age as Dougherty, but he had long hair and wore jeans and a t-shirt that had the image of a couple of big dice ironed on the front, looked like it came from the head shop in the Alexis Nihon plaza.

Dougherty thought Burnside looked surprised to see a Montreal cop in uniform in his office, even if the uniform was just the short-sleeved blue shirt open at the collar, but there were still the handcuffs and the gun on the belt.

He said, "What can I do for you, Officer?"

Dougherty said, "It's not official business, I'd just like to talk to you if that's okay."

"Sure, you looking for tickets to Uriah Heep?"

Dougherty wasn't sure if his little brother would want to see that show or not, or if he'd be allowed downtown while their father was in the hospital, but just in case he said, "I might, yeah."

"Or Elton John, better if you have a date."

Didn't sound like Judy's idea of a night out, big glitzy concert at the Forum, but Dougherty said, "Maybe, yeah."

"The shows are completely sold out, of course," Burnside said, "but for the boys in blue we could find a couple."

"I appreciate that."

Burnside motioned to a chair and started to sit down himself, getting out his cigarettes and lighting one. He blew smoke at the ceiling and leaned back in his chair and waited.

Dougherty sat down in the guest chair and said, "I just want to ask you a few questions about David Murray."

Burnside was about to take a drag on his smoke but he stopped for a second and then inhaled and blew the smoke out in a long stream, making Dougherty think he was buying himself some time to try and make it look like he had to think to place the name.

"David Murray?"

Dougherty was a little surprised that this was the way Burnside wanted to play it, trying to pretend he didn't really know the guy. "Yeah, he was an American living in Montreal. He worked for some of the war resistance organizations, the draft dodgers and deserters. Someone killed him."

Burnside knew, of course, at least Dougherty really got the feeling he did and that it mattered to him, but Burnside tried to shrug it off, leaning forward and flicking his cigarette over the ashtray, saying, "I heard something."

"Someone beat him to death," Dougherty said. "Caved in his skull."

Burnside was nodding and he said, "That's too bad."

"He didn't even fight back."

"Really?"

"It's strange," Dougherty said. "I understand he was involved in some of the benefit shows — Jesse Winchester, I think, and Pete Seeger at Place des Arts?"

"Well, I really just do the rock stuff," Burnside said. "All the big shows, did you see the Stones at the Forum?"

Dougherty said, "I got called in when the bomb went off."

"That was some union thing out of the States, wasn't it?"

Dougherty said yeah, but he could tell Burnside knew a lot more about it than he was letting on.

"Led Zeppelin, that was fantastic," Burnside said. "I do all the big rock shows. When I was a kid I worked for Sam Gesser, you know him?"

"No."

"Old-timer, great guy, he booked all the legends: Sinatra, Louis Armstrong, Liberace. It was in Montreal that he came up with the name, did you know that?"

Dougherty said no but decided to let Burnside keep talking. The guy was so nervous he had to and

Dougherty was thinking that if he was here, Detective Carpentier would let him talk.

"Yeah, he was just a kid then, Liberace, he was playing the Mount Royal Hotel, the Normandie Roof, but he wasn't getting much action. He was Walter Liberace then, that was it, nothing special. But then they came up with the idea to just call him Liberace, put that on the posters and the ads, make him sound a little more exotic, and it worked. He stuck with it after that."

"That was this Gesser guy?" Dougherty said. He wanted Burnside to keep talking, relax a little, let his guard down.

"No, that was someone else, I'm not sure who it was. I got a job as a stage manager for Gesser when I was a teenager, and then Janis Joplin puked all over his shoes backstage at the Forum and I got all the rock acts." He held out his hands like it was a punchline but they were shaking so Dougherty just waited and Burnside said, "He said to me, 'Kid, you can have all the rock stuff,' and here I am."

Dougherty thought about saying something about Burnside's father owning half of downtown maybe being a little bit of it, too, but he instead said, "When was the last time you saw David?" and he could tell Burnside knew exactly when it was by the way he made a big deal about taking another drag and thinking about it.

227

Finally he said, "Quite a while. I don't know exactly."

"You weren't at the party they had for him, at the Yellow Door?"

"I didn't know him that well."

Dougherty could tell it was a lie. He couldn't say exactly how but he knew. He said, "Look, it's okay, I know the guy was bringing in drugs, supplying the bands, I don't care about that," and Burnside burst out laughing, a loud, high-pitched squawk, and looked to Dougherty like he was relieved. "He didn't get landed immigrant status," Dougherty said, "so he worked in the underground."

Burnside pulled himself together but he still had a slight look of amusement on his face, still glad to be talking about drug smuggling. He said, "Officer, I don't have any idea about that. I won't deny these bands and their fans have drugs. Have you been in the Forum for a show? You'll get high just being there, everybody's smoking dope, but that's not my business."

"It's not mine, either," Dougherty said. "I'm trying to find out who caved in his skull."

Burnside nodded, serious again, and Dougherty was thinking the guy's really off guard, time to get something out of him, but now he wasn't sure what it would be. He thought talking about the drugs would've shaken him more.

"He was killed Saturday night," Dougherty said, "September second, the night of the Canada-Russia game, the first one here at the Forum."

"That was a few weeks ago," Burnside said.

"Were you with him that day?"

"What? No, of course not."

Dougherty shrugged and said, "Friday?"

Burnside stood up and stubbed out his cigarette, saying, "Officer, I have no idea why you think I was with David Murray but you're mistaken. I barely knew the man. Now, I'm sorry but I'm very busy. Sophie will show you out."

Then he looked past Dougherty and said, "Sophie!" and when she came into the office he said, "Officer . . ." and when he realized he didn't know the name just said, "The officer is leaving now."

Dougherty stood up and said, "Thanks for your time," and as he walked out of the office looked back over his shoulder and said, "I'll let you know about those Elton John tickets." He really just wanted to get another look at Burnside to see if he was still flustered but he wasn't.

He was scared.

Outside on Greene Avenue Dougherty decided to stop at one of the cafés. When he walked in the young waitress said, "What's so funny, Officer?" and he realized he'd been thinking about it like a detective movie where Burnside would rush out of his office and meet an accomplice.

Dougherty said, "It's just such a nice day," and the waitress said, "It's about time, after the crappy summer we had."

"That's for sure."

Dougherty ordered a coffee and took a seat on the patio, thinking he should enjoy these few days between the wet summer and the coming winter. There was a newspaper on the table, opened to an inside page, and he saw an article with Keith Logan's byline. The story was about what it described as the "thirty-seventh murder of the year," an unemployed longshoreman killed by a shotgun blast. The guy, thirty-four years old, had just stepped out of his gold Cadillac on St. Catherine Street East. Dougherty thought it was funny the way Logan wrote it was "gangland style," but he didn't smile.

And he figured the real murder total was seventy-four, counting the victims at the Blue Bird.

The waitress brought the coffee and went back inside.

So, Burnside and Murray did know each other but now Dougherty was thinking why would Burnside be so scared if it wasn't drugs? He imagined explaining it to Carpentier, saying something about he could tell by the way Burnside reacted — or didn't really react — so he knew it wasn't drugs.

Carpentier would say, "That's not evidence," and Dougherty would say, "But I'm sure."

And Carpentier would say, "But it's not evidence."

Or he might say, "You're becoming a detective."

And then he might say, "Find the evidence."

CHAPTER
SIXTEEN

Friday night Dougherty checked a few of the Irish bars, the Cock 'n' Bull and the Old Dublin and the Black Bull, and then he had a look in a couple of the top-less places, Danny's Villa and the Copacabana on St. Catherine, but didn't find anyone he was looking for so he walked down the hill to St. Antoine and Rockhead's. It was a cool, clear night, summer becoming fall.

Jones said, "No uniform?"

"No," Dougherty said. "I like yours, though, looks like a lawyer."

Jones put his thumbs under his lapels and pushed his chest out. "Dress smart, be smart."

"No more doorman tassels?"

"Low key." He winked.

"All the fire exits clear?"

Jones said, "You know it."

Both men stood silent for a moment, nothing else to say about that.

Blues music pumped out of Rockhead's, a live band, guitar, bass and drums. Dougherty said, "Nice night."

"After such a shitty summer, we deserve a good long fall."

"My favourite time of year."

Jones smiled. "What my daddy said smelled like football."

"He played?"

"In the army."

"My father was a boxer in the navy."

"We miss all the fun."

"Yeah, and we're glad about that."

Jones laughed. "You know it."

Dougherty got out his smokes and held the pack for Jones. "Your father was in the American army, right?"

Jones leaned in to get a light, and then tilted his head way back and blew smoke at the night sky. "Joined up in Brownsville, Texas, where my grandmother lives to this day."

"But you were born here?"

"Yeah. What's it to you?"

"I've been talking to a lot of Americans lately."

"Plenty inside," Jones said. "Up from the air force base in Plattsburgh."

"The ones I've been talking to decided not to join up."

"Draft dodgers?"

"Yeah."

Jones nodded. "We got those, too."

"I haven't met any black draft dodgers."

"Whatever you got, we got."

Dougherty took a drag on his cigarette and said, "You know a guy named Goose?"

"White boy?"

"From the Point, yeah."

"You think he's here?"

"Is he?"

"You're not wearing your uniform," Jones said, "but you're still a cop."

"Hey, it's me, Eddie. We're just talking."

"I know," Jones said, "but the city's getting tense, you know?"

"I know. I don't like it, either."

"The way it is."

Dougherty said, "I'm not a detective yet. I don't have an expense account."

"You've got a telephone."

Dougherty nodded, and Jones said, "You know how to use it when you have to?" and Dougherty said, "Yeah."

"All right." Jones thought about it and then said, "Goose is inside, he's with Manny."

"Manny O'Ree?"

"That's the one. He was stationed at Plattsburgh once, long time ago."

233

Dougherty took a drag and tossed the smoke in the street and said, "You wouldn't bring him out, would you?"

"Now's the time," Jones said, "that you're supposed to say something to me about how I don't want the place getting raided every night, how I don't want the health inspectors coming by every day finding rat shit in the kitchen."

"Is that what I'm supposed to say?"

"If you could make any of that happen."

"The telephone's all I've got."

Jones looked him up and down, and Dougherty was thinking that being able to warn him of a raid wouldn't be enough, but then Jones nodded a little and said, "Okay, wait over there."

A few minutes later, Jones came out of the club with a long-necked, skinny white guy who saw Dougherty and said, "Shit, what do you want?"

Dougherty nodded at Jones and the big bouncer stepped back into the doorway.

"Talk about old times."

"Screw you."

"So, you're working for Buck-Buck now."

"I don't work *for* him," Goose said.

"He's ambitious, though," Dougherty said. "He's going to go far in the organization."

"Yeah? Me, too."

Dougherty wasn't sure what to say then — it wasn't going at all like he'd expected. He thought Goose would deny working with Buck-Buck and the Point Boys or deny there even was an organization, but he was talking about it like he'd got a job at customs and was hoping for a promotion.

Now Dougherty was thinking he could really use Carpentier.

"Well, I really want to know about David Murray."

"What about him?"

Just like that, no pretending he didn't know him or pretending not to remember the name or anything. Dougherty was the one thrown off in this conversation.

"When was the last time you saw him?"

"I don't know, I don't keep a diary, shit."

"He got killed the day of the first hockey game against the Russians, you remember it?"

"Manny won a lot of money that night. Nobody else in town was taking any action on the commies."

"Did you see David Murray that day?"

"No." Goose relaxed a little then, and Dougherty was thinking, It's like the guy has no idea this is a murder investigation.

"The day before was the fire," Dougherty said, and Goose was nodding.

"Yeah, that's what I was thinking. Andy Millington died there, you know that?"

"No. I heard about Alice Bedard."

"Fucking shit. Those guys going to fry?"

"I don't know," Dougherty said. He wanted to say they haven't even been charged yet, the coroner was still having his inquest, but he didn't want to get too sidetracked, and he said, "You see David that day?"

"No, it was the day of the game." Then Goose seemed to snap out of it a little and he said, "How do you know Murray?"

"I don't," Dougherty said. "I'm trying to find out who killed him."

"Well, it wasn't me."

And Dougherty was thinking, Finally this guy gets it.

"Murray was taking dope into the States, right?"

"Jesus Murphy, Eddie, you're stupid."

235

"You guys get it off the boats in the port and he took it across the border?"

"I've never been on a boat in my life."

"But that's the way it works: the Higginses still have the port, right? Italians haven't taken that from you?"

"They have enough trouble of their own," Goose said. "You sure you're a cop?"

Dougherty said, "Yeah." Now he was thinking about the museum robbery and how that crazy idea might be true, that the stolen paintings were being used to buy off one of the Italian guys so there wouldn't be a street war in Montreal.

"So, Murray was supposed to pick up a delivery?"

"He was a funny guy," Goose said. "He was in and out, you know? And you can't be in and out in this business."

Dougherty was still surprised this guy was talking about it like it was any other business, but then to him it probably was.

"You saw him that day, Saturday. Maybe you were the last person to see him alive."

"Couldn't've been," Goose said. "He was going to see someone else after me." He paused and then said, "And then there was the guy who killed him. He saw him, too."

"And you were telling him he had to be in or be out?"

236 out?"

"We were talking about the weather," Goose said.

"Was this in the ghetto," Dougherty said, "by McGill?"

"St. Henri."

"Is that where he was living?"

"Shit, you don't know anything, do you?"

Dougherty said, "I guess not," but now he was convincing himself he was only playing dumb to get Goose talking.

"I think his girlfriend killed him."

Dougherty said, "Yeah?"

"Yeah, the guy was always sneaking around — he had something on the side for sure. And then somebody hit him with a rock, right? And beat him after he was dead?"

"You know a lot about this," Dougherty said.

"More than you. But come on, if I did it, I would have killed him and walked away. Wouldn't you?"

"Unless you wanted to make it look like someone else."

Goose laughed. "You watch too much TV — you're like Mannix." Then he turned and started back towards Rockhead's and said, "Watch out, you'll be that fat guy, Cannon."

Dougherty stood on the sidewalk for a moment then nodded at Jones and walked back towards Peel, feeling like there were things going on all the time he had no idea about, and he couldn't decide if he wanted to try to find out or just drive around in a squad car, break up fights between drunks and someday inherit Delisle's desk.

Too close to call right now.

237

Tommy said, "What's a fag?"

Dougherty said, "What?" but Tommy was looking at him, so he said, "Well, you know how when you like a girl you want to hold her hand and kiss her and stuff like that," and Tommy was nodding and Dougherty said, "but your stomach feels really funny and you can't talk?"

Tommy said, "Yeah," with too much enthusiasm.

"Well, a fag is when a boy feels like that about another boy."

"That's weird."

Dougherty said, "Yeah, I guess."

It was Sunday afternoon, and Dougherty had crossed the bridge to Greenfield Park to watch the game with Tommy and have dinner with the family. Trying to make it as normal as possible but everything was strange with his father still in the hospital. The surgery had gone well, so the doctors said, but they couldn't really be sure until they saw how the recovery went. Triple bypass: there was a lot of artery to heal and then there were all the ribs they had to crack to get in there and dig around.

"Why," Dougherty said, "do you feel that way about another boy?"

"No. Why would I do that?"

"If it's how you feel, it's how you feel," Dougherty said. "You can't pick which girls you like, can you?"

Tommy said, "No, I guess not."

Dougherty was feeling strange. Usually he would have made more jokes about it, maybe picked on Tommy a little, teased him till he got upset, but he was thinking about Judy, wondering if he would pick her as the girl he liked if he had a choice. And maybe thinking about Judy had something to do with why Dougherty actually tried to answer Tommy's question.

The second period was just starting and there was no score. Dougherty was surprised Tommy wasn't watching the game with his friends, but when he'd asked him Tommy said they weren't really interested.

"No one wants to see them lose again."

The series not going at all like anyone had expected.

"At least they're not playing dump-and-chase anymore," Dougherty said. "They're trying to keep the puck."

Tommy said, "Like the Russians."

Dougherty was thinking that was funny, how everybody expected Canada to win eight games easy and now it was us learning from them.

Tommy said, "Damn."

"Who scored that, was it Kharlamov?"

"No, somebody else."

"Yeah," Dougherty said, "they're really leaning on Kharlamov."

"Dryden's playing good," Tommy said.

"Yeah, too bad about that goal, otherwise the defence is really coming together. Hey look, the Russians finally got a penalty."

"The refs are crap."

Dougherty said, "Don't blame the refs — that'll never get you anywhere and thinking about it just throws you off your game."

"But they are crap."

Dougherty said yeah, but he was thinking about Judy again. He was thinking about her all the time now, was seeing her face smiling and laughing in bars they'd gone to, out-of-the-way places, knowing no one would ever recognize them. Dougherty liked the way she was so relaxed and could talk to anybody. Just as much as the way he liked how she got so upset talking about the Milton Park stuff or anything else she was involved with.

And he liked the way she knew exactly what he was going through with his father because she'd gone through the same thing.

"Woo hoo, yay!"

"Nice goal," Dougherty said. "Dennis Hull."

Tommy said, "I wish Bobby Hull was playing," and when Dougherty didn't say anything Tommy said, "And Bobby Orr."

"Look at that, another one."

"Wow, two goals in a minute."

Dougherty said, "This is a rough game, though, they're really taking it to them." It was the kind of play the Canadian announcers were going to call grinding and tough and relentless pressure and old-time hockey and all kinds of things but they'd never say the word dirty. They'd never say the words cheap shots or anything like that.

"Yes!"

"Wow," Dougherty said, "Paul Henderson, I didn't even think he'd get picked for this team."

"This is more like it," Tommy said, "3–1."

"Yeah, let's see if they can hold it this time."

"Wow, look at that," Tommy said.

Dougherty said, "Yeah, little face-wash there."

Bobby Clarke got knocked down and when he got up he shoved his hand into Kharlamov's face and then the two of them were taking punches at each other, but neither one dropped their gloves.

"Come on," Tommy said, "fight."

Dougherty was thinking any idea that this was an exhibition tournament or that it was about bringing people together was long gone. The game was hard fought but chippy — every time two players came close to each other there was shoving and slashing.

"If this was the NHL," Dougherty said, "there would be some fights," and he was thinking it was what this game could use, a couple guys dropping the gloves and going at it, let the rest get back to playing hockey.

Tommy said, "Oh, wow!"

"That's gotta hurt."

Kharlamov was limping then, Clarke had slashed him, a two-hander across the ankle. The Russian skated on one leg towards the bench but slowed down as he passed the Canadian bench and yapped at them.

Every guy was standing up yelling back; the whole arena was going crazy.

Clarke got a two-minute slashing penalty and a ten-minute misconduct.

Tommy said, "Are we going to be short-handed for twelve minutes?"

"No, just the two. Clarke will be in the box for ten more but we'll be at full strength."

The game was still chippy. After Clarke's penalty was over but while he was still in the box serving the misconduct, Dennis Hull got a slashing penalty — Dougherty figured they could call slashing every time two guys came close to each other — and the Russians scored on the power play.

"Oh crap," Tommy said, "3–2."

Near the end of the period Kharlamov, still dragging one leg, almost scored on a power play.

But there were no more goals and the game ended 3–2.

"Look at that," Tommy said, "they're shaking hands with the refs."

"I guess they do that in Europe," Dougherty said. But he was thinking that would be as crazy as a drunk in a bar fight shaking hands with him after he broke it up.

"We're back in it," Tommy said. "Now we just need to win the next two."

"Yeah, that's all," Dougherty said.

"They're coming on now," Tommy said. "They can do it." He was on his feet then, almost jumping up and down, and he said, "I'm going to go play," and ran up the stairs.

Dougherty waited a few minutes, and then went upstairs himself. He was going to make up some excuse and leave, but his mother was at the stove checking on the roast and she said, "Cheryl will be here soon."

"How are you doing?"

"I'm fine."

"I thought you'd want to go see Dad today."

"I'll see him tomorrow after work." She was peeling carrots. "He sleeps a lot during the day."

"You're doing okay?"

"Yes."

"Are you sure?"

"Yes," she said. "I'm fine. *Vraiment*." She gave him a look and walked out of the kitchen.

Dougherty went out onto the back balcony and

had a smoke, and he was still there a while later when Cheryl got off the number five bus and walked up to the house.

He said, "You made it."

"Nice to see you, too." Sarcastic.

Dougherty laughed, but he was feeling odd. Cheryl looked different than he'd expected, more grown-up, no jeans or t-shirt with a dead musician ironed on the front, she was wearing proper pants and a blouse and a jacket. She was carrying a purse.

"You have another one of those?"

He held out his pack and she took a cigarette. "Don't let Mom see you."

"She won't even notice," Cheryl said. "She's got so much going on."

Dougherty said, "She seems okay, considering."

"Really? That's what you think?"

They were sitting in deck chairs on the patio.

"She's worried about Dad, sure," Dougherty said, "but she's handling it. Some of the people I see . . ."

Cheryl took a drag and blew smoke at the sky. "Are they ever in shock, the people you see? And have reactions later?"

"I don't know," Dougherty said, "I'm not there later."

"Exactly."

"Well, what do you think is going to happen? Dad's going to come home and things will go back to normal."

"Normal?"

"As normal as things ever are here."

"She's talking about moving back home."

"She is home."

"Back to New Brunswick."

Dougherty laughed.

"It's true, she's talking about it."

"Well, that's your shock."

"She's talking about Gramma Hébert and Aunt Pauline. She misses them."

"And when she visits in the summer, she can't wait to leave," Dougherty said. "She hasn't lived in the country since she was a teenager. She's always loved it in Montreal."

"She used to," Cheryl said. "Not so much anymore. It's not the same these days."

Dougherty was feeling that way, too, but he didn't want to admit it to Cheryl. He said, "She's just scared, it's understandable. Wait till Dad gets out of the hospital."

"You think everything will go back to normal?"

He looked at his sister, so different than he was used to, and thought he had no idea what normal was anymore.

But he said, "Yeah, I do. I think it will."

SEVENTEEN

Gagnon said, "*Je ne pensais pas que les folkies étaient rowdy comme ça,*" and wiped more blood off his head.

"*C'est pas leur politiques,*" Dougherty said, "it's the two-asshole theory."

They were standing on Dorchester beside Gagnon's radio car, just after midnight and the street was quiet. Dougherty had got there just as the fight was ending. Just as Gagnon started to get the upper hand and one guy ran off.

Gagnon motioned to the guy in the back seat of the cop car and said, "He's the asshole."

"Yeah, but there has to be two." Dougherty was leaning back against his own car and he lit a cigarette. "If two guys get into something — one spills a beer on the other or a fender bender, something like that — if they're two reasonable guys they work it out between themselves, they come to an understanding they can both accept."

Gagnon said, "Yeah," and tossed the blood-covered handkerchief on the street.

"And if one of them is an asshole then they'll come to the same conclusion, it'll just take longer while the asshole yells and screams and gets it out of his system."

Gagnon put his hat back on and said, "Yeah?"

"Yeah, but if they're both assholes then we get called."

"But maybe one guy started it, maybe the other guy didn't do anything."

"Doesn't matter," Dougherty said. "Whenever you show up you have to expect them both to take a swing at you. You're only there because there are two assholes."

Gagnon nodded. "Well, everybody else took off when I got here."

Dougherty was looking at the small group of people standing by the door of the Hotel de Province and said, "Back inside for more peace and love?"

The sign by the door said Jesse Winchester was playing.

"No," Gagnon said, "they all gone. Well, maybe a couple left."

"All right," Dougherty said, "you take this guy back to Ten."

"You coming?"

"I'll just make sure everything is calm now."

Gagnon opened the squad-car door and said, "You won't get overtime."

"I know."

Dougherty waited till Gagnon had driven away and then walked to the side door of the old building, the entrance to the club. There were a few people at the tables near the stage but the show was over and the place was quiet.

A couple people looked over at Dougherty and then looked away. No one was going to start anything.

Except maybe one person he recognized. The one he was looking for. He gave a quick nod and walked away.

Judy lit a cigarette and said, "You ever think about getting a real apartment?"

Dougherty took the match and lit his own cigarette. They were both on their backs in his bed, blowing smoke at the ceiling, and he said, "No, not really," but now he was thinking about that stewardess and her apartment in the high-rise, her car getting broken into and her moving out to Dorval.

"This is worse than student housing. It feels so temporary."

"I took it because it was so close to Station Ten," Dougherty said.

"At least you don't have any roommates."

She took a drag and exhaled.

"I'm hardly ever here," Dougherty said.

After he'd seen Judy in the bar at the Hotel de Province and she'd seen him, Dougherty clocked out and walked the couple blocks to his apartment. Judy was waiting on the steps.

Now she said, "I'm getting tired of roommates."

"But David Murray was never home," Dougherty said.

"We still haven't rented out his room. It's just there and no one's doing anything. We'll be short on the rent."

"You getting tired of doing all the work?"

"I don't do all the work."

Dougherty turned his head a little and looked at her, but Judy was staring at the ceiling, blowing smoke rings.

Then she said, "Yeah, I'm getting tired of doing all the work."

"Where do you think David was staying?"

"I don't know, girlfriend's?"

"Did he have a girlfriend?"

"No." She took another drag and exhaled quickly and said, "It's funny, since he's been killed no one's come forward, you know? Wherever he was sleeping, whatever he was doing, no one's saying anything."

"Maybe he was having an affair, a married woman or something."

"I guess it's possible," Judy said. "Just doesn't seem like him."

"So, the week before, what was going on? I've been looking into it but it just seems so long ago."

"A month."

"Before the Wagon Wheel fire, before my dad's heart attack."

Judy said, "Let me think. End of August? Lot of people were out of town." She took a drag and leaned off the bed to flick ash on the saucer on the night table. The sheet slid off and Dougherty was looking at her naked back, smooth skin all the way down to her butt.

She lay back down on the bed and said, "I remember there was a kind of party at the Yellow Door."

"What for?"

"It was a Monday night, it's usually closed, but Nixon said in an interview on the weekend that he was going to eliminate the draft. People just started showing up on Monday and some people played music."

"Eliminate the draft, sounds like a big deal."

"It's been heading this way, since he put in the lottery."

"Nixon?"

"Yeah."

Dougherty said, "That make a big difference, the lottery?"

"Oh yeah, you should hear these guys," Judy said. "They all know their number, exactly how high it is."

"Must be weird."

"Yeah. And there are about twenty-five million people between eighteen and twenty-five in America, Nixon wants those votes."

"Will he get many of them?"

"More than you might think," Judy said. "The draft has been slowing down, there were only about twenty-five thousand called so far this year."

"Sounds like a lot of guys," Dougherty said, "twenty-five thousand."

"It was two hundred and fifty thousand in '69."

"I didn't realize it was so many."

"You should come to a meeting."

Dougherty smoked and said, "But David wasn't at the party?"

Judy said, "No. It wasn't planned or anything, it was just people stopping by when the news came out."

"The good news."

"Meanwhile the 7th Fleet is still bombing the crap out of Haiphong, so it's not like the war is over."

"Yeah, but John Lennon put up those billboards."

"And there are the ads on TV."

"What ads?"

"Unsell the war, you haven't seen them?"

Dougherty said no, and Judy said, "My favourite is the one with the pie — you haven't seen it? A bunch of people sitting around a table, average Americans, and Uncle Sam is cutting up an apple pie? Everybody gets a really small piece, just a bite, but the general gets a huge chunk."

"Oh yeah," Dougherty said, "maybe I have seen that one, the general's smoking a cigar?"

"Yeah. A lot of people like the motherhood one, the old lady talking about the mother bomb that drops the baby bombs."

"I don't know that one."

"I don't know if they're doing any good."

"Must be doing something," Dougherty said.

Judy took a drag and leaned over and stubbed out her smoke on the plate.

Then she said, "It's like people are just getting tired of it."

"Tired of the war?"

"Tired of protesting."

"You've been doing it a long time?"

Judy nodded a little, serious, and said, "Since Expo."

"Expo 67?"

"It was in all the papers."

Dougherty said, "That's what my dad says about the war — the world war, not Vietnam."

"Mine, too, that's the joke." She turned her head a little towards him and Dougherty smiled and said, "Right."

She held his look for a moment and then turned away, looked back at the ceiling and said, "That's when it started for me."

"Was it the American pavilion? I worked construction on that."

"No, not that one. Do you remember the Christianity pavilion?"

Dougherty said, "I must have missed that one."

She shoved him a little with her shoulder and said, "It wasn't all wild parties and drinking and drugs."

"It wasn't?"

"They showed a movie, just a short one, a few minutes, but it had all these scenes of wars, all these images of . . . violence and suffering and death. It wasn't like any movie I'd ever seen."

She was serious, and Dougherty didn't say anything.

"Women and kids. Men, too, of course, but just average people, you know, just people all being killed. There was a controversy, they said the movie shouldn't be shown."

"But you saw it?"

"I went back and saw it again and again. I wanted everyone to see it — drove my friends crazy."

"Really? You?"

"Hard to believe, I know."

Dougherty waited a moment, thinking about making another joke, saying something to lighten the mood, but he was feeling it, too, the seriousness of the situation, of the world, really, and he said, "But you found people who agreed with you."

"I started at McGill that fall. It's not like in the papers, the campus isn't all protests all the time, but there were some."

"But now," Dougherty said, "they're getting tired of it?"

"People graduate, they move on. People are moving to Toronto."

"Why would they do that?"

"It's changing, too, there are a lot of people there now."

"They put a man on the moon, too," Dougherty said, "I wouldn't want to move there."

"Or they don't graduate and they move on. Roberta and Tom joined the Hare Krishnas."

"Wearing the robes, shaving their heads?"

"People are getting into EST, have you heard of that?"

"Like reading minds?"

"That's ESP. This is some kind of therapy. There are a lot of therapies now, scream therapy, all kinds."

"I guess."

"Lots of splintering," Judy said. "People going their own way."

"You're still protesting the Milton Park development."

"Yeah," Judy said, "that's right, but it's changing."

Dougherty leaned across Judy and stubbed out his own smoke. They looked at one another for a moment, their faces close and neither one saying anything, and then Dougherty rolled back and looked up at the ceiling.

"What do you mean, changing?"

"Well, it's really happening, they started phase one, they knocked down all those houses."

"How many?"

Judy shook her head a little. "Two hundred and fifty-five. That was in July, remember?"

"Yeah, there were some demonstrations."

Judy smiled a little and said, "Yeah, there were." Then she got serious again and said, "But the houses came down anyway. People had been living in those houses for a long time, paying their rent every month, then they just got kicked out and the buildings knocked down."

"When my parents moved out of the Point," Dougherty said, "and bought a house on the South Shore, I was mad, I didn't want to move. I remember we had fights about it. My dad trying to explain to me what a difference it makes when you own your own house."

"How old were you?"

"My last year of high school."

"My parents bought our house when I was a baby," Judy said. "But Montreal is a rental city, all these houses are rentals."

"It's changing," Dougherty said.

"Change is hard for people. Now they're closing all the stores on Park and Jeanne-Mance. They're just going to knock everything down."

"You're still going to protest?"

Judy nodded a little and turned her head sideways. "This is some pillow talk — you trying to be a spy?"

"Come on," Dougherty said, "we've talked about this. I'm just trying to find out who killed David Murray."

"Well, he hadn't been to any meetings in a while so it didn't have anything to do with that. But now that I'm thinking about it, he was the first one to talk about this, about the way things were changing."

"What did he say?"

"I don't remember exactly, but he kind of warned me about the way it was going, the way people were starting to break off into small groups and talk about direct action."

"What's that?"

"You know."

"I don't."

She didn't look at him. "People were talking about Concordia Estates, who owns it, where *they* live."

Dougherty said, "Oh."

"I remember at one of the meetings David said something about that kind of action never working, how it was just what they wanted, how we'd lose public support."

"But some people didn't agree with him?"

"That's right."

"Who?"

Now Judy turned her head and looked at Dougherty. He waited and after a minute she said, "I don't remember."

"You sure?"

"David being killed, it couldn't have had anything to do with Milton Park."

"If people were talking about direct action," Dougherty said, "then anything's possible."

"It was just talk, nothing happened."

"Not exactly nothing," Dougherty said. "Someone killed David Murray."

Judy turned her head away from Dougherty and said, "I can't believe anyone at our meetings had anything to do with it."

"Wouldn't be the first time somebody trying to talk people out of direct action got themselves killed, would it?"

Judy said, "I don't know, would it?"

"Tell you the truth, I don't know."

But it gave Dougherty a few more people to look at.

And then he wondered if Carpentier had already looked at some of them and if some new information or connections might show up out of nowhere, but he didn't say anything about that to Judy.

———

Just after lunch Dougherty walked into HQ on Bonsecours and found Constable Carocchia on the second floor and said, "Hey Tony, I've got a question for you."

"Yeah?"

"Last week of August, what was going on?"

"Are you making a joke, Dog-eh-dee?"

Carocchia wrote the press releases for the police PR department and spoke English, French and Italian. Dougherty didn't think he had a sense of humour.

"I don't remember what the big stories were."

Carocchia said, "Fuck you," and walked away.

Dougherty went up to the third floor and found Rozovsky making notes in the evidence room.

"Any idea why Carocchia would fly off the handle because I asked him about the last week in August?"

Rozovsky looked up from the big leather ledger he was writing in and said, "You're funny, you know that. I don't mean Lenny Bruce funny, I mean . . . yeah, maybe I do."

"What the hell?"

Rozovsky looked at Dougherty and said, "The Mafia release."

Dougherty shrugged.

"Carocchia put out the press release about Saputo."

"So?"

"He put right in the press release that it was well known that members of American organized crime, I think he even used the word Mafia, are often seen at Saputo Cheese."

Dougherty said, "Oh yeah, now I think I remember. That wasn't August, though."

"No, it was back in the spring some time when the release went out but it was August when Saputo was on trial and he wanted Carocchia held in contempt. Guy had to get up and testify."

Now Dougherty was laughing a little and said, "Poor Tony. Well, I guess to him it is well known."

"I'm surprised he's still in PR."

Dougherty said, "You don't make a few mistakes, how're you going to learn?"

"And learn to make the right mistakes."

"So," Dougherty said, "what else was going on in August?"

Rozovsky closed the ledger. "Aren't you all down in Maine, what's it called, Old Orchard?"

"You all?"

"They're calling you Anglos these days."

"What are you?"

"Jews will always be Jews. We're in the Laurentians with Duddy Kravitz."

Dougherty said, "Right. Okay, so were there any demonstrations or anything?"

"Why?"

"This guy, David Murray, he's in with the draft dodgers, he's on the committees, he's organizing stuff, but then a few months ago, I guess around the start of the summer, he drops out. Or he stops showing up at meetings, no one sees him, and then we find him dead on Mount Royal."

"I thought he was smuggling drugs."

"He was, but they said they didn't kill him."

"Oh well, if they say so . . ." Rozovsky's eyebrows were raised.

"I've got some contacts," Dougherty said. "Told me that Murray smuggled drugs from here to the U.S."

"So maybe he screwed somebody on the other side of the border."

"And they came up here and killed him?"

"I'm sure they can find Montreal, it's on all the maps."

"And then find Murray? I can't find anyone who knew where he was, and I know the city."

"Somebody's lying to you."

Dougherty said, "For sure," but he had no idea who it was. He had a feeling it was everyone.

Rozovsky said, "Are you working now?"

"Four to midnight."

"So you've got a couple of hours, go look at newspapers from August, see if there were any demonstrations."

"What kind of pictures did you take then?"

Rozovsky shook his head and said, "I can't do all your work for you," but he was opening up the big leather ledger and flipping pages.

"What's the next step for you?" Dougherty said. "Do you want to be a detective?"

"All those headaches? Working twenty-four hours a day, what for?"

"Don't all cops want to be detectives?"

"Heroes," Rozovsky said. "When you signed up you told them you wanted to help people, right?"

"I guess, yeah, that's what everybody says."

Rozovsky held up an eight-by-ten colour photo and said, "Do you know how much I got for this?"

"Some guys standing around in a parking garage, that what it is?"

"It's Mick Jagger at the Forum, looking at the truck where the bomb went off."

Dougherty squinted and said, "Oh yeah, maybe that's him. Maybe not."

"It's him. This picture went out on the wire, got picked up all over." He put the picture away and held up another. "Guy from the Who, the drummer, I think. Didn't get as much for this one, but it's a better picture."

"It's a guy taking a leak against a wall."

"Got a good one of Alice Cooper — that's a guy, in case you didn't know."

"I knew that," Dougherty said. He pushed aside some photos on the table and said, "Who's that?"

"That's evidence."

"You mean an actual photo you took for your job?"

Rozovsky picked up the picture, a man's face covered in bruises. "That's a good shot, isn't it? The look on his face — I really captured it, didn't I?"

"Can you sell that one?"

"He's a fruit, got beat up outside a fruit bar on the Main."

"Usually those guys don't want the police involved, they don't want to go to court," Dougherty said. But looking at the picture he saw the defiant look in the guy's eyes. Rozovsky really did capture it, the guy staring at the camera, looking for a fight.

"This guy did," Rozovsky said. "There was one other witness, too, said a few guys followed them, calling them names, shoving them and then this guy," he looked at the white sticker at the bottom of the photo, "Pierre Lafontaine, he turned around, apparently, and said something back to them."

"I hope he got a few shots in before this happened," Dougherty said.

"Says he did, but the other guys took off."

"The other guys weren't in the bar? Nothing happened inside?"

"I don't know," Rozovsky said. "I just take the pictures, but there must be a report somewhere — the guy was pretty insistent."

"So they didn't know each other at all? It wasn't anything personal?"

"Well, it was personal to Pierre, here."

"Yeah," Dougherty said, "I guess it was. Thanks." He turned and started out of the office.

"Hey," Rozovsky said, "don't mention it. Whatever it is."

It was personal, Dougherty was thinking. Personal for him.

CHAPTER
EIGHTEEN

It was dark in the lane, no streetlights, just the flash from Rozovsky's camera. "Yeah, I recognize him," Dougherty said, "his name's Greg Herridge, called him Goose."

"Because of his long neck?" Carpentier said. "That's broken?"

"Yeah, that's right."

"Was he with the Point Boys?"

"He sure wanted to be," Dougherty said. "I talked to him a few days ago about David Murray."

Carpentier stepped back to let a couple of guys bring the stretcher through and said, "Oh yes, the draft dodger."

"Herridge knew him, said they smuggled drugs together."

"He told you that?" Carpentier took a drag on his cigarette and exhaled smoke. "So, it's not a complete surprise someone killed him, a mouth like that."

Dougherty could see Goose's neck was broken but he wasn't sure if the black and blue marks all over his face were something that came with a broken neck or if he'd been beaten, too. Carpentier said, "Probably the same killer."

"You think so?"

"Close enough," Carpentier said, "it's a war starting."

Dougherty didn't say anything and then Carpentier said, "You know a lot of these guys, the Irish ones. Maybe you should talk to Ste. Marie."

"I've talked to him."

Carpentier blew out smoke and said, "About working in his squad. Kennedy retired, you know."

"No," Dougherty said, "I didn't know that."

"Well, he's still in the hospital, cancer, but he won't be coming back to work. They'll need an Irish."

"Is that how it works?"

"I'll talk to Paul-Emile," Carpentier said. "So much drug now. Lot of hash and heroin and mescaline, you know what is that?"

"No."

Rozovsky said, "Horse tranquilizer." He stepped out of the shadows and said, "Kids are snorting it."

"Sounds like a party," Dougherty said.

"There's nothing on the ground around here," Rozovsky said, "no bricks or rocks or anything, looks like he was dumped here."

"Why here?" Dougherty said. "What's the message here?"

"Who knows, maybe you'll have to talk to them."

"I'm sure they'll tell me everything."

Carpentier turned to walk away then stopped and said, "*Connais-tu sa famille?*"

"I know his sister, Imelda. His father died when we were kids — an accident at the CN yards, I think. Mother still lives in the Point."

"*Bon*, I'll talk to her."

When Carpentier was out of earshot, Rozovsky said, "Look at that, talking about a promotion."

"You think?"

"He's going to talk to the assistant director."

"He is?"

"Paul-Emile Olivier. Don't you know anything?"

"Right now he's going to talk to Greg Herridge's mother, tell her some other drug dealer beat her son to death."

"That may not be the best part of the job," Rozovsky said. "But you won't have to wear that uniform —" the flash lit up the lane as he snapped a picture " and look so official all the time."

———

"Is this guy a fag, is that what you want to know?"

"Have you seen him in here?"

The bartender pushed the picture back towards Dougherty and said, "Don't recognize him. What did he do?"

"He got killed."

"That's a shame."

Dougherty was pretty sure the bartender had recognized David Murray's picture, the high school graduation

263

picture Murray's mother had given Carpentier.

"And you never saw him in here? Did you see him anywhere?"

It was just after lunch and the place, the Mystique Cocktail Bar on Stanley, across the street from the Stanley Court apartment building where Dougherty had thought about getting a place when he was first assigned to Station Ten, was filling up fast. He hadn't even noticed the Mystique the day he came by to look at the apartments, half a block up from St. Catherine, and he wouldn't have seen the place now if he wasn't looking for it, the plain brown wooden door crammed in between a stationery store and a dry cleaner.

The bartender said, "No."

"You're sure?"

"I'm sure."

Dougherty picked up the picture and said, "He was an American going to McGill." He put the picture back in the pocket of his sports coat and got out his smokes. "Maybe he came in here," Dougherty said. "Maybe somebody followed him when he left, started a fight."

"Does that happen? Do guys follow men coming out of places like this and start fights with them?"

"I've heard it does," Dougherty said.

"You'd think the police would do something about that."

Dougherty turned away from the bartender and looked out at a couple dozen men moving chairs around. There was a small stage against the back wall and on his way in Dougherty had noticed pictures of the performers, drag queens dressed up like Tina

Turner and Mae West, but the chairs all seemed to be facing the end of the bar.

"Is there going to be a show?"

The bartender rolled his eyes and said, "Aren't you going to watch the game?" Then he motioned to the barstool Dougherty was standing beside and said, "You're welcome to join us, but there's a two-drink minimum."

Dougherty lit his cigarette and said, "This series was over when we lost the first game."

"Come on, we win today and we win on Thursday, that's the series."

"We were supposed to win all eight games. Win them easy."

"We have to take what victory we can," the bartender said.

Dougherty said, "Yeah, I guess we do."

Walking out the of the Mystique, Dougherty looked at the bar upstairs, a dance bar called Truxx, and thought about going in, but it looked like it wasn't open in the afternoon. And he didn't think David Murray was really the dance bar type, but this whole wild goose chase Dougherty was on was because he really had no idea what kind of a guy David Murray was. Everyone seemed to agree the guy wasn't the same as he was when he left Wisconsin but no one seemed to know who he was by the time he got killed.

A couple blocks over on Peel, Dougherty went into a bar called the Tropical Lounge. It was older than the brand-new Mystique, probably twenty, twenty-five years in the same location. The first bar in Montreal where men could dance together. Dougherty had been in the place a couple of times on duty, usually because of tourists, drunk, away from home being crazy, getting in fights.

The dance floor of the Tropical was filled with chairs, and men here were getting ready to watch the game, too. Dougherty thought it was funny, if he just looked at the guys and not the decor of the bar it could be the Rymark or Magnan's — bunch of men watching a hockey game. Maybe there were a few more cocktails and fewer pitchers of draught but otherwise it was just the same.

Dougherty walked to the end of the bar and put down the picture of David Murray.

There were two bartenders working, and neither one made a move to come over to where Dougherty was standing. He waited.

The game started on TV.

Dougherty waited.

Two minutes in Esposito took a penalty.

After Canada killed the power play, one of the bartenders, the older one, walked slowly to Dougherty and said, "What'll it be, Officer?"

Dougherty tapped the photo on the bar and said, "Do you know this guy?"

"Just like that? You don't want chit-chat, pretend to be my friend?"

"Have you seen him in here?"

The bartender shook his head a little and said, "Why are you by yourself, where's your partner? How long have you been a detective?"

A huge cheer rang out in the bar, guys standing up and clapping.

The bartender said, "Espo scored."

Dougherty clenched his fists. He wanted to bang on the bar and grab this guy and tell him to answer the damned question, but he also wanted to be calm and cool about it. He didn't know how to play it. He wished he had a partner. He wished he was a detective.

Dougherty said, "You do know him, don't you?"

"I'll get you an O'Keefe," the bartender said. "That seems like you."

Dougherty leaned on the bar and turned around a little and looked at the TV. And he looked at the crowd of men looking at the TV.

One of the older guys said, "This is more like it," and the guy sitting beside him said, "We have our legs, finally."

"If we'd had a training camp, or if this series had been in the middle of the season, the whole thing would have been like this."

"Just took a few games to get into shape."

"I don't know," another older guy said, "these Russians are good. They'd put up a good fight no matter when we played these games."

The bartender came back and put a beer in front of Dougherty. "You want to run a tab, Officer?"

Dougherty was thinking he just wanted this guy to tell him about David Murray and then he'd leave, he didn't want to spend the afternoon watching a hockey game in a fruit bar — no matter how much these guys knew about the game.

But he said, "Sure." Then he said, "My name's Dougherty. Constable Dougherty."

The bartender was probably in his fifties, his short

hair mostly grey, his clean-shaven face lined. He said, "Steve Whitmer," and held out his hand, and when Dougherty shook it he said, "The last rank I had was chief petty officer."

"World War II?"

"The one that was in all the papers, yeah."

Before Dougherty could say anything, Whitmer went off to serve some more guys and the Russians scored.

A few minutes later the Russians scored again to take the lead, 2–1, and the place got tense.

Whitmer brought Dougherty another beer and said, "Why are you looking for this man, Constable?"

"He was killed."

"So why are you the one asking questions?"

The bar exploded with cheers.

"Espo again," Whitmer said. "He's having a game."

Dougherty took a drink and said, "We don't know very much about him. I'm trying to find out."

Whitmer nodded. "So they just sent you."

"No one sent me," Dougherty said. "I'm looking everywhere."

"This your first time in here without your riot helmet and billy club?"

"I've never been here on a raid," Dougherty said. "I've only been here when someone called — breaking up a fight, calming people down."

"But you will be, now the Olympics are coming."

"What do you mean by that?"

Whitmer looked around the bar and said, "Before Expo we got raided all the time. Do you know how many bars like this got closed down permanently then, because the city didn't want to admit we exist? Eight bars shut down, gone."

"That was almost ten years ago," Dougherty said. "Before my time."

"So it's going to happen again, and now it's your time. What are you going to do?"

The period ended and the bar got crowded with guys looking for more drinks. Dougherty got pushed off to the side, but he stayed and drank his beer. He watched the whole second period, no goals, thinking about what he would do if the city tried to clean up again before the Olympics.

And he was thinking that Whitmer, like the bartender at the Mystique, had recognized David Murray.

The third period started and a couple of minutes in, Canada scored, but the Russians got that back a couple minutes later on the power play, and it stayed 3–3, tight-checking game, no one giving an inch, and Tony O and the Russian kid, Tretiak, stopping everything thrown at them.

The place was tense. Every single guy staring at the TV.

With two minutes left, Paul Henderson got around a big Russian defenceman, Tsygankov, and fired it past Tretiak and then fell and crashed the net. The red light came on for a second but then went out.

The bar was silent for a moment, and then the Canadian players jumped over the boards and skated out to Henderson, celebrating, and the bar exploded, guys jumping up and cheering.

Whitmer was by Dougherty then and he said, "This is just like '66 against Detroit, remember? Henri

Richard scored in overtime, crashed into the net, and Toe Blake sent the rest of the team out to celebrate before the refs could call it back."

"I remember," Dougherty said.

Every guy in the bar stayed on his feet for the last two minutes of the game, holding their breath until the final buzzer.

"Jesus Murphy," Whitmer said, "that's two games in a row Henderson scored the winner. Harold Ballard must be going insane." Dougherty didn't get it, so Whitmer said, "Henderson's negotiating a new contract now — that goal will get him an extra twenty-five grand."

Dougherty said, "I guess. He should sign it today, he's never gonna score a bigger goal."

"There's one more game," Whitmer said, "and now it's for all the marbles. You never know."

The bar started to clear out, but a few guys looked like they were going to stay right there for two days until the next game.

Dougherty waited and finished his beer and then got out his wallet. Whitmer came over and said, "I bet this is the last place you expected to watch this game."

"You've seen this guy, haven't you?" He held up the picture and watched Whitmer nod a little.

"Not in here, though, this wasn't really his scene, you know?"

270   "I don't know anything," Dougherty said, and Whitmer said, "Good of you to admit that, Constable, that may help you in your job."

"We'll see."

"People are talking about organizing, forming a committee."

"He was on a committee," Dougherty said, "the War Resisters."

Whitmer smiled a little, sadly, Dougherty thought, but he couldn't be sure.

"No, this committee . . . You remember the 'We Demand' manifesto last year on Parliament Hill?"

Dougherty said, "Not really. There've been a lot of manifestos."

Whitmer laughed at that and said, "I guess so, yeah, everybody has one these days. Well, after that a committee started in Vancouver, GATE, Gay Alliance Toward Equality, and then one started in Toronto, Gay Action Now."

"Those initials don't spell anything."

"They sponsored something back in the summer, called it Gay Pride, lots of people went."

"When in the summer?"

"August, near the end of the month, a big party on one of the Toronto Islands, why?"

"Was he there?" Dougherty was still holding the picture.

"There were a lot of people."

"Out in public?" Dougherty said.

"Better blatant than latent."

"I'm trying to find out who he was hanging around with, what he was doing. His friends, no one saw him for a while."

"He may have been in Toronto," Whitmer said. "I can't say for sure. I can tell you he didn't come to any of the meetings here."

"All right, well, thanks." Dougherty put a couple of two-dollar bills on the bar and started out.

Whitmer said, "We'll see you again, Constable."

Dougherty said, "Yeah, I guess you will."

Outside on Peel, Dougherty checked his watch and figured he had just enough time to get to Station Ten and change into his uniform to start his four to midnight. Walking back along de Maisonneuve and seeing people spilling out of the bars he realized that the whole city was likely going to shut down for the final game.

And then he wondered what would happen if we lost.

Or if we won.

NINETEEN

Dougherty got to HQ on Bonsecours Street just before four and headed straight to the homicide offices on the fourth floor. Carpentier was standing beside his desk talking to Detective Ste. Marie, so Dougherty thought he'd have to wait and stood by the office door but Carpentier said, *"Entrez, Constable, venez ici."*

Ste. Marie said, "We were just talking about your friend."

"David Murray?"

Carpentier said, "Greg Herridge. What did you call him, Goose?"

"Yeah, Goose."

Dougherty saw pictures spread out over Carpentier's desk: David Murray, Goose, the biker who'd been dumped on Atwater and a couple of other guys with their eyes closed who likely weren't sleeping. Not Rozovsky's postcard work.

Ste. Marie said, "He's trying to dump them on me."

"They're all organized crime," Carpentier said, "they're all yours."

"This guy is a biker."

"*Mais oui*, they work for the mob: they're the muscle and the street dealers, they're part of the same war," Carpentier said. "It's all organized crime, that's yours." He looked at Dougherty and said, "Right?"

Dougherty said, "Um . . ." and wished he was anywhere but here.

"It's territory," Ste. Marie said. He picked up one of the pictures Dougherty didn't recognize and said, "Martin Michaud, killed in St. Léonard, *chuté* there, anyway, probably by your Point Boys *en représailles à* whatsisname, Goose?" He looked at Dougherty and then back to Carpentier and said, "You already have the men for the investigation."

"*Le constable n'est pas assigné à mon équipe.*"

"Well, maybe not assigned, but he's working for you," Ste. Marie said.

Dougherty was pretty sure he saw Carpentier shrug but then the detective said, "It could have been the Italians or the bikers, the St. Henri Dead Men, they lost this one, Tremblay." He tapped a picture.

Ste. Marie said, "Could be," and Carpentier said, "Look, if we're going to get a break, it will be from a *stooler* trying to make a deal, so, Robert, I'm just asking you when it comes up, when you've got someone and he says he knows something about any one of these, let me know right away."

"*Bien sûr.*"

Now Dougherty was positive he saw Carpentier shrug as Detective Ste. Marie started to walk away.

When it was just the two of them in the office, Dougherty wasn't sure he wanted to say what he'd come to say, but Carpentier was waiting. "It's possible David Murray wasn't part of this mob war."

"Why do you say that?"

"He may have been involved in something else."

"What?"

Dougherty paused for a few seconds and then said, "He might have been a homosexual."

"So?" Carpentier said. "Homosexuals sell drugs, too."

"But he was keeping it a secret."

"So how did you find out?"

Dougherty said, "I played a hunch," and Carpentier said, "Good for you — you're a detective now."

"Well, we'll see about that."

"Yes," Carpentier said, "nothing is for sure, of course."

"Rozovsky had a picture of a guy who was beat up after he left a bar, a fruit, and he said that these guys usually didn't call the cops."

"The fruit said that?"

"Rozovsky, he said it was unusual that he had to take the evidence pictures, usually there was no investigation, so, I just thought," Dougherty said, "that Murray seemed to be dropping out of everything — his friends hadn't seen him for a while, he seemed to be keeping secrets."

"But that was because of the drug smuggling."

"Maybe, but maybe it was this."

Carpentier said, "And someone recognized him?"

"Yes," Dougherty said. "More than one, really, but only one would admit it. He said they're organizing committees."

"Who isn't these days?"

"Murray wasn't on any of them, but he might have gone to Toronto for some kind of gay party."

Carpentier said, "All right, well, you don't really have enough," and he paused, and Dougherty said, "For a detective to follow it up," and Carpentier said, "Yes, but it's good work, you should keep going with it."

Dougherty said, "You're right, it probably has nothing to do with it. It's probably the drug smuggling. Probably the same guy who killed Goose killed Murray."

"Probably." Carpentier turned back to his desk and started packing up the files, the pictures of the murder victims, and said, "But you keep going. Good work, Constable."

"All right."

Dougherty walked out of the homicide office feeling pretty good, thinking it was probably a waste of time but at least Carpentier was okay with it and then he started to get worried, not knowing what his next move should be.

But really, he knew there was only one next move, only one person to talk to.

Judy said, "What difference could it possibly make if David was a homosexual?"

"It might help us figure out who he was hanging out with."

Judy nodded a little, thinking about it, and he figured she was going to help if she could. When he'd knocked on the door of the house and she'd answered, she wasn't surprised or upset to see him, she wasn't worried anyone would see them together, she'd just said, "Look at you, out in the middle of the day."

Dougherty told her he'd just come from talking to Carpentier, from telling him about this hunch about David Murray.

Now they were sitting in the kitchen at the back of her house, and Judy was saying, "I've heard some talk about a committee being formed."

"Who's doing that?"

"I don't know if I can tell you."

Dougherty said, "What?"

"All the people who live here in this house, everybody I've been hanging out with for years, they don't trust cops."

"There are some cops I don't trust," Dougherty said, "but this is you and me."

"I know that. But what are we?"

"What?"

"You and me, what is this?"

Dougherty said, "I don't know, what's it supposed to be?"

"I don't know."

Dougherty didn't say anything. He hadn't thought about it at all, but he knew enough not to say that, so he waited, and finally Judy said, "Okay, never mind. But this, with David, it doesn't sound like a fight, like a couple would have a fight."

"What do you mean?"

"Well, it just seems so severe."

Dougherty said, "All we know is it happened."

Judy nodded and said, "I might know someone."

"Yeah, we all hopped on Flight 602."

"David Murray didn't take a flight, he drove here from Wisconsin."

Stan smiled a little and said, "It's just an expression."

They were in George's on Stanley Street, a Hungarian coffee shop that Dougherty was surprised to see so crowded in the middle of the afternoon. Judy had set up the meeting and she was sitting across from Dougherty, smoking one of Stan's Gitanes and drinking espresso.

"Flight 602 is the Mohawk Airlines flight from New York to Toronto," Stan said, "so guys use it as an expression for going to Canada. They don't usually fly."

Dougherty said, "Oh," and drank some of his own coffee, regular with milk and sugar.

"And it's a song now, Chicago Transit Authority, I guess they're just Chicago now." Stan drank espresso and said, "'I only wanted to be just a man fulfilled, but a little more free.'"

Judy said, "A little more free."

"I get it," Dougherty said. "Not drafted."

"That's too much government," Stan said. "We're

trying to get away from the communists telling us what to do every minute of the day."

Dougherty was going to say, Yeah, but we have to fight them for that freedom, but he knew Stan would have a better argument, or at least be able to argue all day like the long-haired student he was, probably something about becoming what it is we're fighting against or is it just the same thing in a different disguise, and he didn't want to get into that now, so he said, "You knew David pretty well."

Stan shrugged and said, "Not very well."

"But you were getting to know him better. You were in Toronto with him in August?"

Stan looked sideways at Judy but didn't say anything, and she said, "It's just for the murder investigation, nothing else."

"You know," Stan said, "that a man can be denied landed immigrant status in Canada if he's homosexual?"

"No," Dougherty said, "I don't really know anything about immigration," and Stan said, "Well, that's okay, not many immigration officers know much about it, either."

He motioned around the café with his hands and said, "All these Hungarians, they all came here after their revolution against the Soviets failed, you know about that?"

"A little," Dougherty said, "Ten, fifteen years ago?" He wasn't interested in a history lesson from this guy, but he was learning to listen more and let people tell their stories, it usually loosened them up enough to start talking about what he really wanted to hear.

Stan said, "Nineteen fifty-six, sixteen years ago.

Refugees came to Canada, maybe thirty thousand, maybe more. You notice all these Hungarian coffee shops and restaurants."

"I like the Coffee Mill," Dougherty said.

"On Mountain Street. You like the paprika chicken."

"Yeah, it's good."

"You ever have the schnitzel at the Riviera?"

Dougherty said, "No, but I've had the strudel."

"So, do you think any of the refugees they let in were gay?"

"I don't know."

"Well, I can tell you," Stan said, "if any of them were, they would have kept it a secret."

"Okay." Dougherty didn't really understand what this guy was getting at — of course a fruit would keep it a secret.

"I'm Hungarian," Stan said, "but I was born in New Jersey. It's always hard to find a place to fit in. Am I American? Hungarian? Canadian? Student? War resister?" He paused and then said, a little more quietly, "Gay?"

Dougherty said, "It's not a crime anymore."

Stan shrugged. "It could be again, we don't know."

"Is this what you talked about in Toronto," Dougherty said, "with David?"

"It was mostly a party. David didn't come to the meetings."

Dougherty said, "He went to meetings here, though, in Montreal?"

"A couple, maybe."

Dougherty looked at Judy and said, "He was dropping out of the War Resisters and the Milton Park stuff, but he was doing this?"

"I didn't know," she said. "But I'm not really surprised to hear it. The odd thing was David dropping out of sight, dropping out of the groups. He did like to be involved."

Stan said, "I knew him a little from the resisters but not much. Then I saw him in Toronto."

Dougherty felt there was more to it, more that Stan wanted to say, and he wasn't sure if he should push him or wait. When it seemed like the moment had passed, Judy said, "What is it?"

Stan looked at her and fidgeted with his little coffee cup and shrugged and said, "I think he wanted to be more involved, David. I think he wanted to be more, I don't know, active in the movement? If you can call it a movement."

Judy said, "What was stopping him?"

"His ride," Stan said, "the guy David drove to Toronto with."

"Were they a couple?"

"They were very . . . reluctant to be public about it, how's that?"

"Obtuse," Judy said. "Is that the right word?"

Stan was smiling and he said, "There's a lot of fear. It's a scary thing."

"Who was it?" Dougherty said. "Who was David with?"

Stan looked at Judy and then looked away, towards the kitchen at the back of the dining room.

"Richard Burnside."

Walking on de Maisonneuve Judy said, "You didn't look surprised at all."

"I've heard them connected before," Dougherty said. "I thought Murray knew Burnside because of the drug smuggling, I thought Burnside was supplying the rock bands."

"Maybe that's how they met."

Dougherty started to say something but then he stopped and said, "Hey, Cheryl."

His sister was walking towards him, and she stopped and said, "I don't see any traffic needs directing."

"Did you fall asleep in class?"

"I'm on my way to the library." She motioned farther along de Maisonneuve to Drummond, where the apartment building extended over one lane of the street and made a kind of one-block-long tunnel.

Dougherty said, "You know where the library is?" and Cheryl ignored it and said, "Who's your friend?"

"Judy, this is my little sister, Cheryl. She's just started what we all expect to be a very long career as a student."

"Are you going to McGill?"

"Sir George."

Judy said, "What's your major?" and Dougherty said, "This week?"

"Ha ha." Cheryl looked at Judy and said, "Psychology."

"Cool."

Dougherty said, "Okay, now that we're all caught up," and made a move to walk away.

Cheryl said, "Are you going to see Dad later?"

"Yeah, I start my shift at four, I'll stop in some time after that."

"Mom's going right after work, she'll be there by five thirty."

Dougherty said, "Okay, I'll try to make it then," and started to walk away.

Judy said, "It was nice to meet you," and Cheryl said, "You, too," and they shook hands before walking in different directions on de Maisonneuve.

After a few steps in silence, Judy said, "Sometimes this is such a small town," and Dougherty said, "That's because you're an Anglo and you only use half of it, or less."

"That's not true."

"When was the last time you were east of St. Denis?"

"My grandfather is buried in Hawthorn-Dale, that's pretty far east."

Dougherty glanced sideways at Judy and said, "My grandfather's buried there, too."

"So you've been."

"It's got that big kids' section."

Judy said, "I think that was from a typhus epidemic."

"I bet your father says he'll be happy when the Ville-Marie Tunnel opens."

Judy said, "He may have."

"This city feels more divided."

"More than what?"

"Than it used to, I guess," Dougherty said.

Judy said, "Divide and conquer. We see it in Milton Park all the time. The developers are very good at giving just enough people a little of what they want so we're always fighting with each other and they get what they want."

"So who gets what out of driving the city further apart?"

"Money, power, the usual."

Dougherty said, "Yeah, I guess." He stopped then and said, "I have to get changed and get to work. Do you want to get together later?"

"You mean when you finish, at midnight?"

"After I see my dad in the hospital, we could grab dinner."

Judy said, "You'd be in your uniform."

"I guess it's a big step for you to be seen with me like this."

"It sure is."

Dougherty wasn't sure if she was kidding or not, so he didn't say anything and waited, but she was just looking at him, so he said, "Yeah, I get it."

She nodded a little, and he said, "How about lunch tomorrow?"

"Okay."

Dougherty said, "Okay."

Then as he walked back along de Maisonneuve towards Station Ten, Dougherty was thinking that the Richard Burnside connection was probably enough now for Carpentier to get interested and maybe interview the guy himself. And Dougherty felt one step closer to detective.

CHAPTER
TWENTY

It was almost two in the morning when Dougherty finally got back to Station Ten to clock out, and as soon as he walked into the building, the night shift desk sergeant, Arseneault, told him to phone Detective Carpentier at homicide.

At the homicide office, one of the other detectives answered the phone and said he had no idea why Carpentier wanted him to call, and just before Dougherty hung up the guy said, "*Attends une minute.*" Dougherty waited while the guy talked to someone else, and then came back on the line saying, "Come down to the office right now. He wants to talk to you."

"Who," Dougherty said, "Carpentier?"

"No, the pope, *bien sûr*, Carpentier." He hung up.

Dougherty didn't bother changing out of his uniform, but he walked the couple of blocks to his apartment and got his own car and drove down to Bonsecours Street. On the way through the finally sleeping city, he figured that Carpentier had looked into the Richard Burnside connection he'd given him what seemed like a long time ago, but what was really only about ten hours.

Time flies when you're wrestling drunks out of bars.

Even on a Wednesday night, Montreal was hopping. Late September, even though no one mentioned it, they could feel winter was coming and were getting in every minute of partying before the long hibernation.

At HQ, Dougherty went up to the fourth floor and walked down the hall to the homicide office. He was getting used to it, and starting to feel like he could fit in coming to work here, wearing a nice suit and taking charge of an investigation. He was thinking maybe Carpentier had already brought in Burnside and got a confession out of him and they were going to celebrate.

But when he walked into the office, the detectives standing by the window all had stern expressions.

Carpentier was at his desk, and he motioned Dougherty over and said, "Good, you didn't change — the uniform will help."

"Sir?"

"We have one of your friends downstairs in detention, and I thought maybe you could talk to him. There are a couple of things we'd like to know."

"Is it Richard Burnside?"

Carpentier looked surprised for a second, and then said, "Oh, no, that was a good idea. The two of them were probably *des amoureux*, so to speak, but Burnside wasn't involved in the murder."

"He wasn't?" Dougherty could feel whatever confidence he had coming into the office slipping away.

"That was the night of the first game, remember, the Soviets at the Forum. Burnside was there, with a group of people, then they went out to drown their sorrows."

"He was at the hockey game?"

Carpentier shrugged. "Lots of witnesses. His father was there."

"You talked to him?"

"No, but we did talk to others. Look, Constable, it was a good idea. You did well," Carpentier said, "but that's the way it goes. Now," he picked up a file and handed it to Dougherty and said, "You know Daniel Buckley."

"Buck-Buck, sure."

"He's an informant of yours?"

"We haven't spoken in a while."

"Yes, he's moving up. Ste. Marie tells me these Point Boys are moving a lot more drug themselves now, not just unloading the boats."

"Yeah," Dougherty said, "someone in the Point finally got ambitious."

"Well, there's an opportunity now. In any event, this Buckley seems to be moving up."

"Up to murder?"

"Is that hard to believe?"

Dougherty said, "No, not really."

"It's possible Buckley ordered it, and may have

287

taken part in the murder of Greg Herridge. A kind of house cleaning."

"Shit," Dougherty said, "those guys have been friends their whole lives."

"When you move up in this business, you make new friends," Carpentier said. "It looks like Buckley's new friends were worried that his old friends maybe weren't professional enough."

"That's a tough business."

"It is."

"I thought it was territory, I thought it was revenge for the guy who was killed in St. Léonard?"

"It might be — we aren't positive. What we know is that Buckley called Herridge to meet with him and then he was killed."

"So Buckley did it himself or set him up?"

"*Probablement.*"

Dougherty was thinking this was taking it to a whole new level for Buck-Buck, but he wasn't too surprised. "What do you want to know?"

"We cannot tell Buckley how we know about the phone call. We have a witness but she needs to be protected."

"Has he said anything?"

Carpentier shrugged and said, "He's asked for his lawyer, Howard Shrier."

"Mob lawyer?"

Carpentier nodded. "That's the one. He works for Cotroni."

"Buck-Buck *is* moving up."

"You pretend it is a coincidence that you've been given the job to transport him to Parthenais jail, talk to him and see if he might be willing to make a deal, tell him it would be good for both of you."

Dougherty said, "I can do that," and Carpentier said, "Yes, you can."

———

The guard led Dougherty along the row of cells in the basement that was like a medieval cave: dim lighting, damp and, if it was quiet enough, the sound of rats scurrying around. The guard stopped at the last cell and unlocked it.

Dougherty said, "Holy shit, Buck-Buck?" and hoped he didn't overdo it with the surprise. "They told me I was transporting a murderer."

Buckley was standing up then and said, "Eat shit, Dougherty."

Dougherty laughed and said, "These look good on you," as he slapped his handcuffs onto Buckley's wrists and squeezed them tight, the steel teeth clattering as they closed. "This should be a fun ride," and he gently shoved Buckley's back.

In the parking lot, Buckley stopped by the back door of the police car and said, "Now you're a taxi driver, is that a demotion?"

Dougherty winked as he put Buckley in the back seat. "Watch your head."

He drove slowly out of the parking lot and through the empty streets of Old Montreal, past the construction for the new Ville-Marie Expressway and the big old Édifice Jacques-Viger, dark and looking like an empty castle with its turrets and stone walls, a long way from the fancy hotel and train station it once was,

289

now just a bland office building inside. Almost dawn, the only time the city was ever so quiet.

"Jesus Murphy, Buck-Buck, you killed Goose? Did he fuck your sister?"

Dougherty kept his eye on the rear-view, watching Buckley roll his eyes and look out the window, pretending to be bored, but Dougherty knew he had to be a little worried, probably thinking even if the cops didn't have enough on him they'd fake it well enough to send him down for a few years anyway.

"Naw," Dougherty said, "we'd give him a medal for that."

Buck-Buck was shaking his head but still not saying anything.

"They tell me you're moving up, cleaning house, getting rid of the wannabes and the amateurs, the groupies. I guess Goose wasn't really tough enough, was he?"

Dougherty pulled over and stopped. They were on Notre-Dame, under the Jacques Cartier Bridge.

"He had a big mouth, though," Dougherty said, "that's for sure."

Buckley said, "So do you."

"Nobody listens to me," Dougherty said. "I'm just some Anglo from the Point, like you."

"Not like me, I'd never kiss their asses like you do, you're practically a frog."

"There's a couple guys, maybe one guy who might listen to me. If I said you might be willing to make a deal."

Buckley laughed. Not loud and not hard, but he laughed.

"They're going to put you away for Goose, you know that, right?"

"They've got nothing."

"They'll make it up. If they don't get a deal from you, they'll get a deal from your lawyer, Shrier. It'll stop with you, it'll never get to any of his real clients."

"You have no idea what's going on."

"I know you're going to Kingston for a long time," Dougherty said. "Did you kill David Murray, too?"

"You're funny, Eddie."

Dougherty saw something in the rear-view, though, something in Buckley's eyes.

"Doesn't really matter, they'll pin that one on you, too."

Buckley smirked, dismissed it.

"Two murders, you'll do real time, twenty-five to life."

"Fuck you."

"Goose told me himself — he was working with Murray, giving him a hard time because Murray wouldn't commit."

"Fag."

Dougherty said, "So you killed them both. Shit, you are cleaning house."

Buckley shrugged that off, too, and Dougherty realized that Buckley probably killed Goose because of his big mouth, because Goose talked to Dougherty.

"You're fucking cold, Danny." He slammed the car into gear and hit the gas, squealing the tires and pulling a U on the empty street.

"I didn't kill anybody."

"Who cares."

"If I have to I'll start talking — this'll blow up in your face."

"Sure it will."

"You talk to Murray's boyfriend?"

"Yeah, we did," Dougherty said. "He was at the hockey game."

"So what, guy with his money, his connections."

"Why would Burnside kill his own boyfriend?"

"You're thick, Dougherty, you know that? You think Burnside's rock 'n' roll business is making him any money? You think he clears a cent after paying everybody off he has to pay?"

"So what?"

"So, what do you think his old man would do if he found out he was a fag?"

"Sure, you want me to believe Burnside was worried his father would cut off the money."

"Cut something off," Buckley said. He was smiling. "Look, you're the detective, or you wanna be, I'm just saying that maybe Burnside was the one who wanted Murray to go away."

Dougherty took his foot off the gas and eased it onto the brake. "So he hired you?"

"Me? Jesus Murphy, you don't give up, I'll give you that."

Dougherty stepped on the gas again but it was in his head now, and he was thinking it was possible. It fit with what he'd heard about the Toronto trip, how Murray wanted to be more public about their relationship and Burnside didn't, but was it enough reason to kill a guy?

Well, somebody killed him for some reason.

They were pulling up in front of Parthenais, the smooth glass building that held the Quebec Provincial Police headquarters and three storeys of jail cells on the top. It was only a few years old and had already had a few headline-grabbing escapes.

"All right, you sure this bullshit is the story you want to stick to?"

Buckley was looking up at the cell floors at the top of the building. "I've said everything I have to say."

Dougherty said, "Then I guess there's a few French guys looking forward to meeting you."

He got out and opened the back door of the police car, and Buckley got out saying, "Don't worry about me, Eddie, I *parle* enough *français* to get by."

"Sure you do." Dougherty pushed him towards the building but was already moving on and thinking about what he'd tell Carpentier, how it was probably nothing, just bullshit from a guy scared he was going to jail for a long time.

But they should probably check it out.

———

The sun was coming and the day was starting at police headquarters. Dougherty checked in the car and rode the elevator up to the fourth floor with a couple of secretaries.

The homicide office was busy already and Dougherty felt like he was walking into the middle of something. He saw Carpentier talking to Ste. Marie and waited till they finally looked up and waved him over.

Ste. Marie said, "*Qu'est-ce qu'il dit?*"

"*Rien,*" Dougherty said. "*Rien de nouveau.*"

Carpentier said, "He doesn't want a deal at all?"

Dougherty wasn't sure if he should answer in French or English but he said, "He's still saying he had nothing to do with it. Now he's saying Richard Burnside had David Murray killed."

Ste. Marie shook his head and said, "*Encore l'histoire de chantage, tabarnak.*"

"He tried to sell us some bullshit about Burnside being blackmailed," Carpentier said. "Threatening to go to his father."

"Yeah, that's what he said. You're sure it's bullshit?"

"Yes, we checked," Carpentier said. "He's just throwing shit out there now. *Bien*, that's the way he wants it, fine."

The detectives turned back to one another, and Dougherty felt dismissed. He waited a few seconds, and then there was no doubt, they were finished with him, so he turned and walked out of the office.

A couple of men in their fifties wearing nice suits were coming into the office, and Dougherty could feel the place tense up. He heard Carpentier say, "*Bonjour, Paul-Emile.*"

On his way down the hall, Dougherty saw Rozovsky go into the evidence room, and he followed him. "Hey Peter, do you have any idea what's going on?"

Rozovsky had a cup of coffee in one hand and a bagel in the other, and he said, "Gearing up for something big, it looks like."

"The assistant director is here and some other guy."

"Marcel Plante," Rozovsky said. "From the mayor's office. All kinds of bigwigs coming in."

"And me getting the bum's rush out."

"So, what do you want with all that *tsuris*."

Dougherty said, "All that what?"

"Trouble. Whatever they're doing it's way above our pay grade — we'll find out about it when they want us to find out about it."

"I'd like to know now."

"Oh, that's right, you're ambitious."

"I just want to know what's going on."

"Soviets are favourites today," Rozovsky said. "Bookies are giving 6–7 odds."

"That's the best you can get?"

"Bet five bucks on Canada, you win six."

"If we win."

———

Dougherty got his Mustang out of the parking lot by city hall and drove up the hill, thinking Rozovsky was right, he didn't need the *tsuris*, he wasn't a detective, maybe he never would be, so what. He was a good constable, he liked the job and someday he could take over the desk from Delisle.

He drove slow past Station Ten, looking at the squat concrete building, almost out of place with all the old brownstones but a couple high-rises had gone in on de Maisonneuve and Sir George Williams was taking over more old houses, so nothing was out of place anymore. Or everything was.

Dougherty was thinking that his father was still an installer — he'd never moved up into management. Then he had an image of him in the hospital bed hooked up to the ventilator, shit, Dougherty'd almost forgotten. He thought about going to the hospital right now but he couldn't.

He just drove, no destination in mind, just feeling the road passing under his wheels. He drove right past his apartment — his temporary room as he'd told Judy, and that's what it was, as temporary as everything else in his life — and then he was thinking about Judy and her causes and her fights and her workboots.

He pulled a U.

Dougherty said, "Sorry, I've been working all night — I didn't have a chance to go undercover," and Judy looked at him standing in her doorway in his uniform and said, "That's okay, it looks kinda good on you."

"I was just going to grab a bite, you hungry?"

"You're not going to watch the big game?"

"I don't think we can avoid it no matter where we go."

They went to the Hollywood Deli, just outside the student zone, a little farther into the east end, and there was a TV mounted on the wall behind the cash and a crowd starting to gather in front of it.

On the way over, Judy had told Dougherty that the new batch of freshman who'd moved into the house at the beginning of the month probably wouldn't care about his uniform anyway, and he'd said, "Not activists?"

Now she was saying, "Not really, they talk the talk but I don't think they can walk the walk."

"It's not easy."

Judy said, "No."

"And how do they pick a cause?"

"It's as hard as picking a major." She was smiling.

A man said, "*Tabarnak,*" and Dougherty turned to see it was a bus driver standing and looking up at the TV, a brown paper bag in his hand.

"Yakushev."

Looking through the glass door of the diner, Dougherty could see the bus idling on the street but it appeared to be empty.

Judy said, "Every September I think about going back to school. It's in the air, you know."

"You mean do a master's degree?"

She smiled like he was cute and said, "No, finish my bachelor's. I turned on, tuned out and dropped out."

"That must have gone over well with your folks."

"After my father's heart attack?"

She drank coffee and then held the mug in both hands, looking over the top of it at Dougherty. He looked back and didn't say anything for minute. He didn't feel like he needed to say anything and that felt good.

The crowd by the cash watching the TV was getting restless, feet shuffling and hands tapping on the counter.

Dougherty said, "How far are you from graduating?"

Judy shrugged. "Depends what I pick as a major."

"You didn't pick one?"

"I picked a few," Judy said, "I just haven't settled on one yet."

A cheer from the crowd.

Dougherty looked up at the TV and said, "Esposito."

"He's one of ours?"

"I don't think they have Italians in Russia," Dougherty said. He put a glob of mayonnaise on one of the triangles of his club sandwich, took a bite and then said, "What's your major now?"

"Political science."

"Politics isn't an art anymore, now it's a science?"

"Everything wants to be a science now."

The waitress came to the table and asked if they wanted anything else, and Dougherty looked past her to the TV, trying to see how much time was left in the game. He said, "Just some coffee," and looked at Judy.

"That's fine, thanks."

Then Judy said, "I'll be right back," and Dougherty watched her walk into the back of the restaurant to the washrooms.

Outside Dougherty could see the bus still idling and the street still empty.

After a couple of minutes, Judy came and sat down saying, "It's like the city has stopped."

Dougherty said, "Yeah," and then there was another groan from the crowd, another Russian goal, and Dougherty said, "This could be a long night."

"How long will the game last?"

"After the game," Dougherty said. "Bars are full now, and it'll only get worse. People will either be drowning their sorrows or celebrating."

"So?"

"There'll be fights, there'll be car accidents, all kinds of stuff. We'll be busy."

"I guess," Judy said. "I never thought of that."

"I never did, either," Dougherty said. "Not really. I

mean, I didn't think there'd be so much of it; I didn't think that's what this job was."

"What did you think it was?"

"I don't know, the poster just said, *Fascists Wanted*, I thought we'd wear black shirts and get free beer."

Judy said, "Funny."

A cheer from the crowd, banging on the counter.

Dougherty said, "2–2 now."

"You do seem good at it," Judy said. "Being a cop."

"I'm getting kind of tired of wrestling drunks."

"What do you want to do?"

"I don't know," Dougherty said. "When you join up you tell them you want to help people, that's what you say and you do mean it. And you do, sometimes, you do help people, but then it's also a job, you know, so you want to get promoted and get a raise and all that."

"They aren't mutually exclusive."

He smiled at her and said, "No, I guess not, but I just didn't think by now I'd still be doing this."

"Who does? Look at me: the first time you arrested me I was with the Workers' Coalition, and now it's the Milton Park Defence, and there've been some others in between."

"The first time I arrested you — that sounds funny."

"It's losing its charm."

"So, how do you do it? All these causes, all these fights? You don't always win."

"Almost never," Judy said.

The whole restaurant seemed to let out a sigh and relax at the same time, and Dougherty glanced up at the TV and said, "There's the first period." He motioned to the waitress and said, "*Café, s'il vous plaît.*"

Judy said, "I don't expect to win every battle. It's like you — you don't expect to wipe out all crime."

"No, I'd be out of work."

"Ha ha, but you want to do some good where you can."

"Yeah," Dougherty said, "I guess that's it."

The waitress put a couple of cups of coffee on the table and said, *"Trop de pénalités,"* and Dougherty said, *"Plus le match progresse, meilleurs on est."*

"Les autres, aussi."

"Nous sommes en forme maintenant — ce n'est plus l'été."

The waitress said, *"Ça c'est tu penses,"* and went back to standing in front of the TV with the rest. The bus driver was sitting on a stool at the counter.

"I guess that's it," Dougherty said, "you do some good where you can."

"Is this about David Murray?"

"It looks like we got the guy who killed him," Dougherty said, "but maybe not enough evidence. He'll go to jail for something else, and not for long enough."

"I know it sounds dumb when I say it," Judy said, "but it won't bring him back."

"I still want the guy to pay for it."

"Hey, lots of criminals go free," Judy said. "Richard Nixon is going to get re-elected."

Dougherty drank coffee and didn't say anything.

"At least Richard didn't have anything to do with it."

"No," Dougherty said. "Poor guy, just caught up in it."

"In the murder?"

"Well, the guy who did it, guy named Buckley, he's trying anything he can: he tried to pull Burnside into it, said someone was blackmailing Richard, threatening to get his father involved."

"His father, why?"

"Just to muddy the waters, I guess. He's just throwing shit at the walls, hoping something sticks. He's got a Mafia lawyer now, and that's their strategy: stall, delay, file motions every day, trivial crap, bring up anything that'll be a distraction. Imagine what would happen if the papers started talking about Richard Burnside's gay son being blackmailed?"

"That might still happen."

"Yeah, it probably will."

"Someone should tell Richard," Judy said, "warn him it's coming."

"Someone?"

Judy said, "Yeah, it might be doing a little good where you can."

Dougherty knew she was right. She was right about a lot of things.

They left the Hollywood Deli in the middle of the second period. The teams had traded goals and it was tied 3–3. Judy said she was going to use the time while the city was quiet to put up some posters about the next Milton Park Defence Fund concert at the Yellow Door, and Dougherty asked her if she had a permit.

She kissed him good-bye and held him for an extra moment, and he liked it. The more time he spent with her the better he felt.

301

Another thing in his life he wouldn't have expected and had to learn to accept.

Driving across town, he had the game on the radio in his car, and the Russians scored two more, the second period ended with them up 5–3 and Dougherty figured he would be in for a long night, drowning sorrows probably leading to more fighting than celebrating.

Probably.

He turned onto Greene thinking Burnside wouldn't be in his office, he'd be in a bar somewhere watching the game, but Dougherty wanted to try to talk to him, let him know what was coming. Then a man ran across the street.

Richard Burnside.

He jumped into a car parked at the curb, pulled a U and raced past Dougherty.

He had a gun in his hand.

CHAPTER
TWENTY-ONE

The gun was a lousy Saturday Night Special, a little snub-nose .22 that Dougherty thought probably wouldn't even fire, but Burnside was standing in the middle of the living room, aiming it at an old man sitting in armchair in front of a TV, so he said, "Richard, over here."

Burnside looked over his shoulder but kept aiming at his father. "Go away."

Dougherty said, "It wasn't him."

"It was." He looked back at his father. "You killed him."

Dougherty said, "Who told you that, Richard?"

The old man had turned around in the chair and was looking at Richard. His mouth was open but he wasn't saying anything.

Burnside said, "You got one of your thugs to do it, beat him to death."

"No," Dougherty said, "he didn't."

"Shut up!"

Burnside turned and pointed the gun at Dougherty. "You don't know anything."

"Danny Buckley told you, didn't he? He's lying."

Now Burnside was looking over his shoulder at his father and he said, "I paid them off and they went to you anyway."

"No, son," the old man said. "No one came to me."

"Liar!"

The big house was empty, and Burnside's voice echoed.

The hockey game was playing on the TV, the sounds of whistles coming from the crowd in Moscow, the way they cheered.

Dougherty said, "No, Richard, this is bullshit. We caught the guy who killed David. He killed another drug dealer, too, a guy named Herridge, Goose Herridge. He told you he went to your father because he's desperate."

Now Dougherty could see Buckley in Parthenais coming up with this idea, probably had it in mind for a while, saving it in case he thought the cops were getting close to him. Fucking Buckley, too clever for his own good.

"He's a criminal," Dougherty said, "he's a liar, he'll say anything, he'll try and blame everyone else."

Burnside was thinking about it, Dougherty could see that, and maybe he wanted to believe it. He hadn't shot his father, and now he was still pointing the gun at

Dougherty, but his hand was shaking and the moment seemed to be passing.

"We arrested him last night," Dougherty said. "He's in Parthenais jail. Did he call you this morning?"

"I didn't know who it was," Burnside said.

Now Dougherty could see how Buckley thought it would work, if Burnside killed his father, or tried to kill him, it would be a sensational story, headlines and TV news and all the police attention. Lawyers and psychologists and deals, and no one would be interested in a drug dealer from the Point. Buckley probably thought it was his ace in the hole.

"He had pictures of you and David in Toronto."

"Yes."

"And David didn't care, he didn't care who knew."

"He wanted people to know," Burnside said. He was shaking his head and smiling a little. "He wanted everyone to know."

Dougherty took a few steps towards Burnside, saying, "He was tired of fighting the big battles, always for someone else. He wanted a little something for himself."

"He wasn't selfish," Burnside said. "He just wanted to be . . . himself, who he really was."

Dougherty was close enough to reach out and take the gun from Burnside's hand. "I know."

The old man clicked a remote control in his hand, and the TV shut off. He struggled to his feet and said, "What's this about, Richard?"

"A friend of mine was killed, Dad, murdered. I thought, you . . ."

"But why?"

"Because . . . we were . . ." His head fell back and he said, "David is dead and I can't even say it." He looked at his father, who was standing now, leaning on the chair looking back at him, waiting.

Burnside said, "I'm a homosexual."

The old man nodded a little and said, "Like your uncle Ned."

Burnside said, "What? Uncle Ned killed in the war?"

Dougherty took a few steps back, and the old man said, "Officer, would you be able to dispose of that," motioning towards the gun in Dougherty's hand.

"Yeah, sure."

"Fine. I think we can manage now."

Dougherty said, "Right," and nodded at the old man and at Burnside and walked slowly through the living room, seeing the big fireplace for the first time, the painting above it, the bookshelves — the whole room looking like something Dougherty'd only ever seen in the movies.

Outside, the street was quiet. The middle of the afternoon and no one was around. Dougherty wasn't sure what to do. He leaned against his Mustang and laughed a little, feeling the tension flow out of him. He laughed harder, shaking his head and looking at the gun in his hands and thinking, Holy shit, he could have killed me.

And in the strangest way he liked it. He liked the feeling that he'd done something, done like Judy said, a little good somewhere.

He got in his car and drove down the hill, past the big old stone Westmount houses with their manicured lawns and hedges and even trees that had been sculpted, the houses getting closer together and then some old apartment buildings as the street levelled off at Sherbrooke. Then he was thinking he could just drive a few more blocks to the Royal Vic and stop in and see his father, but then he thought, no, wait till the end of his shift and have a real visit, sit down and really talk.

And then Dougherty wanted to call Judy: he wanted to see her and tell her everything, he wanted to share it with her, and that surprised him. Made him feel good.

He drove past the empty Forum and along de Maisonneuve, lined with office towers and tall apartment buildings. The place was deserted. Not just quiet because people were at work — it was eerie quiet like that National Film Board movie Dougherty'd seen, *23 Skidoo*, about the neutron bomb that wiped out all the people but left the buildings intact.

Pulling into the parking lot behind Station Ten, Dougherty saw the attendant's booth was empty, and when he got out of his car he'd never heard the city so quiet. He stood there in the parking lot for a minute listening, not hearing anything.

Crazy.

And then screaming. Cheering and hooting. Horns.

A moment later, car horns started blaring.

Dougherty ran into the station house and it was packed with cops, all of them on their feet cheering.

307

Delisle grabbed Dougherty and shouted, "You believe it!? What a goal!"

"What?"

"Henderson, unbelievable, he score with thirty-four seconds left, *trente-quatre*, we win!"

Dougherty didn't get it — Henderson had scored the winner, that was the game before — but Delisle was gone then, moving through the room, slapping backs and shaking hands and Dougherty noticed the beer in his hand, every cop in the place had a beer in his hand.

The TV they'd set up for the game was showing the replay, and Dougherty realized it was a different goal, Henderson had scored another game winner, the series winner.

Dougherty walked back outside, and now the city was the way he knew it best — celebrating.

CHAPTER
TWENTY-TWO

The squad room was crowded, there must have been twenty-five cops in it, mostly older guys, detectives in wrinkled suits smoking cigarettes and listening to the *directeur*, the top man in the police force, René Daigneault, explain how the new task force was going to be set up. It was going to be called the *Commission d'enquête sur le crime organisé*, and already Daigneault was calling it CECO.

Standing at the back of the room by the door and only hearing half of what Daigneault was saying, Dougherty was just happy to be in the room.

There was grumbling and a lot of foot shuffling when Daigneault talked about the Caron inquiry in the '50s and how nineteen cops and the *directeur*, Albert

Langlois, were charged with conspiring with organized crime and fired and it only settled down when he said that wasn't going to happen this time.

"*Cette fois, nous allons après les vrais criminels*, the big boys."

Dougherty saw Carocchia looking doubtful and wondered if he'd get to write press releases about any of this.

There were a few women in the room, too, a couple Dougherty recognized from the Social Squad who knew their way around.

It was looking like it could be a real inquiry, a real investigation.

And it was another temporary assignment for Dougherty, but this time he felt he could make it work.

When Daigneault finished his speech and got a round of applause from the cops, they divided up into smaller groups, and Dougherty pushed through the crowd to where Ste. Marie was sitting on the edge of a desk. He said, "*Ça regarde bien.*"

Ste. Marie smirked a little, and Dougherty heard Carpentier say from behind him, "It always looks good in the beginning, Constable."

Dougherty turned around and Carpentier said, "Detective-Constable."

"It's temporary," Dougherty said, but he liked hearing it.

Carpentier said, "It will be permanent by the end of this assignment." Then he looked at Ste. Marie and said, "Going after the big boys."

Ste. Marie didn't look too impressed.

"Maybe you'll get Cotroni."

"Maybe."

"But you won't be getting Rizzuto."

"Bastard."

"He's gone," Carpentier said to Dougherty. "Looks like South America — Colombia or Venezuela."

"I guess he's got those paintings," Dougherty said, "from the museum."

"*Il va revenir*," Ste. Marie said. "He won't be able to stay away."

"Yes, for sure. So, did you hear, charges laid today in the Blue Bird fire."

Dougherty said, "All three guys?"

"Yes, each one charged for thirty-seven murders."

"*Mon Dieu*," Ste. Marie said. Then he stood up and said, "*Bon, au travail*," and walked towards the other senior detectives planning their squads.

Carpentier said, "This is a good assignment for you, Dog-eh-dee."

"Thanks. And thanks for making it happen."

"You worked for it. So now," Carpentier said, "a not-so-good assignment. We're also making a murder charge today against your old friend Buckley, for Greg Herridge and David Murray."

"That's good."

"Yes, but I was wondering, would you like to call Mrs. Murray?"

Dougherty thought, No way, no one wants to phone a woman to tell her about her son's murder, but he said, "Yes, I'd like to be the one."

"Good." Carpentier handed him a piece of paper

with a phone number on it and said, "Come on, use the phone in the homicide office."

Dougherty followed him and realized it would be his first assignment as a detective-constable.

Judy said, "Just let me get these on," and Dougherty watched her go to the back door where her workboots were sitting on a piece of newspaper. But she reached past the boots and picked up a pair of black shoes.

"This is just like how we met," she said. "The first time you arrested me, you remember?"

"I remember."

She was walking past him then and said, "That's how I'm going to tell our kids how we met."

Dougherty followed her out of the house to where she was standing beside his car and before he could say anything — and there was a lot he wanted to say — she was holding up a record album and saying, "Alice and Ian? A bootleg?"

"It's for my brother."

"He's going to love it."

In the car, Dougherty said, "You sure you want to do this? Sunday dinner in Greenfield Park? We have to cross a bridge, you know."

"Sure," Judy said.

Dougherty put the car in gear and pulled away, thinking he had no idea how it was going to go, but it felt right.

AUTHOR'S NOTE

A Little More Free uses many historical events to tell its story. Most Canadians my age or older can remember where they were when Paul Henderson scored the winning goal in the final minute of the final game in the Summit Series (I was in a grade seven classroom in Centennial Regional High School), but not so many of us seem to remember where we were for the first game of the series (my brother's apartment in Moncton, New Brunswick — he was on duty that night with the RCMP, but he stopped in a few times for updates).

The fire at the Wagon Wheel nightclub, usually referred to by the name of the club on the main floor of the building, the Blue Bird Café, is also not so well known. Most of what's described in this book actually happened. In August 2012, a permanent memorial for the thirty-seven victims was unveiled in Phillips Square. (The building that housed the Wagon Wheel and the Blue Bird Café no longer exists.) A story from the Canadian Press looking back at the original story said, "Somehow, it barely made a ripple — not even in the local media. The death of working-class kids in a country-and-western bar happened to have occurred on the eve of a far more famous event that captured the nation's imagination: the beginning of the 1972 Canada-Soviet hockey series."

Also, the Montreal Museum of Fine Arts was robbed, although that happened in the early hours of Monday, September 4, not Sunday. The stolen paintings and jewellery have yet to be recovered.

Montreal had been awarded the 1976 Summer Olympics in 1970 and was watching closely, along with the rest of the world, as eleven Israeli athletes were murdered in Munich in September 1972.

There are no reliable figures for the number of Americans who came to Canada rather than be drafted into the American armed forces to fight in Vietnam, or who simply came to Canada to continue to protest what they saw as an unjust war. The numbers range from 60,000 to a quarter of a million and include men and women. The term "draft dodger" has generally been replaced by "war resister," as most of the people who came to Canada weren't avoiding the draft but were protesting the war. There are a few very good books on the subject, but it is still a contentious issue and more needs to be written, I think. A good place to start is Jack Todd's 2001 memoir, *The Taste of Metal: A Deserter's Story*.

Claire Helman's 1987 book *The Milton-Park Affair* offers some very good background on the story of what was, at the time, as the subtitle says, "Canada's largest citizen-developer confrontation." The mass arrest of fifty-six people protesting the development was a turning point in 1972. Phase One, what is now the LaCité complex, was built but plans for more towers and more destruction of existing homes was stopped. After decades of expropriation for the construction of new buildings, expressways and Expo (the destruction of Griffintown may or may not have been a result of Expo), the people of the Milton Park Citizens' Committee should be remembered.

Of course, *A Little More Free* is a novel and many of the characters are entirely fictional. Any mistakes in the research are entirely mine. I'd like to thank everyone who helped in the research of this book:

My sister, Susan Bentley, and my cousin Linda McFetridge, who had both been to the Wagon Wheel and remember the tragedy well, and the many, many people I pestered with questions: Randy McIlwaine, Michel Basilières (whose father appears in *The Milton Park Affair*), Roy Berger, Jacques Filippi (who continues to do what he can with my awful French), Peter Rozovsky, Dana King, Keith Logan, Kristian Gravenor and everyone at ECW Press: Jack David, Michael Holmes, Erin Creasey, Crissy Calhoun, Scott Barrie at Cyanotype (for the fantastic cover), Rachel Ironstone, David Caron, Jenna Illies and, for the incredibly thorough and thoughtful editing that made this book what it is, Jen Knoch.

And, of course, my wife, Laurie Reid.